Captured by Storms,
The Keizer House, #2

FRENZY

of the

STORM

Sequel to
Storm at Keizer Manor

RAMCY DIEK

Frenzy of the Storm, a sequel

First Edition, Frenzy of the Storm

Captured by Storms, The Keizer House, Book # 2

Book Cover design by Damonza.

ISBN—Paperback 979-8-9891302-0-7

Acknowledgments

If it wasn't for the many requests, this sequel to my first novel, *Storm at Keizer Manor*, wouldn't exist. Thank you so much for asking.

Thanks beta readers, Catherine Van B., Becky C, and editor Kelley Davis from Kokua Editing Services. I appreciate your feedback, suggestions, friendship, and encouragement.

Damonza, once again, the cover is gorgeous.

And big hugs and admiration for my editor, Shelly Stinchcomb. Without your continuous support and expertise, none of my stories would have come alive. I'll always be grateful that you believed in me.

Rolf, my husband, thanks for being my rock for over forty years. Keep on rocking!

Captured by Storms,
The Keizer House,
Book # 2

FRENZY

OF THE

STORM

Prologue

September 28, 1864

FROM HER BEDROOM WINDOW on the second floor of Keizer Manor, Annet watched white cumulus clouds develop over the dunes in the near distance. Her throat tightened as they rapidly changed color. They'd experienced a strange and unstable autumn at the coast this year. Hot days filled with sunshine, blue skies, and high temperatures had turned cold and gloomy in the blink of an eye. Rain had fallen from a cloudless sky, sometimes accompanied by thunder and lightning flashes. The unpredictable weather unsettled her. How would a meteorologist explain the rapid changes in the atmosphere, she wondered. Global warming, climate change, El Nino, La Nina, or something in between?

Unable to tear herself away from nature's disturbing display, she stared at the darkening sky. Her blouse stuck to her back and tiny specks of perspiration beaded on her forehead. With her hands, she fanned herself in an attempt to cool down, her thoughts going back to that dreadful day when her life had changed dramatically. To that day in her past when two worlds collided and the universe swallowed her up and spat her out, shattering her perceptions, beliefs, and existence. So much had happened since then. Fleur engaged, Frank at university, and Violette...

A jagged streak of lightning cracked against the sky and jolted her back to the present.

"This can't be real," she cried out, and pressed her hands against her throat.

In the few moments her mind had wandered off, the wind had picked up, pushing clouds inland at an increasing speed. The last rays of sunshine had lost their fight, and the eerie purplish glow of the sky was alarming. Her fingers twiddled with the gold necklace around her neck. The clouds seemed brownish green instead of gray, and strange shafts of pale pink and orange light streamed up the sky in waves. Was her imagination playing tricks on her, and was she seeing things that weren't there?

Pull yourself together, Annet, she thought, forcing herself away from the terrifying view. This storm is just like all the others, showing off its power with crackling lighting flashes, tumultuous thunder, and torrential rain. But only until the heavens part and the sun triumphs again, its battle temporarily lost before it returns in full glory, with long rays of brilliant yellow light, wiping away all evidence of the storm's frenzy.

A deep rumble in the distance made her rush back to the window. A few seconds later, lightning splintered the claustrophobic dark sky. Dread spread through the pit of her stomach. The oppressive humid air became hard to breathe. She would never dare to open the window and let the cool, ocean air in. Even a tendril of this storm entering the house could be disastrous.

With her right palm against the cold glass, she watched the storm batter the familiar landscape. Rain came down in sheets. Dune grasses and bushes took a severe beating, jerking back and forth. Branches were ripped off the small trees and disappeared. Heavy gusts whipped and thrashed everything that came in its wake, and the noise overhead increased until it sounded like an entire squadron of military jets flying overhead. Her legs trembled as panic settled in her chest. This couldn't be happening. Not again.

Overcome with terror, she watched dark green and purple clouds with eerie shafts of light streaming upward morph into deep blue, violet, and orange. She had lived through a storm like this before, caught in the center with her boyfriend Forrest, and she had never seen him again.

Something unexpected and terrifying caught her attention. She pressed her nose against the glass and narrowed her eyes. It looked like a piece of cloth, thrashing around between the nearest dunes across the yard, like a bedsheet on a clothing line, or a flag on a flagpole, the fabric light-yellow, like Fleur's dress. *Like Fleur's dress?*

Forgetting her fear, Annet threw the window open. Fine sand blasted against her cheeks. Thrashing rain soaked her hair in seconds.

"Fleur!" she shouted, her voice barely detectable above the tumult. "Fleur! Hurry back inside! Fleur!" She couldn't hear her own cries over the explosive storm. It was useless. She slammed the window shut and hurried down the stairs toward the family room, calling out her daughter's name. "Fleur!"

Frank, her twenty-two-year-old son, peeked up from his book when she rushed in. "Mother, your hair is soaking wet. What happened?"

Violette sat on the floor, stacking blocks into a multitude of towers. "Mommy?"

Raindrops slid down Annet's neck into the fabric of her blouse. She didn't even notice. "Where are Fleur and Jeremiah?"

"They had a fight," Frank replied.

"A fight? About what?"

Violette's eyes widened in alarm at the panic in her mother's voice.

Frank scoffed. "Over a card game. Fleur exploded, flung her engagement ring at his head, and told him she never wanted to see him again. After Jeremiah left, Fleur went upstairs."

"I heard you yelling," Alex said behind her. Her husband had just walked in, his eyes searching hers. "Is it the storm?"

He reached out to her and for a fleeting moment, Annet allowed herself to be pulled into the comfort of his loving embrace. Then she pried herself loose. "I have to find Fleur."

Alex grabbed her arm before she could walk away. "There's nothing to worry about," he said. "I just talked to her."

With the doorknob in her hand, Annet turned around. "What did she say?"

"That she couldn't marry a man she didn't respect. I let her rant and rave, and then told her not to make such an important decision until she took command of her emotions." He gave his frantic wife a warm and encouraging grin. "She thanked me with a big hug, told me she loved me, and headed to her bedroom."

"I'm sure you're right, but I still want to check on her," Annet replied.

She rushed up the stairs, the turmoil inside of her raging in sync with the storm outside.

"Fleur, can I come in?" Without waiting for an answer, she walked in.

The room was empty.

Chapter 1

Present Time

DISMAYED, CASSIUS REWICK sat in his cluttered office. He wiped the perspiration off his forehead and buried his fingers in his curly hair. Tomorrow was his sixty-third birthday, the average age for government employees of the Abernathey Research Center to retire. An hour ago, he'd met with his boss and longtime friend, Commander Milton Lee Thornton, who'd brought up the subject. He rested his elbows on his desk and buried his fingers even deeper into his short crop. For him, birthdays had stopped having any meaning after his wife Javina passed away three years ago, taking with her all the trips they'd planned to make in retirement. Retracing their roots to Africa, going on wildlife safaris, a visit to the pyramids in Egypt, a cruise on the Mediterranean, and so many more adventures. A deep sigh escaped his lips. Without his wife, and his only brother having passed last year, he didn't have anyone left. Not even a faraway cousin, niece, or nephew. How would he possibly be able to fill his time?

"Why would you think I'd want to retire, Milton?" he'd asked. "I'm not ready. Besides, you're two years my senior, and you're still working."

Milton had laughed without mirth. "Yes, that's true, but I would have stopped years ago if it wasn't for all the alimony I still have to pay." His two failed marriages had cost him dearly. "Don't worry, Cassius. I'm not asking you to turn in your keys. I only needed to verify you're still on board. Changes are looming, by orders from above, and I wasn't sure you'd want to be a part of it." Milton had handed him a document. "Read this. I'm sure it'll get you worked up."

Cassius picked up the pages in front of him and read them for the third time.

Internships have become a valued and vital part of many degree programs, and students recognize the multitude of benefits they can gain from hands-on experiences in the real world. Numerous branches in the government already collaborate with universities all over the United States. Heemstead University has reached out about the possibility for a mechanical and electrical engineering internship program at Abernathey Research Center (ARC).

With the current climate changes and the warming of the oceans, opinions have shifted and interest in our work is renewed. As an underutilized and modern state-of-the-art facility, a young and eager student could bring many benefits to ARC.

The document ended with a very important sentence:

With the aid of an intern, older developments could be revisited, utilizing the funding already in place.

Cassius knew exactly to what specific older development they referred, otherwise Milton wouldn't have bothered to bring it up. He leaned back in his chair. Start the project back up after having it simmer on the back burner for twenty-four years? With the aid of interns? Warning bells went off in his head when he thought about the accusations ARC had been the target of after Annet Sherman disappeared. They rang so loud that the noise overpowered the stirring of excitement in his gut. No. It was too dangerous, too experimental. He had to talk the Department of Defense out of it.

He pushed the disturbing papers to the side and opened his lunch bag. The cheese and tomato sandwich he'd prepared for himself that morning looked unappetizing. After one bite, he threw it in the trashcan. He needed fresh air to clear his head.

The narrow hallway outside his office led to the back entrance of the building. He opened the door and narrowed his eyes against the bright light. The sun shone brilliantly in a blue cloudless sky, and the salty ocean air filled his lungs as he breathed in and out. He loved that smell, and the view over the dunes never failed to calm him down. He longed to walk to the ocean, like he used to, if only his arthritic knees didn't crunch and growl in protest with each step. Two total knee replacements were in his near future.

When he reached the end of the parking lot at the eight-foot chain-link fence, he turned around and gazed back at the research center where he'd worked for the last thirty-three years.

The drab two-story building with the brown siding was marred by a chaotic collection of antennas, satellite dishes, and powerful generators. People wondered what could possibly be happening inside such a small facility to warrant that much equipment. That's because they didn't know about the existence of the two sublevels, where he'd engineered and built the Scientific Magnetospheric Ionospheric Thermospheric Storm Research Machine. The full name was too long for anyone to remember, let alone pronounce it, and all the ARC employees referred to it as SMITS, the driving force behind Abernathey's existence.

With his hands in his pockets, Cassius paced along the fence, reminiscing about the years gone by and the joy and anguish his work had given him. For the first ten years, it had been his dream job, his brilliant career and salary surpassing anything he'd ever imagined. Like everything else in this world, nothing lasts forever, and from one moment to the next, he'd hit rock bottom. "Javina," he whispered to his late wife. "Am I nuts to listen to Milton and even contemplate going back down that same road and restart the project?"

Knowing he wouldn't be able to resist the challenge, all Javina would have done was smile, and despite his concern, he grinned. *You knew me so well*, he thought, her loss a constant pain in his heart. Slightly revitalized, he turned on his heels and went back inside.

"What a gorgeous day," Darlene said. She sat behind the reception desk at the main entrance, the phones quiet as always, the only visitors an occasional sales agent or delivery person. *It used to be so different.* He scolded himself for going down memory lane once again.

"Spring is definitely in the air," he commented.

He bypassed the stairs and took the elevator down to sublevel 1. The door opened to a hallway, and he flipped several light switches. The green carpet on the floor was dull and threadbare, the white paint on the walls yellowish and scuffed. The building had seen better days. He passed four small offices. They had been empty for years, and the doors were closed, some of the name tags of former employees still remained.

At the end of the long and narrow corridor, he stopped in front of a metal door that displayed a Maintenance sign. Like most doors in the building, it was electronically secured. His hand shook nervously as he fumbled for the keycard hanging from the lanyard around his neck. After touching it to the security panel, a green light lit up and he gained access onto a small landing. The sound of the heavy metal door closing automatically behind him bounced off the plastered walls in the cold stairwell, shutting out the outside world and closing him in. He headed down the stairs, his footsteps sounding hollow on the concrete steps, the air stagnant and stale. He cleared his throat. The air conditioning hadn't been turned on in ages and the ventilation system was probably dusty and invaded by pests.

At the bottom of four short stairs was a small hallway with a second security door. As he slid his card and accessed sublevel 2, the entire length of the hallway in front of him was lit by outdated fluorescent light bulbs. Some of them buzzed, others flickered. If he was going to work down here, they needed to be replaced with LED bulbs.

Despite his effort to keep his face impassive and his feelings impartial, he trembled. Because of controversy and lack of funding, Abernathey had been forced to abandon the classified work that had taken place down here. It had been the darkest day of his career.

He slowed down to suppress his mixed emotions and take in the moment, everything around him still as familiar as his favorite worn-out corduroy dress pants.

By the time he reached the control room, his initial doubt and regrets faded, trading places with a nervous excitement of starting the project back up. Technology had advanced so much in the last two decades. What if he could figure out how to control SMITS's powerful, unleashed forces? It would be revolutionary, mind-boggling, world changing.

Anticipation of getting back to work hummed through his body when he slid his access card for the third time. The door to his old sanctuary clicked open and the lights came on automatically. From the threshold, he took in the enormous space and workstations; the smell of oil, grease, and old electronics still hanging in the air. He breathed in through his nose and out through his mouth, savoring the old smell as long suppressed memories swooped through his mind. How he'd enjoyed working here, his life vibrant, the visions of what he could accomplish endless. And the pride he'd felt being in control of all the decisions, with no one second-guessing his expertise or looking over his shoulder, telling him what to do.

So much had changed since they'd stopped the entire project and let most of his old coworkers go. The only ones still there were Milton, Darlene, the two maintenance guys, and the janitor. Even the security guards had been laid off, all of them replaced by the tall chain-link fence that surrounded the entire property, a gate, and motion detection security cameras with infrared night-vision. Nothing and no one could go in or out without being recorded. Not even the seagulls or the occasional rabbit.

Reminiscing about the past, he sat down behind his old desk and removed the plastic cover from the computer. A coating of dust puffed into his face. He turned away and sneezed. Besides Milton, three co-workers, and himself, nobody had been allowed entry on sublevel 2. Not even a cleaner. His research had been too classified.

With his hands folded in his lap, he leaned back in his chair and looked around. It would be too much work for him to tidy up the entire floor, upgrade the computers and internet, replace the lights, clean the ventilation system, and so much more. Before he could even contemplate getting back to work, they would need to hire an entire crew of highly qualified and cleared personnel.

The loud ringing of his old desk phone interrupted his thoughts. Confused as to why the phone would be ringing in the abandoned room, he picked up the receiver.

"I knew you would be down there," Milton said on the other end of the line, his voice pleased. "What are you thinking?"

They knew each other so well. "Torn, for sure," he replied.

"I hear you," Milton chuckled. "Listen, I realize this might move faster than you're prepared for, but there's a young man in my office who's studying mechanical engineering in Heemstead and wants to major in climatology and alternative energy. He's eager to apply for the internship. Do you want to meet him?"

Milton was right. This was moving way too fast.

On his way out of the control room, Cassius stopped at the five-by-eight window that allowed a good view into the mechanical room. For at least five minutes, he stared at the radio transmitters, the wall of computers, and multiple air conditioning units. They surrounded a huge rectangular object, hidden from view and protected by thick ecru blankets. The object had been the focal point of his life for more than ten years, while he had practically lived down here. Now, it appeared forlorn and abandoned, almost haunted.

Did public outcry over the extreme weather conditions being experienced around the globe get through to the higher-ups? Had they finally realized that something had to be done? That it would be smart to use existing facilities and rekindle important work from years past? He shrugged and securely closed each door behind him on his way to the main part of the building and Milton's office. Who knew how the government worked?

"Two important meetings in one day?" Darlene commented when he reappeared.

Distracted, he stared at her and blinked. "What did you do to your hair?"

Darlene touched her purple hair that she'd tied up in a messy bun on top of her head. "What are you talking about? I've had it colored for more than two weeks."

"Sorry, I didn't notice before. Looks good," he mumbled, and chuckled sheepishly.

"Grrr...," Darlene growled. "It's about time we see some

young blood livening up the atmosphere in this stuffy place." She pointed with her head toward Milton's office. "Look at that cutie in there."

Through the window, Cassius noticed a tall young man dressed in a pair of black slacks and a crisp white button-down shirt. It seemed he'd tried to tame his brown tangled locks with a wet comb. He hadn't succeeded.

Cassius lowered the corners of his mouth in a frown. "An intern. People and their crazy ideas."

"You immediately take that scowl off your face, Cass," Darlene countered. "That young man is nervous enough without seeing a big old Black man shooting daggers at him."

The door opened, and Milton stepped out. "Cassius, I want you to meet Mr. Emmett Castella."

The applicant had followed Milton out into the hallway and extended his hand with a bright smile on his face. "I've heard so much about you, Mr. Rewick," he said. "It's wonderful to meet you."

"You have?" Cassius replied, taken aback.

"Of course. Your work at the Abernathey Research Center has been the focus of my study, and I would be honored to work with you."

This kid knows about flattery, Cassius thought.

"Emmett is twenty-three and lives in Heemstead," Milton added. "Over the years, he's come out to Dunedam and the coast often."

Emmett nodded enthusiastically. "I have. I love the ocean and the dunes, and come out here all the time to hike, surf, hang out. I have a motorcycle, so transportation won't be an issue."

"Come, I'll show you around," Milton said and turned around.

"Again, an honor to meet you, sir," Emmett said to Cassius before he hurried after Milton.

Deep in thought, Cassius watched them walk away.

Chapter 2

Forrest

"LET'S GO, HANK," Forrest said to his twelve-year-old golden retriever. The old dog raised his head, looked at him, and closed his eyes. Each night, it got harder and harder to get Hank to go out for his evening walk.

"Come on, buddy, you know you have to go," Forrest continued, poking him gently with his foot. He waited while Hank got up on all fours. "Just to the coach house and back. I promise." The dog's nails clicked against the white marble floor in the hallway and out onto the terrace. Forrest closed the door behind them and took the steps down to the driveway. Hank followed down the wooden ramp. At the bottom, he sniffed the planter box, like he did each night.

With melancholy, Forrest thought about the wonderful years they'd had with him. He loved that dog and seeing him struggle pulled on his heartstrings. "You're doing good," he said, petting him.

It was a warm spring evening. Stars twinkled in the night sky, and the solar lanterns along the driveway cast a welcoming, warm lighting in front of them. Hank disappeared between the nearby bushes. When he reappeared, they strolled for several minutes until they reached the two-story coach house. The lights were on, and he could hear someone strumming a guitar inside. It had to be Rix, his tenant, neighbor, and longtime friend.

"Let's go back," he said to Hank and turned around at the loud roar of a motorcycle in the distance. He stopped and watched the driver slowly make his way down the long driveway. Emmett, Rix's oldest son, was coming home.

"Hey, how are you?" he said when the BMW came to a stop, the motor idling. "Do you want me to open the garage door for you?"

The young man nodded with a smile. "That would be great. Thanks." He revved a few times and pulled into the garage.

Forrest followed him inside and waited until Emmett shut down the engine and took off his helmet, revealing a mess of tangled brown hair. "You're home late tonight," he commented.

Emmett hung his helmet from the handlebar and stepped off. In his motorcycle boots, he stood several inches taller than Forrest. "Just working late," he replied and rolled his shoulders.

Forrest grinned. The chubby toddler, wild boy, and lanky teenager he'd seen grow up had transformed into a good-looking young man. A man who was going to college and had taken on an internship at Abernathey Research Center.

"Are they any closer to get SMITS up and running?" he asked.

Emmett furrowed his brow and glanced at Forrest.

"Although I would love to, you know I can't talk about what goes on there. It's classified, and I could lose my new job after barely working there for one month."

"Come on, Emmett. It's common knowledge that the government has rekindled research at Abernathey by special funding for SMITS," Forrest said gruffer than he'd wanted. He massaged his forehead to ease some of the tension that had built up inside him. "It's been in the paper and on their website, and all I want is an update."

Emmett fumbled with the zipper of his leather jacket, avoiding Forrest's inquisitive gaze. "I'm really sorry, man. But it's a risk I can't take."

"Look," Forrest went on. "I appreciate your continued interest in what happened to Annet all those years ago, but Abernathey's involvement has only been based on suspicion and speculation." Although it wasn't a lie, his gut told him they were somehow involved. Annet had disappeared in the close vicinity of the government research center, and they'd found one of her black high-heeled shoes nearby. But without proof or anyone coming forward to talk, no one had pursued the suspicions.

Emmett kept staring at the ground. Then he sighed. "I understand what you're saying, and I get how much this means to you. Hell, ever since I was a teenager and heard about the unexplained circumstances surrounding Annet's disappearance, I've been fascinated by the fact that Abernathey might be responsible. It's the reason I chose to study mechanical engineering and alternative energy and jumped on the chance for that internship. But still, everything there is shrouded in secrecy."

They both watched Hank sniffing around until he lifted his hind leg and peed against the daffodils.

"Forrest, you know how long and extensive the clearance process was, and I can't jeopardize it," Emmett said, suppressing a yawn. "Just know that if there's anything I can tell you, I will." Then he grinned. "Even if it wasn't about Annet and all of that, I enjoy working there. Cassius Rewick is a kind and intelligent man who works harder than anyone else. And I love the experience it offers. Being able to put on my resume that I interned at one of the government's most classified research centers will impress any potential employer in the future."

Hank weaved himself around Forrest's legs. Emmett wasn't the only one who was tired and wanted to go to sleep.

"I totally understand," Forrest said with resignation. The boy had matured into a bright, determined young man who followed his dreams by working hard in the field he wanted to pursue, and he admired that Emmett was conscientious and followed the rules. "Have a good night."

Forrest closed the garage door and followed the stone walkway through the rose garden back to the main house on the Keizer Estate. It had been a busy day at work. Like Emmett, he was tired.

"You're ready for bed?" he asked Hank and opened the door for the slow-moving dog.

Inside, he took in the entrance hall. Unlike the rest of the house, it still held its former grandeur, with the circular marble staircase and wrought iron spindles. In a chair, next to the carved marble fireplace that featured leaves, roses, lion's paws, and intricate swirls, he noticed his youngest daughter. The lamp next to her reflected off her shiny, long blonde curls.

"Why are you still up, Caro?" he asked the twenty-one-year-old.

"Just studying," she replied. "It's almost the end of winter term, and there's still a lot I need to finish."

"Studying educational psychology is not easy, I know," he replied.

Caro made a face. "You better tell Josie that."

Josie, the oldest of his two children, enjoyed hanging out with a multitude of friends, unlike her more serious and reclusive younger sibling.

Forrest noticed the pain in Caro's blue eyes. "What happened?"

She let out a sigh and closed her book. "My dear sister made fun of me tonight because I didn't want to join her at karaoke."

It was normal for young adults in their early twenties to go out and meet friends, and it surprised him that Caro had no interest at all. Raising two daughters had its difficulties. "It's Friday night, sweetheart, and she only wants you to have fun."

"Singing in a bar is not fun for me." Caro grumbled in her adorable, girly way, making him laugh.

"Don't stay down here too long. It's getting late." He squeezed her shoulder encouragingly before heading up the stairs.

In his bedroom, he unbuttoned his shirt, kicked off his shoes, and sank down on the antique four-poster canopied bed with the carved figures and bulbous legs. Kara, his wife, had wanted to get rid of the oak monstrosity, feeling she had to share the sheets with ghosts from the past. Fortunately, she had grown to love the solid piece of nineteenth-century craftsmanship and changed her mind.

He checked the time on his phone. Kara usually didn't come home this late after a business meeting. He wrote her a quick text asking when she expected to be home, fell back on the mattress, and closed his eyes. Immediately his mind reverted to Emmett, Abernathey, and SMITS, the images of two women with long blonde hair and blue eyes dancing behind his eyelids. The familiar sadness that gnawed underneath the surface for the last twenty-four years stuck its ugly head back up. His unsettled emotions had been worse since Emmett had started working at Abernathey. Why was he feeling troubled and anxious? He had much to be grateful for – a job he loved, an amazing wife, two smart and gorgeous daughters, and he lived on an estate. *What more could a man ask for?*

He forced his thoughts in another direction and got ready to take a shower. Instead of going into the bathroom, his feet took him into the walk-in closet, where the cardboard box on the top shelf drew him closer. It was filled with letters he'd read so often that he knew them by heart. As if his hands were guided by some ghost from the past, he took the box down and sat on the bed. He hesitated to open it. What waited for him inside wouldn't cheer him up. It would be better to put it back, take that shower, and hope Kara would be home by then. Her loving presence never failed to chase away his dark mood, her smile enough to brighten his day. Instead, he took the lid off and stared at the wrinkled and tear-stained letter on top. It was dated October 30, 1864, the ink smudged, blurring out several words.

Sweet Forrest,

I don't even know where to start. My heart is broken and my despair suffocating.

A week ago, Alex and I drove to Keizer Manor. Frank and Violette came along, and so did Fleur. She'd invited her fiancée, Jeremiah, to spend the day with us before we closed the house for winter. The weather has been unpredictable of late, and while a sudden violent storm raged outside, Jeremiah and Fleur got into a fight. Jeremiah took off on horseback, and instead of going up to her room, Fleur followed him.

From that moment on, the writing almost became illegible, but he knew what it said. Fleur had disappeared in the storm, just like Annet had years before. His eyes went to the bottom of the page.

I still desperately hope she'll be found or will return. But if she traveled through time, she could be anywhere.
Please, Forrest, try to find her.

Annet

His throat closed. If Fleur, his oldest daughter, had traveled back through time, just like Annet, she would have landed in the year 1664. He'd researched and researched, only realizing that records from those days were nearly impossible to find. Not knowing what happened to her had gnawed at him ceaselessly for decades.

The bedroom door opened, and Kara walked in. Quickly, he dropped the letter and put the lid back on the box. "Sorry," he said, getting up to kiss her. "I was just reminiscing."

Kara wrapped her arms around his neck, a teasing twinkle in her eyes. "I just talked to Caro. She told me you were in a pensive mood, even forgetting to give Hank his evening snack."

He pulled her slender body close and nuzzled the sensitive skin of her neck. "I ran into Emmett during my evening stroll with Hank. It bothers me that he's working on that machine."

She freed herself from his arms and walked to the window overlooking the woods behind the estate, the trees dark silhouettes against the night sky. "You remember Detective Jaeger investigated Abernathey's potential involvement in Annet's disappearance several times, right?"

Of course, he knew. The last time he'd spoken to Jaeger was a few years ago. The dedicated detective had still hoped to find out the truth before his retirement and they'd gone to Abernathey together to talk to Cassius Rewick. It hadn't delivered results, the former vibrant research center now appearing like a neglected and tired office, and Rewick himself gray-haired and old.

Forrest joined her at the window. "Yes, he told us about their former DOD-, Air Force- and Navy funded atmospheric research program that was supposed to improve communication and surveillance systems, and that they used these high-power transmitters to heat the ionosphere. It only confirmed my suspicion. People shouldn't mess with nature. Look at what's happening now. Forest fires everywhere, hurricanes and tornadoes getting more frequent and stronger than ever. Not to forget the unprecedented floods and record-breaking temperatures all over the world."

Kara took his hand in hers and squeezed it. "All we can do is try to do our part, by recycling, eating less meat, taking the bicycle instead of the car." She yawned. "Sorry, I had a good meeting tonight, but it wore me out."

Forrest turned around to face her, gazing deep into her eyes. "I'm sorry that I delved back into the past."

She gave him a warm smile, her brown eyes filled with compassion. "I understand this is about Fleur and not Annet. So don't worry."

He buried his hands in her light brown hair. "I love you so much. Don't you ever doubt it."

Chapter 3

Cassius

THE NUMBERS ON THE PRESSURE VALVE in front of him blurred. Cassius blinked a few times. It didn't help. He checked the wall clock. Close to 9:30 pm. It had been another long day for him and his small crew. One of many since Abernathey Research Center had received the grant from the government, to revive the highly classified work in the basement.

Ramon Ensenada, the electrical engineer, and Adam Devries, a computer scientist, had gone home fifteen minutes ago. Both men had impressive credentials, an array of degrees, and cleared by the DOD. After the nondisclosure documents were signed that enabled them to gain access to sublevel 2, they'd gone to work, upgrading the computer systems, and replacing the outdated and dried out wiring and mechanical parts. Another crew, under direction of Commander Milton Thornton, worked on the connected mechanical equipment outside. Exposed to the elements, the array of satellite dishes, generators, transmitters, and towers had endured years of neglect and most needed to be overhauled, replaced, or repaired.

"How many amps, Emmett?" Cassius asked, a tiny screwdriver in his right hand.

Emmett shot up in his chair. "Sorry, what was that?" he said, suppressing a yawn and rubbing his eyes.

Cassius moved away from the machine and placed the screwdriver back in the exact spot where it belonged, with careful precision. Nothing was allowed to randomly lay around. Order, punctuality, and cleanliness were priorities in the control room, offices, and shop. "We accomplished a lot today," he said. "Let's go home before we both fall asleep."

The young intern rolled his shoulders and turned off the computer. "Thank you, sir. I'll see you tomorrow."

Cassius watched him head to the door. The young man was dedicated, smart, and eager to help.

"We have to double check all the connections and filters, and Ramon needs to replace that faulty transistor, but I think we might crank SMITS up for the first time tomorrow."

Emmett stopped in his tracks and turned around. "Really, Mr. Rewick? That would be fantastic!"

The unbridled enthusiasm Emmett exhibited matched his own. "See you tomorrow."

The aim of SMITS was to study the solar radiation ionized part of Earth's upper atmosphere, and to influence the levels of radiation and quantity of hydrogen and helium. With NASA launching two new satellites over the next several weeks, contact with SMITS would be restored, and a multitude of atmospheric researchers could keep track of any development.

After another anxious week, they had finally received the go-ahead and all authorized personnel had gathered in the basement.

"Are you okay, Cass?" Milton asked, tension written on his face, his white mane a disorderly mess. "You seem a bit flushed."

The air on sublevel 2 was filled with nervous excitement, expectation, and anxiety. Cassius found it difficult to breathe. The last time he'd cranked up the machine, it had caused the shutdown of the entire project, and someone had disappeared. How could he be sure none of that would happen this time?"

"I'm fine," he replied, opening the two top buttons of his white shirt. "All of SMITS's crucial parts have been replaced, the measurements and outputs have been checked three, four, five times, and there's nothing else we need to do. The final moment has arrived."

The entire crew closed in on him, surrounding him. It almost became too much.

"We'll start SMITS at the lowest capacity." The nervous twitch in his left eye caused him to blink several times. "Please, give me a little space, guys. I can't think with everyone breathing down my neck."

Milton sagged down in one of the office chairs, rested his elbows on the armrests and steepled his fingers. "We understand the pressure, my friend. If you need more time, just let me know."

To release his anxiety, Cassius paced in front of his desk. His fingers moved in rapid tempo, as if he was playing the piano at top speed. "Well, maybe I should double check..."

Milton coughed excessively loud. "Are you ready or not? Because I don't have all day."

"Just push the button, Mr. Rewick," Ramon encouraged him, dropping a screwdriver from his hand onto the floor. "It'll start up just fine. No worries."

Cassius stopped in front of him. "Put that screwdriver where it belongs."

Tension mounted as they watched Ramon bend over and place it in the toolbox.

"When you're done pestering your employees, I'll start a countdown, Cass," Milton spoke out loud. "You're ready? Ten, nine, eight, seven, six, five, four, three, two..."

At the word GO, Cassius pushed the red button. Lights flickered, dials on various gauges turned, mechanical parts whirred, and rotating components spun until the loud grinding of bigger moving parts overpowered all other sounds.

"Monitor the pressure meters, Emmett!" Cassius yelled over the noise, pointing to the backside of the machine. "I see a drop of oil coming from that valve, Ramon. How is it looking at your end, Adam?" He frantically walked back and forth, trying to check everything that could go wrong.

"Everything is functioning as it should," Adam replied, running between several computer screens.

"All readings are accurate at my end," Emmett reported.

"I'll adjust the frequency a bit, Mr. Rewick. It seems a bit on the high side," Ramon reported. He clicked away on the keyboard that was hooked up to the machine with several cables. "It's going down and responding nicely."

A few minutes later, Milton got up from his chair and

slapped Cassius on the shoulder. "It looks like everything down here is going according to plan, so you can let go of that fear."

Cassius let out a sigh of relief. "So far, so good, I guess." He walked over to his desk, picked up two walkie-talkies and handed them to Milton. "Time to head upstairs and meet up with the rest of the crew outside."

As discussed during the team's planning sessions, Milton and Adam would go outside after the startup to join the rest of the crew, to check if the satellite dishes and mechanical arms on the roof moved smoothly, while the towers submitted their high-frequency radio waves. The radar detection system, determining the range, angles, and velocity of all objects involved, also needed to work properly. And the direct satellite connection with the National Weather Service had to be double-checked.

Ten tense minutes later, the two-way radio in the control room crackled, and they heard Milton's voice loud and clear. "All is well. Congratulations!"

To celebrate the outcome, Milton ordered pizza and beer, and everyone gathered in the lunchroom on the main floor. There were at least thirty people – scientists, engineers, office workers, and military personnel. Security at the research facility had increased considerably over the last three months. The gate was now monitored by a security guard, and everyone had to show an access pass to get in. Armed soldiers patrolled the surrounding area on a regular basis, and sometimes a helicopter would land on the new concrete pad next to Abernathey.

Cassius declined the second piece of pizza Milton offered.

The slice of pepperoni pizza he'd already eaten and the effect of his first beer in months bothered his stomach. "Excuse me," he apologized.

"Where are you going?" Milton asked.

"The bathroom," he replied, his answer drowned out by a burst of laughter. Everyone was celebrating. Rightfully so.

Inside the toilet stall, he sat down with his elbows on his knees and his chin resting in the palms of his hands. He slowly breathed in and out. It had been a heck of a day. He was exhausted.

The door of the bathrooms opened, and two men came in, talking. "Aren't you as excited as we all are?" he heard one of them say. He recognized Ramon's voice.

"Of course," the other man replied. "It's just that I had expected something to happen, but nothing did."

There was laughter. "Like what?" Ramon asked. "Did you expect the heavens to open with a deluge of rain and lightning flashes? Or a tornado knocking down the towers and satellite dishes?"

"Something like that," came the soft reply.

Cassius was sure Ramon was talking to Emmett.

"Are you referring to the disappearance of that woman and the time travel fairytale from decades ago?" Ramon went on. "That was all Cassius's fault. If he hadn't messed up by cranking the pressure up way too high, that would never have happened. Just talk to those military guys. They'll confirm it."

A sheen of sweat formed on Cassius's forehead. He'd hoped people would have forgotten about that crazy rumor over the years. Apparently, they hadn't.

Chapter 4

AGITATED, CASSIUS STOOD in the middle of the supply room. Since his first conversation with Milton about revisiting SMITS, gnawing apprehension and doubt had kept him from enjoying his work. He'd tried to ignore his premonition, and fortunately over the last few months, everything had gone smoothly. The prospect of succeeding with his revolutionary work sometimes made him forget his concerns, until they started SMITS up and the power kept fluctuating. Ramon and Adam concluded a valve on one of the controllers had failed and needed to be replaced. He'd hoped to find a new one in the storeroom. Not finding it added to his uncertainty. *It could be another omen.*

The door opened and Emmett peeked in. "Do you need help, Mr. Rewick?"

Every time he recalled Ramon and Emmet's conversation in the bathroom, his normally calm and optimistic disposition shattered. The guilt he felt and had tried to dismiss for so long flared up. The remote possibility that he was responsible was still a foreign concept and the likelihood unbelievable, but the doubt was always there.

"I'm glad you could join us this morning," he remarked with a sardonic undertone.

"Sorry I was late," Emmett apologized. "We celebrated my mom's fiftieth birthday last night, and I overslept."

Cassius had tried to avoid a one-on-one with Ramon or Emmett, not sure how to handle Ramon's suspicion and Emmett having learned of it. Distracted, he kept on searching for the valve. "This could be it," he mumbled, opening a small brown box.

Back in the main shop, he joined his team at the plastic folding table set up next to SMITS. On top of the table stood a metal tray holding all the parts from the failing controller.

"Emmett, we need to replace the faulty valve with this brass one. It's a vital component that, coupled with the electric actuator, provides the precise flow control we need," Cassius explained, stepping back into his role as teacher. "Adam, file the required paperwork, update the inventory, and order another one. Here's the box with the part number."

The three men worked for several hours, and Cassius explained along the way each necessary step until the parts tray was empty and they were done.

"Clean up the tools and folding table while I call the DOD," he ordered.

Ten minutes later, Emmett and Ramon joined him in the control room. "We received the green light for the test run," Cassius said, hanging up the phone.

Emmett threw his right fist in the air. "Yes!" he shouted, coming across as overenthusiastic.

His enthusiasm lightened Cassius's austere and pensive

mood. "Since you're so overly excited, why don't you do the honors?"

Emmett's eyes lit up. "Me? Seriously? That's awesome."

"I need you to gradually crank up the power when I say so, because with Adam gone, I have to check the readings on the computers in here."

"Not a problem," Emmett replied, and almost ran into the adjacent workshop, leaving the connecting door open so they could talk.

Soon, the familiar grinding and whirring sounds vibrated the air as SMITS started up and came back to life.

"Looks like it's holding steady," Cassius concluded after a few tense minutes, his eyes glued to the monitors in front of him. "Now, slowly move the lever up until we reach thirty, Emmett."

"Everything is good on my end," Ramon reported.

"Perfect. Bring it up to fifty, and stop there," Cassius ordered, deep in concentration. "Before increasing the power even higher, I want to double-check the heat sensors."

He returned to his desk a few minutes later. "All the gauges are in the green and the readings are to specs. Gradually give it another forty points until you reach ninety. That's more power than we've given it so far."

With his eyes glued to the controls and computer readings, the steady beeping and whirring computer part of the background noise, Cassius's confidence grew. "Another ten, please."

"You got it. Up to one hundred now," Emmett announced.

The loud ringing of the landline penetrated Cassius's concentration. He picked up. "What?" he shouted.

Then he shot to his feet in alarm. "Are you saying the readings are negative instead of positive? That's impossible."

Wild-eyed, he dropped the phone on the desk and rushed over to Emmett's side. "Oh, my God. It's true. The numbers are red instead of green and completely inaccurate and out of whack. Emmett, why didn't you tell me? Turn it down. Turn it down!"

SMITS screeched to a halt, the sudden silence gloomy and foreboding.

Chapter 5

Fleur

OCTOBER 23, 1864

Violette giggled. "I'm winning."

"Yes, you are," Fleur said and smiled down at her ten-year-old sister.

"Right," Jeremiah snickered. "Cheating you mean."

Fleur threw her betrothed a disapproving glance.

"What?" he whispered.

That angered her even more. How could he be so childish? "It's only a game," she hissed.

Jeremiah leaned over in her direction. "It's impossible I'm losing for the third time," he growled. "You must be duplicitous. It's not right." With one angry swipe, he pushed the playing cards off the table. They flew through the air and landed on the floor.

Violette brought her hands to her mouth, her eyes huge in disbelief and condemnation.

"Why did you do that?" Fleur yelled.

Jeremiah got up from his chair and tugged on the pointed bottom hems of his tan striped vest. "Because I'm done playing with cheaters."

Fleur sprung up and placed her hands on her hips. "You scared Violette and are such a bad sport. I never ever want to see you again, Jeremiah McDougal!"

In the darkening room, her small figure looked pale and fragile, but what she lacked in physical strength, she made up with ferocity. "I hereby declare our betrothal dissolved!" She pulled the ring off her finger and threw it at his head. It landed on the floor, in between the scattered cards.

"Nothing would make me happier," Jeremiah sneered, casting her a disdainful glance.

"You're a liar, Jeremiah," Violette joined in. "We don't cheat!"

Frank got up and walked over to stand next to Fleur, balling his hands into fists and glaring at Jeremiah. "I think it's best if you leave before I throw *you* on the floor."

Jeremiah's eyes flitted from one member of the Keizer family to the other. The three of them formed a united front against him. With a condescending scoff, he turned around and grabbed his coat from the back of his chair. "It's like everyone says, you're all crazy," he mumbled on his way to the door. On the threshold, he stopped and glared over his shoulder. "Just like your witch mother!"

The door slammed shut behind him, the sudden silence in the room only disrupted by the wind howling outside.

"He's quite the friendly chap, isn't he?" Frank grinned,

Jeremiah's departing insults still hanging in the air.

Fleur flashed him a scowl, then shook her head and turned her attention to Violette. "I'm sorry you had to witness that, sweetheart."

"I'm fine. I won!" Violette replied laconically, giving them a victorious grin. She jumped off her chair and started picking up the scattered cards.

Frank and Fleur gazed at each other. While they were still a bit shaken up, their sister had already forgotten about the scene.

"That's what they call moving on." Frank chuckled and dropped his long body on the couch.

Fleur couldn't help but smile. It wasn't in her nature to stay angry. A pull on her skirt made her glance down. Violette stood next to her and held up her hand, the forgotten engagement ring sparkling on her right index finger. "Can I keep it?" she asked, a pleading expression on her cute little face.

"No, you can't," Frank said. "It either has to go back to Jeremiah or Fleur."

"Not to me," Fleur stated, straightening her back. "I made up my mind. The betrothal is cancelled." She gathered up the skirts of her gorgeous, yellow dress and headed towards the door.

"Don't go outside," Frank yelled after her. "A storm is developing."

Their entire lives, they were forbidden to go outside whenever it rained. It drove her batty. "I don't care. I need air," she replied, picking up her pace.

In the hallway, she ran into her father, his clothes covered with paint, a brush in his hand. "Did I just hear Jeremiah take off on horseback?" he asked.

"I broke off our engagement," Fleur replied and walked past him to the front door.

"I hope you're not planning to go out," Alex Keizer warned. "Look at the sky. Your mother is already upstairs, checking the windows."

"I wouldn't dare," Fleur replied, and detoured towards the staircase. "I'll just go up to my room and read a little."

The tension in her father's shoulders eased. He was so easy to read. "Darling, if you want to talk, I hope you remember I'm here for you."

Her father always claimed he'd never loved another woman than her mother. What did he know about matters of the heart, she thought, giving him one of her sweet smiles. "Of course. Thank you, Papa."

Halfway up the stairs, she waited until she heard her father close the door of his workshop. It had been a hot and muggy day, and it was stifling inside, the air suffocating. She needed cool and fresh ocean air to revive her spirit, if only for five minutes. At the bottom of the stairs, she took off her shoes, crossed the marble tiled floor as quietly as possible, and opened the front door just far enough so she could slip through. Jeremiah was already long gone, the only proof of his departure the fainting hoofprints in the sand.

"Farewell, my dear," she whispered. The wind picked up her words and carried them away, over the distant dunes, into nowhere.

On bare feet, she stayed close to the building, hunching down below the windows to stay out of sight. When she reached the corner of the manor, she took off running into the dunes.

Immediately, a gust took hold of her long skirt. The yellow fabric flapped behind her as she battled against the ferocious wind. Gasping for air, she reached the dunes and crouched down between the first several rows of dense brush. Her heart fluttered in her chest, draining her energy. She folded her hands and pressed them against her chest in the hope of calming down. It was all Jeremiah's fault. If he hadn't behaved so childishly, she wouldn't be so worn out.

The first raindrops fell and penetrated the delicate fabric of her puff sleeves. *You have a weak immune system and should be careful,* she heard her mother's warning voice in her head. *Eat your vegetables, stay inside, and wash your hands to get rid of germs.* Germs. Nobody even knew what those were.

She stood and tried to shake the sand off of her wet skirt. The storm was moving in rapidly, and the temperature plummeting. Time to head home. A sharp pain in her heel made her glance down. She'd stepped on a rock with her bare feet. Careful not to step on any other rocks, she rounded the first bushes until the odd color of the surrounding light made her look up. The sun was nothing more than a pale ball of light in the sky, and strange wafts of fog blurred her vision. She blinked a few times and turned in the ocean's direction. The clouds rolling in over the dunes were the strangest shade of brown and transformed into an unnerving deep dark green. She'd never seen anything like it. With her arms wrapped around her waist, her dress heavy from the rain, she gazed up at the sky, mesmerized by the mysterious display of colors. *Father would love to paint this.*

A steady rumble coming from the distance shook her out of

her trance. It was time to rush home. This was getting scary. She shielded her eyes from the rain and looked around. Her throat constricted. In the vast storm-battered landscape surrounding her, nothing seemed familiar anymore. Where was Keizer Manor?

Close to a panic, she took several unsteady steps in the hope of latching on to something recognizable, like the graveled road, the windmill, or the wooden shed where they kept the garden tools. Nothing. How could this be possible? She hadn't wandered that far away from the house. Hopelessly disoriented, she thrashed around the dunes. A sharp twig caught her skirt. "Let go," she shrieked, and jerked the fabric free, tearing it. "No, not my new dress." Hot tears mingled with the rain on her face. It had taken weeks before the tailor finally had it right. Now it was ruined.

A jagged flash of lightning lit up the purple sky, terrifying her. "Mother! Father!" she cried out. "Where are you?" The roaring grew louder, vibrating the air until it pulsated through her entire body. Terrified, she swayed back and forth, her lungs on fire, her breaths nothing more than short white puffs. It all became too much when the sand moved underneath her feet, like the waves of the ocean. Afraid to fall, she sunk down between the tall dune grasses, sand blasting her bare skin and entering her eyes and ears. What was she going to do? Shivering, she wrapped her arms around her trembling legs and pressed her head between her knees, praying with all her might that it would soon be over.

Hurricane-force wind pulled on her clothes and the pelting rain lashed her body while the horrifying rumble around her increased until the world exploded with deafening violence. Then everything turned black.

Chapter 6

FLEUR'S ARMS AND LEGS twitched involuntarily. Her head exploded and waves of nausea took over her body. She rolled over, coughed, and swallowed, trying to keep from vomiting. All her muscles protested under the slightest movement. A deep moan escaped her throat. The storm was over, and she had survived. It didn't matter. She'd never felt so horrible in her entire life.

Curled into a ball, she drifted back into unconsciousness until convulsive spasms wracked her body. She opened her eyes and noticed a square building and light coming from several directions. Still in the grip of her nightmare, her brain couldn't comprehend what was before her. She shut it out and focused on her right arm. It had fallen asleep. In the hope to restore blood circulation, she rolled her shoulder and then vigorously rubbed her hands together. Her fingers were blue and numb, and she didn't have any feeling in her bare feet. With all the strength she could muster, she unfolded her thin frame until she sat up on the unfamiliar hard black surface. Disoriented and dizzy, she waited until the tremors subsided and the pounding in her head became tolerable, her mind gradually remembering what had happened. The storm, the thunder, the sensation of getting ripped apart. Her heart fluttered in her chest. If she didn't get up to find help, her body would shut down like it had done once before. A surge of adrenaline washed over her, and the world came back into focus. She reached out to the strange iron wires close by, woven into a never-ending square pattern, held up by round posts. Her fingers wrapped around them, and her body shook as she pulled herself up.

Lightheaded, she clung to the fence until her rapid breathing slowed down and she gained a semblance of control over her movements. Muttering silent prayers, she took in the windowless two-story building not far from her. It only had one door, and on both sides, rectangular glass lights cast a bright glow over several white posts and a strange-looking metal carriage on four wheels. The sign on the door read AUTHORIZED PERSONNEL ONLY, in bold red lettering. It appeared to be a factory or office, and she didn't recognize any of it. Still clinging to the fence, she suddenly heard a sound and noticed the door open. Mortified, she stared at a dark figure with a huge round head, shiny black coat, and tall boots as it stepped outside. Without noticing her, the monster headed towards a low building where it climbed on top of something with two wheels, with hands just as black as the rest of him.

It didn't surprise her to see a Black man. With the civil war raging and tearing the country apart, many former slaves were on the run, trying to find refuge in the North. Especially since the latest battle at Jonesborough when the Union Army had occupied Atlanta, at the expense of over three-thousand lives. Her mother said the Union's victory would secure the reelection of Abraham Lincoln and help end the war. If she could only believe what her mother said.

A sudden thunderous roar broke the evening's silence. Immobilized by fear, Fleur knelt down with her back pressed against the fence. She tried to make herself as small as possible, her eyes darting back and forth in search of a place to hide.

The figure and its apparatus backed away from the building, a white cloud of smoke billowing from its rear. It came to a stop and then sped forward, the noise deafening. Primal survival instinct took over, and in a complete panic she fled away from the monster on two wheels. With her bare feet hitting the pavement, she kept on running until she reached a small building. Gasping for air, she came to a stop and leaned against the brick wall, her last strength depleted.

"Where am I?" she cried out in terror and sagged to the ground, her ailing body not supporting her any longer. "Mom, Dad, please help me." Her slender shoulders shook violently. "I don't know what to do."

"Are you alright?" someone asked.

Through her wet, disheveled hair, she peeked up into the kind face of an older Black man. He stood only a few inches away, his hand stretched out in front of him, offering assistance. "Come, let me help you get up."

Fleur pushed her wet hair away and stared at him through a cloud of vulnerability and weakness. "Something has gone terribly wrong," she whimpered, her hands moving powerlessly. "I don't know where I am."

"You must be one of Lucia's friends," the man said, reaching for her elbow. "Do you want me to get her? She lives right next door."

Fleur allowed herself to get pulled up. "I'm not familiar with anyone named Lucia," she replied, leaning heavily on the man's arm. Her insides wouldn't stop shaking, her thoughts a jumble of anguish and apprehension.

"Well, someone must have let you in because otherwise you couldn't be here. Was it Adam? Or one of the security guards, maybe?"

The man let go of her arm. Immediately, Fleur's knees buckled, and the man grabbed her before she could fall. "You're so pale," he said. "This is my house. Why don't you come inside, and we'll figure this out." There was genuine concern in his voice.

With his arm around her waist, the man guided her inside his home. As soon as they entered, the entire room was flooded with light. She blinked several times, letting her eyes adjust.

"Why don't you sit down," he said, helping her ease down on a blue couch.

"My dress is wet and covered with sand," she protested meekly, her teeth chattering. "I'm making a mess."

He glanced at the wet trail her saturated dress had left on the floor. "Did you get caught in that thunderstorm? Oh, dear. Let me get you a blanket, and I'll crank up the thermostat. We have to warm you back up."

He left the room and returned with a colorful quilt. "How about a cup of tea?" he asked, wrapping it around her shoulders. "I was just about to make one for myself."

While he walked back and forth, Fleur took in her surroundings. Instead of curtains, the windows were covered with ugly white vertical slats. A large rectangular piece of black glass was mounted against the wall, with wires hanging from the bottom. On top of a small desk stood another rectangular piece of glass on a small stand, surrounded by papers and unfamiliar objects. From the ceiling hung a lighted glass dome with five pieces of flat wood coming out from the center. She massaged her forehead and temples to alleviate the pounding pressure.

"I hope you like regular black tea. It's all I have," her host said, placing a steaming mug and a saucer with shortbread biscuits next to her on a small table. He sat down in one of the matching blue chairs. "My name is Cassius Rewick. I'm an engineer here at the Abernathey Research Center. Are you visiting someone today?"

Fleur could barely stay upright, the weight of everything that had happened pulling her down into an all-encompassing tiredness. "No," she whispered, and struggled to pull the heavy quilt closer around her shivering body.

"There must be someone I can call," he pressed on.

Shriveling within herself, Fleur stared at him. "I'm so tired and cold. Can you try to reach my parents? I want to go home."

"Of course," Cassius replied. He pulled a small flat box from his pocket. "Do you have a phone number?"

With her eyes half closed, Fleur swayed back and forth. "My name is Fleur Keizer. We're staying at Keizer Manor. Just off the Dune Road."

Cassius's jaw dropped. "Fleur Keizer? Are you joking?"

The outburst jarred her out of her slumbering state, scaring her. "I'm sorry," she quivered. "I got caught in an unexpected storm outside our home and didn't mean to trespass."

"No, this can't be," her host moaned, hiding his face behind his hands. "It can't be."

Several minutes went by, the silence in the room heavy and palpable. "Please, sir," she whimpered. "If it's not too much trouble, could you take me home?"

He finally looked up, a pained expression on his face. "I'm sorry for my rude behavior," he apologized, avoiding her pleading eyes. "I was taken by surprise. That's all."

The sudden change in her host's behavior worried her. "Do you need to ask permission from your owner first?" she asked, the tea forgotten on the table.

His dark brown eyes grew large. "My owner? What are you talking about?" Then he emitted a short laugh. "Darn. I'm in serious trouble." He got to his feet and started pacing the floor, his hand raking over his tight, short curls.

Fleur pushed the quilt from her shoulders and tried to get up. "I apologize. I must go," she said, feeling like she was going to faint.

He stopped in front of her. "No, please, Fleur. Don't get up. I can see the tremendous strain your body is under. You need to rest while I try to figure this out."

Chapter 7

FLEUR SPENT THE ENTIRE NIGHT on the couch in a near-comatose state. Her wet, yellow dress lay in a heap on the floor. As soon as Cassius had left the house to go to work, she'd peeled it off and changed into the pants and shirt he'd provided her with. The shirt hung from her shoulders, and she had to hold up the pants to prevent them from falling on the ground. With the quilt tightly wrapped around her body, she'd fallen asleep immediately.

At the sound of footsteps and the closing of a door the next morning, she stirred, sensing something wasn't right. She opened her eyes and gazed around the brightly lit room. Memories of what had happened rushed over her, and the items in the room blurred as her eyes overflowed with tears. Filled with self-pity, she hid underneath the quilt and cried until the pillow of the couch was soaked and she had no tears left. Exhausted, she lay there for several minutes with her hands folded, her eyes puffy, barely able to hold it together. Until her mind cleared a little, and the dark clouds of hopelessness lifted.

Alright, she thought, playing with the light switch of the lamp on her nightstand, turning it on and off. *It's obvious you landed in the future, and that isn't so terrible.* Growing up, her mother had told her many stories, about electricity, telephones, automobiles, airplanes and so much more. Although it was hard to believe any of it had been true, she'd enjoyed listening to her mother, like her peers had enjoyed listening to folklore and fairytales. It also meant the people here would be able to help her find her way back, because this was the future where everything is possible.

Embarrassed by her childish behavior and humiliating crying spell, she pushed the quilt away. It was time to face the facts, since crying and moaning wouldn't solve anything. Besides, the man who had found her seemed nice, allowing her to stay in his house, offering her tea, and giving her time to rest.

She pushed herself up. Sun poured into the room between the vertical slats in front of the windows. It had to be mid-morning, and she'd probably slept for at least twelve to fourteen hours. She wiggled her toes and listened to her heartbeat. It sounded stronger, and her headache had subsided. Grateful she'd survived the power that nature had lashed out during the frenzy of the storm, she got up. She didn't seem to have any lingering effects, and everything worked. Holding up the pants, she walked around the house until she found the bathroom.

In awe, she stared at the toilet, sink, and shower. In her mother's stories, she'd raved about showers, bathtubs, and warm water coming out of the walls. Fleur had to look at this disturbing and scary event from the bright side, since she was able to experience some of those luxuries and oddities herself. All she had to do was pretend her life had become a fairytale, just like in Snow White, Rapunzel, and other beloved stories written by the Grimm brothers.

In front of the mirror over the bathroom sink, she stared in shock at her tear-swollen face and red-rimmed puffy eyes. "You look dreadful and nothing like Cinderella or Sleeping Beauty," she cried out.

A dusting of sand fell from her hair when she touched the tangled mess. Not wanting to see the disconcerting image of the thin, pale, and worn-out young woman, she turned away to use the toilet. In most households, they used dried corn cob leaves or straw to wipe their bottoms, while the upper-class preferred the use of newspapers and magazines. Here, she knew they used the roll of thin paper hanging from a holder on the wall. Figuring out how the shower worked was easy, too. She stripped and stepped in, the amount of hot water and the strong jetting spray a pleasant surprise, the water stinging her skin. It felt good, invigorating, and brought her back to life. She used a liquid from a bottle called Shea Butter Shampoo to wash her air and stayed under the spray until the water cooled off. Wondering where all the water going down the drain disappeared to, she wrapped herself in the towel she'd found in one of the cabinets. It was soft and fluffy and smelled like lavender. Such luxury. From a hook on the door hung a bathrobe with purple flowers. She swathed it around her small frame and almost disappeared into it. With appreciation, she knotted the belt at her waist. It felt comfortable and much better than the pants.

A knock on the door made her jump in alarm.

"Fleur? Are you all right in there?" a man's voice asked. "I came over to see how you're doing, and if you're hungry."

She had no idea how long it had been since she'd eaten her

hosts butter shortbread biscuits with tea, and she was ravenous.

"I'm doing fine," she replied and opened the door, the smell of fresh brewed coffee and bacon wafting in her direction.

At the sight of her, relief appeared on his concerned face. "There are several hairbrushes and combs in one of the drawers. Use anything you need," he said. "But don't take too long. Breakfast will be ready in five minutes."

After he turned around and left, she brushed her hair, rinsed out her drawers and camisole in the sink, and hung them out to dry over the shower curtain rail, hoping he wouldn't come in and see them.

With nothing left to do, she walked to the tiny kitchen. Cassius stood behind the stove, monitoring sizzling eggs and bacon, although she didn't see any flames beneath the pan.

"There's silverware in the drawer to my left," he said, and motioned with his head. "If you can grab forks and knifes, we can eat." Two slices of toast popped out of an unfamiliar metal device. He grabbed them and put them on two plates. Then he divided the eggs and bacon and carried the plates into the dining room that also served as living room. Cassius's house was small.

"I hope you like coffee." He handed her a plate and a steaming mug.

Since the start of the Civil War, blockades cutting of trade had made good coffee scarce. "I love coffee," she replied and sat down. "Thank you. I appreciate your hospitality."

He looked away, a split second of discomfort showing on his face. "Please, don't let it get cold," he said, and took a huge bite of his scrambled eggs.

Fleur dove in. The bacon, eggs, and toast were delicious, and the coffee better than any she'd ever tasted. "This is delightful,' she said between bites. "Do you have chickens?"

He stared at her for a moment and then shook his head. "No, I don't. Do you?"

"No, we don't have chickens either. We always go to the Jonkers' farm for eggs," she replied, and although she knew the answer, she blurted out. "Are you familiar with their dairy farm along the Dune Road?"

With his fork halfway to his mouth, Cassius stared at her. "Never heard the name," he replied.

"But you are familiar with Keizer Manor?"

He nodded.

When she finished her food, she exhaled and stared at her empty plate, gathering the courage to ask the question that burned on the tip of her tongue. "I'm in the future. Am I right?"

Cassius put down his fork, heaved a sigh and leaned back in his chair, his dark eyes troubled.

"I was outside in the dunes and believe that wicked storm transported me here," she continued, trying to be nonchalant about it while, in fact, her nerves were jangled.

When he didn't answer and just sat there, shaking his head and giving her a sad stare, she doubted if he had any idea what she was talking about. "You must believe I'm crazy for saying that," she said, close to tears.

Across the table, he reached for her hand. She immediately pulled her hand back and folded her arms, mustering bravado. "I know I'm right and thought you understood." Then, her sudden courage left her. "Please, forget about what I said."

He studied her for several seconds and then grimaced. "How

did you know?"

Immediate relief washed over her. She'd read the situation right and somehow, he knew and understood. "Can you help me get back home?"

He took a sip of coffee, then another. "You're obviously a smart young lady, and I'm so sorry this happened to you." He dragged a hand over his face and sighed. "I take full responsibility for what happened and will do everything in my power to fix my mistakes and get you home. But I have to be honest. It won't be easy."

His words about taking responsibility and making mistakes took her by surprise. "Do you mean you're to blame for what happened to me?"

Cassius slumped in his chair, his skin color turning grayish, the twitch in his left eye and the lines on his face more pronounced. "Yes, I am," he confessed. "It's all my fault."

Still reeling from Cassius's revelation, Fleur studied her image in the mirror. Cassius had given her a small stack of clothes, including underwear and socks. "These are from Lucia, the girl next door," he'd explained. It felt strange to wear a button-up shirt with long sleeves and a pair of pants, but they fit perfectly. So did the ugly, red plastic shoes Cassius called clogs. They'd belonged to his wife, Javina.

Back in the living room, she sunk down on the couch. Although she felt better, her brain was on overload, the strange environment and worries about what was to come exhausting her energy. She also missed her family and knew they would be terribly worried, unable to find her. Thinking about them brought her to tears. She lay down and pulled the quilt up to her chin. With Cassius gone for several hours, it would be nice to close her eyes... She dozed off, but soon began to toss and turn fitfully, with images of deserted landscapes and torn up bodies filling her dreams.

When she woke up, Cassius sat in his recliner, watching her. "How are you feeling?" he asked.

Warm and flushed from her restless sleep, she sat up and brushed her curls back from her face. "Still tired," she admitted.

"While you slept, I cleaned out the guestroom. You should be able to sleep more comfortably there. It will also give you more privacy."

"You didn't have to go through so much trouble, because I won't be here for very long," she replied, and added barely audible. "I hope."

Cassius stood. "I promise, I'll do whatever I can to make that happen, but it's not all up to me." He waved in the hall's direction. "Come, I'll show you where your room is."

She followed him into a small room with a two-person bed, nightstand, closet, and a window overlooking a driveway and fence, with the dunes behind it. On the walls hung several paintings and a picture of a much younger Cassius next to a short, smiling Black woman. The picture was glossy and clear, and the colors so vibrant that it almost seemed they could come alive and start talking.

"That picture was taken on our thirtieth wedding anniversary," Cassius said, and cleared his throat. "I arranged for someone to take your dress to the dry cleaner and asked them to make necessary repairs. It should be as good as new in a few days."

Fleur walked over to the window and looked outside. She'd disappeared in October, but it seemed to be springtime, with the nearby bushes already green and lush, and colorful flowers she'd never seen before blooming in a planter box next to the fence.

"When you're ready, I hope you'll want to join me for lunch. I opened a can of chicken soup and could make toast."

She nodded quietly and joined him several minutes later. They needed to talk.

Chapter 8

"I'LL TRY TO EXPLAIN what brought you here," Cassius began after he finished his soup. "But stop me if I get too technical and you don't understand."

Unlike her friends, Fleur had always had an interest in history, science, and the universe. She preferred nature walks and books over clothes, hairstyles, and romance. Her different view of the world had been instilled by her eccentric hard-working mother and painting father, who lived in the same house, but were each absorbed in their own universe. Nobody understood their unconventional lifestyle. Including Jeremiah. *Would he be worried when he heard she'd gone missing, or would he care at all?*

"As I explained earlier today, we're on the property of the Abernathey Research Center. For the last thirty-plus years, I've worked here with my friend and boss, Commander Milton Lee Thornton. Our work initiated and funded by the government, to research high-power radio frequencies, solar radiation, the ionosphere, and the neutrosphere. Twenty-four years ago, an unexplained phenomenon caused public outcry," he said, giving her a nervous glance. "Concerns were raised that our work was developed for military purposes and warfare, and not for science. Fabricated stories spread over the internet like wildfire, and along with internal concerns, the government stopped the funding. Subsequently our work and research came to a halt. The only reason they didn't shut the facility down completely and kept it running with a bare minimum of employees was to maintain the radar system that uses radio waves to detect objects and terrain." He shifted in his chair. "Until four months ago, when the government asked us to rekindle our work to research the current climate changes, like the warming of the oceans, wildfires, flooding, tornadoes, hurricanes and drought."

It sounded like gibberish, and all Fleur could do was gape at him. "Are you trying to explain that wildfires and the government are the reason I'm here?"

At her remark, a flicker of surprise appeared on his face. "Simply said, yes." He chuckled, easing some of the tension. "But it leaves out that I was the man in charge, and it will be up to me to rectify my horrible mistake."

"I trust you, Mr. Cassius," Fleur said. "But there's something I would like to find out. Did the Union win the Civil War under President Lincoln and end slavery?"

Cassius burst out laughing. "You're a remarkable young woman and don't cease to surprise me. Yes, he did. The Civil War ended in 1865."

Her mother had told the truth, Fleur thought. "I'm very happy for you." She smiled feebly, hiding a yawn. Although she'd slept most of the day, she was worn out. "If you don't mind, I would like to rest for a while."

With immediate concern, Cassius stood. "Of course. You've been through a lot, and there's so much you have to adjust to. Take all the time you need."

Fleur took a long breath and pulled herself up using the table, her knees weak.

"But before you go, I need to ask you something. This morning I had several meetings about what happened to you with Milton, the Department of Defense, and my staff. There's still a lot that we need to discuss and work out. Until we do, could you please stay inside?"

Dizzy and slightly nauseous, she nodded. "Of course." She reached out to the wall for support and headed into the bedroom.

A terrifying noise from outside awoke Fleur with a jump. She covered her ears, her heart fluttering erratically in her chest, until the noise subsided, and then stopped. Curious, she stepped out of bed and opened the curtain. To her left, several men dressed in green with rifles hanging from straps on their backs, surrounded an elongated metal carriage with big windows in the front and four blades on top that slowly circulated. One of the carriage doors opened and two men stepped out. The dress coat of the second man was decorated with medals, flags, and stripes. He seemed important. She waited until they disappeared, leaving only one man behind who started walking around the carriage, inspecting it.

A knock on the door startled her. Had these men come to see her? On bare feet, she walked to the front door and opened it.

A young man, about her own age, stood outside carrying a small box. "My name is Emmett, and I wanted to say hi." He bowed slightly at the waist. "I hope I didn't disturb you."

He was by himself, his brown hair a curly mess, his eyes examining her with concern.

"I'm bringing donuts," he continued, holding up the box. "Can I come in?"

Fleur hesitated. She was by herself, and it wouldn't be appropriate. Especially not since he seemed her own age.

"Don't worry, I don't mean any harm."

He shifted from one foot to the other and seemed nervous. "Let me explain. I work with Cassius Rewick and heard you're here. I thought you might be lonely and would appreciate some company."

Against her better judgment, Fleur stepped back to let him in.

"I know this is all new to you. Shall I help you make tea or coffee?" He pointed in the direction of the kitchen.

Still hesitant, Fleur followed him. She'd never received a visitor while dressed in a shirt and pants before and wondered what he thought about her casual outfit.

Emmett filled a kettle with water and placed it on the stove. Next, he opened several cabinets in search of mugs and a box of tea bags.

"I sometimes hang out with Lucia and Adam who live next door. The layout of their house is the same. That's why I know my way around," he explained. "Hey, check out those donuts. They're from the local bakery. Which one do you want?"

Fleur looked inside, the sweet smell of the colorful pastries filling the air. "I want to try that pink one with the colorful pieces on top."

"Good choice. The ones with the sprinkles are the best." He tore a piece of paper towel off the roll and handed it to her. "Here, so your hands don't get sticky."

"Thanks," she replied, watching him take out a brown one covered with colorful sprinkles and immediately sink his teeth into it. She followed his example, the taste unlike anything she'd ever had before.

He grinned, but then became serious. "This morning, they called us in for a private meeting with Milton and Cassius," he said. "Everybody had to sign an updated nondisclosure agreement. After I did, I almost fell off my chair. Darn, Fleur. I'm so sorry this happened to you. If I'd only paid closer attention, I would have noticed SMITS's readings were in the negative and out of whack, and none of this would have happened."

It surprised her how readily people took responsibility in this era.

"The donuts are only my first attempt at getting forgiveness, because the least I can do is try to make your stay a bit more pleasant." The water boiled, and he poured it into the teapot. "Let's head into the living room. If you take the mugs, I'll bring the rest."

Fleur sat down on the couch. "I'm glad you came. Everything is so overwhelming. Like that machine out there. It was so loud."

"That's a helicopter," he explained. "It's like a plane, but instead of wings, it uses those spinning rotor blades to fly. And those things out there in the parking lot are cars used to drive around in. I prefer riding my motorcycle. I can show it to you later."

At the sound of music coming from his pocket, he pulled out a small rectangular device and held it up against his ear.

"Hey, Mom," he said. "Yes, I called earlier to tell you I won't be home for dinner tonight. We're off a bit early today, and I'm going to hang out with Adam." He spoke for another minute, pressed a button, and jumped to his feet. "This is my phone. Scoot over, and I'll show you how it works."

They talked and laughed and finished their tea, his uplifting company almost making her forget about the disturbing situation she'd landed in.

The opening of the front door made them both look up.

"What are you doing here?" Cassius's voice thundered in the small room.

Emmett flew up from the couch, his face beet red. "I'm sorry, sir," he apologized and scurried over to the door. Before he walked out, he turned around and waved. "Nice meeting you, Fleur."

With Emmett gone, Cassius deflated and sunk down heavily in his recliner, leaning his head against the back of the chair. He seemed to be exhausted.

"Did you get bad news?" Fleur asked, realizing her sudden appearance had to cause him a lot of stress if he was indeed to blame.

"This afternoon, the Secretary of Defense Austin McConnohie arrived by helicopter. I was convinced he would fire me on the spot, my mistake costing me my home and pension." He dragged a tired hand down his face. That seemed to be one of his habits. "Instead of firing me, he demanded to see yesterday's security footage."

Before he could continue, Fleur raised her hand. "What's security footage?"

Cassius thought for a moment. "It's like when someone takes hundreds of pictures in a row and when you look at them, they show you exactly what took place."

"I understand," Fleur said.

"All of our cameras are motion activated. That means if someone walks by, they start recording. The footage shows that you appeared out of nowhere seconds after SMITS ran at full capacity. Shortly after, the recording stops and doesn't start back up until two hours later, when you regain consciousness and drag yourself up on the fence. Then we see the backdoor open and Emmett walking out before he climbs on his motorcycle and drives off. That's when you ran toward my house. You must have been terrified."

Had it only been twenty-four hours ago? It seemed so much longer.

"After watching the footage from several other cameras, the Secretary wanted to go over it for the second time, while in the meantime, I still dreaded the worst. Milton probably saved my job. He told the Secretary that history has repeated itself, but instead of sending someone to the past, SMITS transported someone to the future, its forces working in the opposite direction because of a faulty controller. He went on to say that this is groundbreaking technology that will rock the world."

"After a few minutes, the Secretary looked at me and said, Mr. Rewick, we give you full authority to do what's necessary to get Ms. Fleur Keizer safely back home."

Chapter 9

STILL UNSTEADY ON HER FEET and with the niggle of a headache behind her eyes, Fleur followed Cassius out the door. She'd had a good night's sleep and felt stronger to face this unfamiliar world, especially since she was wearing Lucia's blue pants and flowery top instead of her own yellow dress that would have stood out in this era. Emmett had worn the same kind of pants and his shirt had a simple straight cut, just like hers.

"I'm sure you're nervous to meet so many new people," Cassius said. "Remember that I'll take you home the moment you feel overwhelmed."

He was like a mother hen, protective, helpful, and considerate.

"I'm glad we talked so extensively last night and that you showed me those videos on your computer. They gave me a better understanding of everything that has changed."

They'd sat behind his computer for hours, watching videos on YouTube about the moon landing, traffic jams, doctors in hospitals, the Beatles and Garth Brooks, cruise ships, trains, and whatever else he could think of. They'd switched to several historical documentaries about the Civil War and the Second World War and ended with the weather forecast. It had boggled her mind to see for herself everything her mother had talked about so frequently.

They crossed the parking lot and reached the building. Two men in uniforms waited at the front door, their curious eyes on her. One of them opened the door so they could enter. "Good morning, Miss," he said.

"Good morning," she replied, immediately overcome by the group of twenty or more people waiting in the hallway. One of them waved at her. It was Emmett. She waved back, his presence slightly calming her jittered nerves.

An older man wearing a coal gray suit and a white dress shirt stepped forward, bowing slightly at the waist. "Miss Keizer," he said. "Welcome to the Abernathey Research Center. My name is Milton Lee Thornton. I'm the commander in chief and fully at your service, as is the rest of the team."

"I didn't know the entire staff would show up, and I apologize," Cassius said close to her ear.

Milton turned around and straightened his back. "Everyone back to work," he commanded.

Throwing her curious glances, the employees spread out, some of them leaving, others lingering.

"Before you show Miss Keizer around, let's talk in my office for a few minutes," Milton said, crossing the hallway.

They passed a round glass reception desk. Behind it stood two women. "This is Darlene, our receptionist and administrative assistant," Cassius said, introducing the older woman with the purple hair. Fleur had never seen anything like it.

The other woman was much younger. "What are you doing here, Lucia?" Cassius asked.

"No worries, Cass," she replied, holding up both hands in mock defense. "This is only the entry hall, and I won't spill the beans about the ugly fake flowers decorating the counter to anyone." She stuck her nose in the faded arrangement of plastic carnations and pretended to sneeze. Then she grinned at Fleur. "If you need more clothes, knock on my door. I'll be home all day."

"Thank you," Fleur said and quickly followed Cassius down the hall into an office.

Commander Thornton closed the door behind them and pointed at the two chairs in front of his desk. "I would like to explain the course of action over the next several weeks," he began, tossing out words like oxygen, earth's atmosphere, ionospheric heater, and radio waves around. "We won't try to send you back until extensive testing has proven it's safe to do so," he concluded, and waited for her reaction.

Confused and at a loss for words, she stared at him. "What's an atmosphere?"

Five minutes later, they left Milton's office and headed down the hall to a door where Cassius slid a card through a box on the wall.

"Now that everyone knows I'm here, why do I have to stay inside the fence?" she asked, gradually becoming curious to see more of this future world and unhappy to stay locked inside.

A green light blinked, and Cassius opened the door, revealing a stairwell. "It's for your own protection, Fleur, because if people outside of the gate find out who you are and what happened to you, they will never leave you alone. Inside the gates, you're safe, because nobody can enter without proper authorization. Do you understand?"

Of course, she understood, but not being able to leave made her feel like a prisoner. "Before I go home, I want to visit Keizer Manor and see the changes in Dunedam and Heemstead," she stated as she followed him down another corridor and two flights of stairs. In the bottom hallway, he stopped to open another door. "I want to walk through the dunes and experience what it feels like to ride in a car. You can't deny me that." She sunk her front teeth into her bottom lip, determined not to let this unique opportunity get taken away from her.

Cassius turned around to look at her. A deep sigh escaped his lips. "You're so understanding and seem to adapt so quickly to your new environment that I forgot how young you still are." Then he nodded. "You're right. I'll talk to Milton and make him understand."

Down another hall, Cassius's small crew, comprising of Ramon, Adam, and Emmett, met them. They immediately bombarded her with questions.

"I have a twenty-two-year-old brother and a baby sister," she replied. "I'm twenty-three. My birthday is on January 5. Yes, Alex Keizer, the painter, is my father."

The next hour dragged on, the constant attention and questions, the workshop, mechanical room, computers, equipment, and the machine they called SMITS draining her energy. Bleary eyed and in a daze, she struggled to stay upright.

Emmett was the first one to notice. "Fleur, you're so pale. Are you okay?" He rushed over to her side.

"Just tired," she said, leaning into him, her breathing labored.

Emmett wrapped his arm around her waist, supporting her. "Let me take you home. You need to rest."

When she woke up several hours later, Cassius was waiting for her in the living room.

How long had he been sitting there, she wondered, feeling guilty for invading his home and causing problems. "I'm feeling much better," she said. "You don't have to worry."

"Maybe so," he replied. "But since we don't know what the effects of time travel on the body can be, we want to have you examined by a doctor."

Over the last ten years, people had constantly worried about her health, and she didn't need a stranger mingling in her affairs. "My mother had no ill-effects," she snapped, tired and cranky.

To move the conversation in another direction, she looked at the two plates with sandwiches on the table. "Did you prepare lunch?"

"I thought you might be hungry," he said, inviting her to join him.

While they ate, Cassius tried to lighten the mood, making small talk, but nothing he said brightened her spirits, and she was relieved when he went back to work. But with him gone, the walls of the house caved in on her. Glum and forlorn, she headed outside, kicking a few small rocks around. Then she remembered Lucia had invited her to visit and look at clothes.

She walked to the house next door and knocked. When nobody answered, she peered through the window and noticed Lucia in the living room, jumping around, her ponytail bouncing up and down. The girl immediately got sight of her and hurried over to the door. "Sorry, I didn't hear you knock," she said, removing a small device from each ear. "I was exercising and listening to music."

Nothing surprised Fleur anymore. "What kind of music?"

"Just some popular electronic dance music from various artists, like Cretia Azul and The Junkies." Lucia grabbed a towel and dried her face and neck. "You've probably never heard of them. That's okay. I'm sure it must be difficult enough for you to be here and it's a real honor to meet you. Wow, I still can't believe the big honcho called me into his office this morning to sign all that paperwork. Did you know you're top secret? Pretty cool, if you ask me." She stopped talking only long enough to take a sip from a bottle. "I like the way you have your hair, hanging loose like that. I had no idea it was so long. You're also very pretty, but I already knew that. Take a seat if you want. Can I get you anything? A beer? Wine? Soda? We have it all."

Fleur had never heard anyone talk so fast. She couldn't understand half of it.

"Sorry for rattling on so much," Lucia grinned. "You're a bit of a celebrity and I'm actually a bit nervous to meet you in real life. Jeez, how will I ever be able to keep myself from talking about it? It's all I can think of."

The girl's nervous energy was contagious and exactly what she needed. "How were you able to get those tight-fitting garments on?" she asked, every contour of Lucia's curves clearly visible.

"I'm wearing leggings, a sports bra, and an athletic workout shirt," Lucia explained, showing how stretchy her clothes were. "Very different from the Victorian dresses, corsets, hoops, and petticoats you're used to, right? But wearing those must be so badass. Being all ladylike, fanning yourself, and walking around with a parasol."

"It's nothing like that," Fleur objected, howling with giggles as Lucia paraded around the room, pretending to be a prudish Victorian matron.

"Come, let's go to my bedroom. Those jeans look great on you, so let's see what else I have you can borrow."

The house was laid out exactly like Cassius's house, only furnished much differently, with colorful curtains, wicker furniture, house plants, and lots of pictures on the walls.

"Do you prefer dresses or pants?" Lucia asked, opening her closet. "What do you think of this red dress? It's made from fake crochet lace, with a round neck and short sleeves." She pulled it out and held it up in front of Fleur. "Great, it falls just below your knees. You want to try it on?"

Within half an hour, they'd gathered a small stack of clothes on Lucia's bed, talking as if they'd been friends forever.

"Are you sure I can borrow all of these?" Fleur asked.

"Absolutely," Lucia nodded. "It'll only be for a few weeks, right?"

Chapter 10

AT THE END OF THE AFTERNOON, Fleur headed back home, carrying two dresses, three tops, a light jacket and a second pair of jeans. She immediately noticed Emmett lingering around.

"What are you doing here?" she asked, happy to see him.

"Just checking up on you. See how you're doing," he replied. "Here, let me take that from you."

She handed him the small stack of clothes and grinned. "You're very kind. Thank you."

Fleur opened the door and Emmett followed her in. "I'm only staying for a few minutes," he said, the heels of his tall black boots loud on the vinyl floor. "Cassius is still mad at me for hanging out here, and I need to get back into his good graces."

"Do you always wear such heavy boots?" she asked.

"No, not always," he replied, putting her clothes on the table. "But I'm joining a friend of mine for a motorcycle ride along the coast."

It was the second time he talked about his motorcycle, making it clear how much he loved it. "Can you show it to me?"

As he walked out in front of her, she admired Emmett's blue

pants that fit tightly around his well-shaped behind. She wondered how he would look in the high-waisted, fitted pantaloons Jeremiah liked to wear, with a short double-breasted coat, or in a black three-piece suit. She was sure he would be devastatingly handsome.

"I have a classic 2020 Harley Davidson Fat Bob 114," Emmett said with pride when he stopped next to a two-wheeled vehicle. "I know it's old, but it has a mind-blowing performance and handles extremely well. Do you like the aggressive look of the exhaust and tires, or is it a bit too much?" He took his helmet off the steering wheel, put it on his head, and climbed on his Harley, making Fleur realize it had been Emmett she'd seen driving off on the day of her arrival, and his big round head had been a helmet.

"Tomorrow is my day off, and I hoped to pick you up and go for a drive. Would you be interested in that?"

"I'm not sure," Fleur replied, still terrified of the machine and remembering that she wasn't supposed to leave the compound.

"Think about it," he said, starting the engine. With a wave of his hand, he drove off, leaving her behind in a stinking cloud of exhaust fumes.

It had been a difficult and emotional day, and as she watched Emmett disappear out of sight, a wave of sadness and longing for home crashed over her. She put her hand to one of the light posts to steady herself. This world was so loud, with the constant zooming of lights, machines, devices, and equipment. And outside, cameras whirred, wires crackled, equipment grinded, and engines roared. It was overpowering and shutting her down.

She doubted if she could last another day, let alone several weeks.

Back at the house, she fell asleep as soon as she closed her eyes, and didn't wake up until early the next morning, her stomach growling. She'd missed dinner and went in search of food. In the nearly empty fridge, she found a piece of cheese and a small bag of carrots. Next, she turned on the coffee machine. Waiting for it to brew, she sat down at the dining table where an envelope with her name on it grabbed her attention. She opened it and pulled out a nametag hanging from a lanyard.

"That card will allow you to get in and out of the compound," Cassius said, coming down the hallway from his bedroom.

"Are you saying I'm allowed to leave?" she said, full of excitement.

Cassius grinned. "Yes, you are. As long as you promise not to tell anyone who you are and where you're from."

It felt like her shackles had fallen off, her sadness and misgivings from the other day forgotten. "Thank you so much," she said.

Cassius disappeared into the kitchen and returned with two mugs filled with coffee. "I also wanted to tell you I made an appointment at the hospital. They're expecting you on Monday afternoon for a complete physical exam."

After a refreshing shower, Fleur changed into her new clothes, her pants snug, the flowered top soft and comfortable. At the sound of a loud engine, she hurried to the door and opened it at the same time Emmett shut the motorcycle off.

When he noticed her, he held up a second helmet. "I stopped by just in case you changed your mind."

"Let me grab my jacket," Fleur said, and rushed back inside. With the lanyard around her neck, she reappeared a few minutes later.

"Where do you want to go?" he asked, helping her secure the helmet on her head.

She climbed on the back. "I want to go home."

At fifteen miles per hour, Emmett chugged over the parking lot towards the gate. After it closed behind them, he increased his speed gradually to twenty miles per hour.

Fleur wrapped her arms around his waist, her knuckles white and her body stiff. To her, Emmett was driving so fast, and she was scared. They drove for approximately a mile before she relaxed a little, Emmett's strong body warm and comforting. Suddenly, she stood up on the foot pegs, causing him to swerve. He quickly slowed down and came to a halt. "Everything alright?"

Fleur took off her helmet and laughed. "It's Keizer Manor. You brought me home," she cried out happily. "But why are there so many cars?" There had to be close to one hundred of them, maybe more.

"That's because it's a museum now, and Alex Keizer's paintings attract more than one million visitors a year," he explained.

Tears of regret and shame welled up in her eyes. "Why didn't I believe my mother?" she spoke softly to herself. "Can we go inside?"

"Of course." Emmett started the motorcycle and slowly

FRENZY of the STORM

drove closer to the museum until he found a place to park. After securing the helmets, they took the steps onto the terrace and joined the line at the entrance.

"What's everyone waiting for?" Fleur asked, staring up at the familiar building. Although it felt like coming home, everything was so different, with people crowding around, multiple security cameras attached to the walls, and information signs on either side of a brand-new front door. Entrance ticket for one adult, thirty dollars, she read.

"We have to pay to get inside?" she whispered close to Emmett's ear, struggling to understand. "But I don't have any money."

Emmett pulled out his wallet and showed her a card. "Don't worry about it. I have a debit card and you're my date."

"Debit card? Date?" There was still so much she needed to learn.

The line moved fast, and soon they entered the hallway. Fleur couldn't believe how much it had changed, with a ticket counter to her right, a glass wall separating the entrance from the rest of the house, and showcases displaying vases, statues, and other artwork from various artists. "That used to be our living room," she told Emmett, pointing with her index finger in the giftshop's direction.

Emmet quickly glanced over his shoulder to see if anyone had overheard what she said. "I hope nobody listened," he whispered, frowning. "You have to be more careful, Fleur. We can't afford to attract attention." He pulled a baseball cap from the pocket of his leather jacket. It had the Abernathey Research Facility logo embroidered on the front. "Here, put this on, just

· 83 ·

in case someone might recognize you."

She threw him a puzzled glance.

"Upstairs, there's a room solely dedicated to paintings of you, and you could be recognized. We can't risk it." He handed their tickets to the museum guard. "Where do you want to go first?"

Fleur slowly followed him, troubled and dejected. "I don't think I want to go inside anymore." Her soul cried out for her parents, her brother, and sister, and she recognized she wouldn't find anything here. Instead, she felt lonelier than she'd ever been. "All of the change... like this peculiar glass wall. I don't understand."

Emmett moved in closer. "As part of the climate control inside the museum, they put this wall up," he spoke near her ear. "It's to prevent the salty ocean air from further damaging the paintings. Come. It'll be alright."

He seemed to know a lot about it, and she wondered why.

Emmett loosely wrapped his arm around her shoulders and guided her towards Storm Hall, dedicated to her father's masterpiece *Lost in the Storm*. Emmett had told her it was the museum's major attraction. It had always been her least favorite place in the house, the painting disturbing, the stained-glass windows casting a sinister light. Sometimes they played with hoops and knucklebones in the enormous space, or chased each other around, the echoing sound of their footsteps on the rust-colored tiled floor adding to her discomfort.

"If you insist," she shrugged, staying close to him, in search of mental support.

The solid oak door of Storm Hall opened, and another

visitor politely held it open so they could enter. To her surprise, the room was inviting and warm, with indirect lighting drawing attention to the painting and several other exhibits set up inside.

"Newly installed LED lighting avoids ultraviolet radiation without the former concern of discoloration or damage, bringing the paintings alive," Emmett explained, guiding her along several displays. One of them was dedicated to the history of the paintbrush, referring to sticks, bones and feathers that had been used by their ancestors, and how it evolved from there on. The next display was a large glass case filled with antique dolls, all beautifully dressed in the clothes of Fleur's time.

"Emmett, do you see that doll with the cream-colored dress?" she whispered in his ear, feeling warmth rising up her neck. "That's Annabelle. She's mine. And that one there, with the straw hat and red painted lips? That's Desiree. She belonged to my sister, Violette." Still with his arm around her shoulders, Emmett moved in closer.

"I haven't seen Annabelle in years," she reflected. "My mother must have put her away in a safe place, because her clothes and hair are still pristine."

"It says these dolls are donated by Caroline Rothchild, one of Alex Keizer's direct descendants," Emmett said, reading the small sign.

"One of Alex Keizer's descendants?" Fleur said, the idea of meeting a relative stirring her imagination. "Do you think it would be possible to meet her?"

Emmett's arm fell from her shoulders. "We have to look into that."

His cool response tempered her enthusiasm. "I'm sure we

could trust her to keep quiet," she said, pressing the matter.

"Of course," he replied, turning his attention to the next exhibit.

If there's one descendant, there might be more, Fleur decided, her mind made up to talk to Cassius about it. Deep in thought, she trailed behind Emmett, the next two exhibits going by in a blur. At the end of the room, they joined a large group of visitors admiring *Lost in the Storm*.

Subtle lighting brought out every detail, the flash of lighting above the desolate landscape, bright and angry. The long white dresses and hair of the slender young woman and small girl, drenched, the light reflecting in each raindrop.

Oh, Mother, why didn't I listen to you? Fleur cried out quietly, a deep regret laying like pain against her heart. *Why was I so unwilling to believe you about so much?* Clutching her elbows, she stood there for several minutes, mesmerized, until a grim determination filled her. *I'll come back to you and apologize,* she vowed. *I promise.*

Biting back tears, she turned away from the haunting scene and headed toward the door.

Emmett had stayed quiet while she'd struggled not to break down and followed her. "I'm sure this must be difficult for you," he said in the hallway.

She nodded. "It's like coming home to an empty house, when you couldn't wait to see your family."

"I'm sure it's even more difficult than that." His smile was full of compassion and understanding. "But I'll be here for you, if you allow me, and I'll try to help you through all this."

Grateful for his kind words, she let him guide her through

her father's former workshop, the stately dining room, and the kitchen that now served as restrooms. What used to be a storage room had been transformed into an elevator, and they'd emptied the library and drawing room of furniture, displaying more of her father's paintings. Most of them she'd never seen before.

With her emotions in a tangled mess, they headed up the stairs to the second floor where she braced herself for another surprise, shock, or disappointment. So much had changed inside and out, and she didn't understand why she subjected herself to this mental torment.

"All of the paintings in the museum have been restored and are under constant surveillance by cameras," Emmett said, acting as her tour guide while they walked through several of her family's former bedrooms. They were filled with more paintings. Other visitors surrounded them wherever they went, admiring her father's work and commenting on each brushstroke, display of light, or minor detail. It was eye-opening. The beauty of the paintings and her father's talent only becoming apparent to her today, among strangers. *I'll have to apologize to my father too,* she admitted to herself. She hadn't appreciated his work as she should have and only saw it as a frivolous hobby, like everyone else around her had. It almost made her wonder if this trip to the future was meant to happen, forcing her to reflect on her own failures, misgivings, and disrespect for her parents. The idea of being here solely to learn one of life's lessons was another blow to her already tenuous self-esteem and added to her misery.

Emmett's voice interrupted her dark thoughts. "Did you know your mother left letters hidden inside *Lost in the Storm*?"

"Letters?" she squeaked, swallowing hard. "For whom?"

He shook his head. "I've never read them."

For the second time, he avoided a straight answer. His evasiveness grated on her frazzled state of mind. "Why do you have so much knowledge about the museum?"

Her question sounded like an accusation, and she read shocked surprise in his hazel eyes. Then he pulled on his bottom lip, thinking over how to respond.

She suppressed the desire to cross her arms and pressure him for answers with a penetrating gaze, like her private tutor used to do. Instead, she asked softly. "What are you hiding from me?"

Emmett's shoulders dropped, as if he was giving up. "From my neighbor. He has worked here for the last twenty-four years and became the director for collections and exhibitions after Dan Mockenburg retired."

The information meant nothing to her, and she headed further down the hallway until they reached her bedroom. Emmett placed his hand on her arm. "Do you think you'll be okay going in there?"

She knew she wouldn't be but nodded. "I'll be fine."

There were several other visitors inside, talking amongst each other. She didn't even notice them, her eyes focused on the four life-size paintings along the wall where her bed used to be. She'd never seen any of them before and placed both hands in front her mouth to keep from breaking down, her bottom lip quivering and her throat closing up.

"Emmett," she mumbled and reached for him. Protectively, he wrapped his arm around her trembling body as she took in every detail of the paintings of herself, in her yellow dress.

"They're haunting and disturbingly beautiful," a visitor next to her commented.

Her father had painted her from memory. Two of them in front of Keizer Manor. The other two of her running through the dunes, her dress caught by briars and her hair soaked, with ominous green and brown clouds in the sky, lightning all around her, and waves of purples and pinks floating on the horizon. He had painted her exactly as she'd felt, the terrified expression on her own face piercing her heart. Struggling to breathe and gasping for air, she pressed her hands against her chest and felt the rapid, fluttering beat of her troubled heart.

Emmett moved in a little closer. "Come, let's go."

With his arm around her waist, he supported her down the stairs and into the entry hall. "Maybe you should sit down a few minutes," he said with deep concern. "You're so pale. I'm afraid you could pass out."

She almost fell into the hard plastic chair he'd led her to, an all-compassing exhaustion taking hold of every part of her being. Her breathing was shallow and fast, and the pressure in her swollen ankles and knees worse than ever before.

Emmett sat down next to her. "I'm sorry if it's been too much. I should have realized."

She gave him a faint smile, massaging her painful knees. "It's not your fault."

They sat quietly for several minutes until she gradually regained some of her strength. "Here's your hat back," she said, her long blonde curls cascading down her back. "I don't think I need to wear it anymore."

He put the hat inside his pocket. "They sell drinks, pastries, and other snacks in the giftshop. Can I get you anything?"

"Water would be nice," she replied, embarrassed he'd witnessed her mental breakdown and seen her weakness. She felt irritable. *Why couldn't she be like everybody else? With endless energy, a steady heartbeat, and strong muscles?* At twenty-three, she hadn't asked for a body that fought against itself, with arms and legs twitching uncontrollably, a debilitating fatigue, and pain in her chest making it difficult to think, the struggle to stay alert crumbling her entire being.

Emmett appeared, carrying a bottle of water and two cups of coffee. "I thought some caffeine might perk you up a little." He handed her a cup. "I also bought two chocolate croissants. They're my favorite."

Quietly, they sat next to each other, sipping their drinks, and enjoying the sweet pastry, until an animated group of visitors returned from their tour through the museum. Most of them disappeared into the giftshop, except the elderly lady with a walker.

"Is it okay if I sit next to you for a few minutes?" she asked. "I can't keep up with the younger generation anymore."

"Of course," Fleur replied, making a bit more room so she could sit next to her. "Did you enjoy your visit to the museum?"

The lady chuckled, struggling with her walker until it stood just right. "I live close by in Dunedam and have been here many times through the years. How about you, dear? Is this your first visit?"

The question took her off guard. "Maybe.... Probably," she stammered.

Her answer drew another smile. "I understand how it feels."

The kind woman extended her hand. "My name is Andrea Overton, and I'm here with my daughter's family. They're celebrating their twentieth wedding anniversary this weekend. Mind you, she got married at twenty-one, had her first child at twenty-two, and her second one only a year later. Sometimes these children move so fast."

"Andrea is my middle name," Fleur replied, nodding as if she understood what the woman was talking about. "It's wonderful to meet you."

"Are you okay, Grandma?" a girl asked, joining them.

"I'm fine, honey," Mrs. Overton replied. "Just visiting with this kind young lady here."

The girl peered at Fleur and then at Emmett. "Hey, Emmett," she said. "What are you doing here?"

Another girl with long brown hair accompanied by two boys about her age walked out of the giftshop, laughing, and joking, and headed in their direction.

"These are my grandchildren," Mrs. Overton said with pride.

Emmett took Fleur's arm, almost pulling her out of her chair. "We have to go."

Flabbergasted, Fleur looked into his panicked eyes. "Why? I don't understand."

Instead of answering, he pushed her towards the exit.

"Hey, Emmett?" the girl with the long brown hair yelled behind them. "You're coming to the party this afternoon?"

The next moment, they were outside.

"Thank you for taking me, Emmett," Fleur said after he

dropped her off at Cassius's house.

On the short way home, her arms clinging around his waist, she'd thought about the girls at Keizer Manor. They seemed to know him well, and she wondered why he refused to explain who they were. "Are you going to that party this afternoon?" she asked, struggling with the chin strap on her helmet.

He reached out to help. "Probably not."

Because of his full-face helmet, she could only see his eyes and had no idea what he was thinking.

He gave her an awkward half-hug. "Can I call you tomorrow?"

She didn't understand what that meant but was too tired to ask more questions. "Of course."

The front door opened, and Cassius stepped out with a deep frown on his forehead. "Where have you two been?" he asked brusquely, clearly distraught. "I was worried."

Emmett climbed back on his motorcycle. "I took her to the Keizer Museum. Sorry, Mr. Rewick."

The lines in Cassius's face deepened. Shaking his head, he turned around and headed back inside.

Fleur hurried after him. "I asked him to take me there, but don't worry. I wore a hat and didn't speak to anyone."

Although she knew that wasn't completely true, she found her brief conversation with the elderly lady too insignificant to mention.

He glanced at her drawn face, his expression one of deep concern over her well-being. "You don't look good, Fleur. Was it too much for you?"

It was hard to think with her brain in a fog, and silent tears rolled down her cheeks.

Cassius took a step forward and pulled her in a comforting hug. "I'm so sorry I did this to you, but promise it'll be all right," he whispered, his hand rhythmically stroking a calming hand up and down her back to soothe her the way a parent would. "Please, let me know what I can do to make your stay tolerable."

Grateful for his support, she leaned against him, seeking refuge against the deluge of her troubled emotions in his caring presence and compassionate words. "I'm so tired and miss my parents and home."

Shortly after, he released her from his grip and offered her his handkerchief, his kind, brown eyes reflecting understanding. "Let's get you to your room so you can get some rest."

Several hours later, she woke up to the smell of food.

"I had pizza delivered," Cassius explained, opening the big square box on the table. "I didn't know what you like, so I ordered half pepperoni and half Hawaiian."

Recognizing he had waited for her to wake up, making sure she was okay, and that he had ordered food touched her deeply. Cassius Rewick was a good man, and although he was to blame for the difficult situation she was in, she couldn't be mad at him. He hadn't done it on purpose and on every occasion possible he'd apologized, his kindness and concern for her welfare and safety genuine. "I'll be happy to try both flavors," she said. "Thank you so much for being thoughtful."

The rest of the evening, she sat behind the computer, awkwardly pressing keys as she learned how to use the machine to access historical information she could share once she returned home. "Rosa Parks was a Black activist in the civil rights movement. Did you know that?" she asked Cassius.

Cassius was lounging in his recliner, reading a book. "Absolutely," he replied from behind his reading glasses. "So were Harriet Tubman, Frederick Douglass, and Martin Luther King Jr., to name a few."

She'd heard secret whispers about Harriet Tubman. "Were they all former slaves?"

He put his book down. "The earlier activists were enslaved people – what we call them now– but since then, many more Black people have become influential leaders. Take for example Oprah Winfrey or Barack Obama, our first Black president. But what brings on your interest in my people's history?"

Fleur swiveled her chair away from the computer. "My parents are part of the underground railroad and help enslaved people flee to Canada. What they do is illegal." Only thinking about it made her heart thud in alarm. "By law, citizens are compelled to assist in the capture of runaways, and they risk imprisonment and hefty fines for doing otherwise. Once home, I can assure them they won't have to put themselves in danger much longer." Then she remembered, her mother already knew.

"Your parents did the right thing," Cassius said. "You can be proud of them."

Fleur gazed at her hands, her fingers cold. Yes, she was proud of her parents, but the idea of them in prison scared her to death.

Chapter 11

Forrest

With a large carrot cake, a bowl of potato salad, and two bouquets of fresh-cut flowers in the trunk, Forrest, Kara, and their youngest daughter, Caro, drove to his parents' house. Against all odds of lasting this long, his sister, Jackie, and her husband, Geoff, were celebrating their twentieth wedding anniversary today, and Forest and his family had to be there at two to get everything ready for the surprise party. Their neighbors, Rix and Skye Castella, and their youngest son, Finn, followed in their own car.

They parked along the street and carried everything inside the house. No matter how old Forrest got, it felt like coming home. "Mom, Dad," he yelled. "We're here."

Instead of his parents, one of his sister's closest friends appeared, with her husband in tow. "Your parents joined the rest of the family on the outing to Dunedam and the Keizer Museum," she explained, drying her hands on a towel.

Even though Forrest had worked there for so many years, his

parents had never shown much interest in visiting the museum since that horrible day Annet disappeared. "They did?"

"Well, they pressured your father to chauffeur since he has that big SUV that seats eight. And your mother joined them because Geoff's mother came along too and asked her."

That explains it, Forrest thought.

The doorbell rang and several more friends walked in, bringing with them a salad, a tray of sandwiches, and bottles of wine. Not much later, he heard his father's SUV pull in, followed by the slamming of doors and a multitude of voices.

"Oh, my word! What are you all doing here?" his sister, Jackie, cried out, entering the house.

"Happy anniversary, Jackie and Geoff!" they all cheered.

Surrounded by the people he loved and cared about, Forrest laughed and joked, and ate and drank too much. The only person missing was Emmett.

"I haven't seen Emmett," he said to Rix. "Is he busy at work?"

Rix took a gulp of beer and wiped his mouth. "That boy is always rushing off. He's often on a motorcycle ride with his friends John and Titus, studying, or working overtime. But most of the time I have no clue where he is." Rix grinned. "He's almost twenty-four and you understand how it goes when they grow up."

Forrest knew everything about it. His oldest daughter Josie was always gone too, and it worried him all the time.

"I believe we saw him at the museum this morning," his mother said, joining the conversation. "But he seemed in a hurry to leave."

"You're talking about Emmett?" Josie laughed, her voice

loud. "I know why he was in a hurry. He hasn't dated anyone since he broke up with Erika several months ago and must have met a new girl. I don't think he wanted anyone to see him."

"My brother dating another girl?" Finn asked, immediately interested. "Anyone we know?"

"She looked familiar, but I couldn't place her," Josie replied, holding up her empty glass. "Hey, Finn, can you pour me another glass of wine?"

The next day, Forrest headed to the coach house.

"Hi Skye," he said when she opened the door.

She stepped aside to let him enter. "That was a fun party yesterday afternoon. Did you by chance bring my wooden cutting board? I forgot all about it."

Forrest shook his head. "I don't know anything about it, but maybe Kara does."

He entered the living room and found Rix and Emmett on the couch, watching the basketball playoffs.

"Who's winning?" he asked, sinking down in a recliner.

"The Golden State Warriors," they replied in unison.

With his mind elsewhere, Forrest watched the game, absentmindedly drinking his beer and eating popcorn.

Emmett and Rix high fived when the Warriors won by a narrow margin.

"Hey, I heard you were at Keizer Manor yesterday?" Forrest commented after they celebrated. "Why didn't you ask me for free tickets?"

"I didn't think about it," he replied.

"Yeah, I hear you've been busy lately. Any new developments

at work?"

Emmett dropped his shoulder, releasing a deep sigh. "Please, can't you let it go for once?" Flashing an annoyed scowl, he turned away. "Mom, did you do laundry? I'm out of clean socks."

"No, I didn't," Skye replied.

"All right, then I'll start the machine," Emmett said and rushed out the door.

Emmett's abrupt behavior didn't go unnoticed. "I'm sorry," Rix said. "He's under a lot of stress lately."

Ever since Emmett had started his internship at the Abernathey Research Center, Forrest's interest in the research had increased, almost to the point that Kara called it unhealthy and obsessive. "Is this work related, you think?" he asked Rix.

Rix leaned forward and placed an elbow on each knee, his hands dangling between his thighs. "Look, Forrest. You know Emmett can't talk about anything that goes on in the belly of the beast and your constant pestering is pissing him off." He straightened his shoulders and looked him straight in the eyes. "As a matter of fact, if I'm honest, it's bothering me, too."

"Damn," Forrest whispered, recognizing all too well his friend was right to call him out. He shot to his feet. "I'm sorry. From now on, I'll leave it alone."

Rix walked him out. "I wish they'd never gotten that grant to rekindle their research," he said. "It's taken a toll on Emmett and this last week, he's been locking himself up in his bedroom as soon as he comes home and doesn't want to eat. He behaves like a lovesick teenager, or someone who's on the verge of a burnout."

"Fleur," Forrest mumbled, thrashing around in bed. "Where are you?"

In the throes of his lingering nightmare, he woke up in a sweat.

Kara turned around to look at him, the room still dark. She reached out to him, feeling the dampness of his skin. "Was that a nightmare?"

He covered his eyes with his arm, waiting for his head to clear. Then he reached out to Kara's hand and put it on his chest. "I dreamed Fleur was here, but even though I tried to find her, she was beyond my reach."

Kara snuggled closer against him. "Now that you've come to realize your preoccupation is starting to interfere with your friendship with the Castella's, maybe it's time to let it go."

There were no secrets between them, and when he'd come home, he'd immediately told her about his confrontation with Rix.

"I guess you're right," he sighed and puffed up his pillow before he tried to fall back asleep. The minutes on the clock ticked away as he tossed and turned between the wrinkled sheets, trying to remember the details of his dream. The loud beeping of the alarm startled him. Without realizing it, he'd fallen back asleep.

Groggy, he forced himself out of bed and into the shower. By the time he reappeared, Kara had opened the curtains, her gorgeous body stirring his desire. Instead of giving in to his longing, he slipped on his underwear and got dressed.

At the bottom of the stairs, he ran into one of their tenants. "Good morning, James," he said. "Enjoy your Monday."

"Same to you, Forrest," James replied on his way out.

Just like Caroline Rothchild had before them, they relied heavily on rental income to maintain the estate and pay the taxes. Over the years, they had remodeled extensively and built four separate apartments on the second floor, each one with its own kitchen and bathroom. Rix had done most of the work, his skills as a handyman invaluable.

An hour later, Forrest drove to work, turning everything over in his mind as he had done since waking up from his nightmare. Was it time to let Fleur go, like Kara suggested? Should he stop hoping that one day she'd appear? At the thought, a shiver ran through him. Through the years he'd seen his daughters grow up. In his mind, Fleur had been there too, seeing her mature along with them, as an older sister. Would he be able to let go of that vision? Then he recalled Annet's desperate letters and knew with one hundred percent certainty she never gave up, never stopped searching, and never stopped hoping. And he knew he wouldn't either.

He pulled into the empty parking lot of Keizer Manor. At this early hour, only the two security guards were there. He unlocked the side door of the Manor, walked into his office, and sat down, a stack of mail on his desk. Mondays were always packed with catching up after a busy weekend. A sticky note on the screen of his computer told him one of the security cameras on the second floor had failed and needed to be checked out. A phone message told him several people had inquired about the job opening for janitor, and another that he needed to put a call in to the mayor's office about the upcoming trade event.

Several hours into the morning, he noticed the beginning of

a headache and rubbed his temples to stave it off. When it didn't help, he got up and headed to the meeting room where they usually had a pot of fresh coffee.

"It was fun to meet your family here last Saturday," his secretary remarked when he walked by her desk. "Your parents looked wonderful and so did Josie. She has grown so much, I barely recognized her." He'd left entry tickets for his family and their relatives at her desk, his assistant welcoming them as special guests.

"Thank you for making them feel welcome and special," he said. "I appreciate it."

"It was the least I could do," she laughed.

With a steaming cup of coffee, Forrest returned to his desk, the sudden need to watch last Saturday's security footage too strong to resist.

He entered his login to access the security system, not sure what he hoped to see. From the home screen, he scrolled to history and opened the folder from Saturday. Each camera had a name, and he clicked on the footage from the camera pointed at the entrance, scrolling down to eleven o'clock, the time he assumed his family had arrived. With his elbows on his desk, his chin resting in his palms, he watched the stream of visitors enter through the door, either making their way to the ticket counter or heading straight to the security guard with their prepaid tickets. Ten minutes into it, he discovered Emmett, his unruly dark curls easy to recognize. Next to him, he noticed a young woman with long blonde hair cascading down her back. She was dressed in blue jeans, a simple brown top with two white buttons, and a light jacket. He noticed they whispered into each other's ear, both glancing back and forth. Next, he saw Emmett pull a baseball cap from his pocket and hand it to her. The young woman gathered her hair before she put it on. A few seconds later, they walked out of the camera's view. He watched for five more minutes until his family arrived and then they too disappeared out of view.

Usually, it took visitors less than two hours to see each room in the museum and he fast forwarded ninety minutes. Shortly after, Emmett came back into view, his arm wrapped around the young woman's waist, supporting her. He helped her sit down in one of the empty seats. She seemed distraught, massaging her knees as if they were in pain. At 12.45, she took the baseball cap off and handed it back to Emmett, who, shortly after, got up and returned with two cups in his hand. Glued to the screen, Forrest watched them eat and drink until his mother appeared and took a seat right next to them. He took a deep, shaking breath, wishing he could zoom in, the camera too far away to distinguish their features.

The door to his office opened and his assistant came in. "I assume you want today's mail," she said, walking toward his desk. She opened one of the letters and spread it out in front of him. "You may want to read this first. It's a certified letter from the IMLS about the grant we submitted." She took a step back and studied his computer screen. "Hey, I didn't know Caroline came to the museum, too. Why didn't you leave me a ticket for her?"

"Caro didn't need a ticket, because she stayed home and helped set up the party," he replied, taking an even closer look. "So that can't be her."

Then it hit him why he'd obsessively watched the footage, his brain overnight combining tidbits of information. She looked so familiar, Josie had said. And his mother's words, that her middle name was Andrea, like hers. And Emmett, begging him to stop questioning him, the boy clearly distressed.

"What the heck," he mumbled, studying the pixeled image of the girl from mere inches away. Was he going out of his mind, and imagining things only because he wanted them to be true?

Chapter 12

Fleur

STILL TIRED FROM THE PREVIOUS DAY, Fleur rested on the couch. Cassius had stayed home the entire morning and Emmett had called, asking how she felt. She hadn't been in the mood to see anyone and waved him off when he asked if she wanted him to come over. But when Cassius went back to work in the afternoon and Emmet met up with friends instead of coming to see her, she felt lonely and regretted her decision.

She wandered through the house, but her ankles and knees felt weak and sore, and her breathing was shallow. On edge, she sat back on the couch, and folded her hands, murmuring a prayer for help from up above, the discontent in her tormented and troubled heart too much to bear. "Please, Lord, give me patience and strength, and guide me through this arduous challenge."

When she woke up from her slumber, she picked up one of the magazines Lucia had given her to read. It was filled with articles about fashion, beauty, exercise programs, and ways to lose weight, among advertisements for perfume, lipsticks, shoes, and leggings. She leafed through it, learning that her Zodiac sign was Capricorn and that passionate energy lingered in the air, with people eager to hear her words, helping her to win hearts and minds. Nothing about it could be more wrong, and that thought fueled her loneliness. Cassius had left her his phone in case she wanted to get in touch with him while he worked on SMITS. She picked it up, tempted to call Emmett, the only one who may enjoy hearing from her. Instead of reaching out to him, she curled up underneath the quilt and closed her eyes, unable to fight her debilitating fatigue.

On Monday, Cassius asked her if she wanted to join him in the research center for a meeting. With another long and lonely day stretching out in front of her, she gladly followed him to work.

"With SMITS back up and running and all the readouts promising, we can perform the first array of tests," Cassius explained along the way.

In the meeting room, they joined Commander Thornton, Adam, Ramon, Emmett, and several other employees, including Darlene, who took notes.

After welcoming everyone, Milton started the meeting. "Under normal circumstances, we would never unleash the forces of the machine on a human being without months of extensive testing on objects and possibly animals, until all questions are answered, and success is guaranteed. Right now, we're only grasping in the dark and in order to safeguard Fleur's speedy return, we need to mimic the exact same circumstances under which she arrived. Cassius and I discussed testing items that weigh approximately the same as Fleur. Those objects need to be placed roughly eighty feet from the back door, close to the fence. That's the spot where she appeared."

He moved some papers around. "Concern has been raised about Fleur's health. We can't unleash forces on her body she might not be able to withstand. Therefore, the DOD won't consider sending her back until she's undergone a complete physical examination and is medically cleared by a physician."

They were talking as if she wasn't there. Annoyed, she interrupted him. "I'm seeing the doctor this afternoon."

Despite her frustration, her voice was soft and shaky, and Cassius nodded in agreement. "That's correct. I'm taking her in around one."

Fleur met Emmett's concerned eyes from across the table. "Why didn't you tell me?" he mouthed.

"There's nothing to worry about," she replied.

"Let's continue," Milton said. "Cassius, what did you find out?"

Cassius opened the folder in front of him. "A male chimpanzee weighs about 110 lbs. So does an adult north-pacific giant octopus, an Anatolian shepherd dog, and several other breeds of dogs. None of those animals will survive in the dunes, and I would like to suggest using goats. They eat just about anything, including blackberry bushes, and will probably survive anywhere. We could have them here by tomorrow."

"Good work," Milton replied. "That means that a week from now, we could theoretically consider sending Fleur home."

Only one more week, Fleur thought. "That's marvelous. Thank you, sir."

A knock on the door interrupted the meeting. One of the guards walked in. "Mr. Rewick, Sir. There's a man at the gate insisting to see you."

"What's his name?"

"Forrest Overton, Sir. What do you want me to tell him?"

Cassius glared at Emmett, the atmosphere in the room suddenly filled with tension.

"Tell him I'm in an important meeting and ask for his phone number, so I can call him later today."

The guard straightened his back. "Yes, sir!"

After the door closed behind him, Milton slapped his hand on the table. "What's that man doing here?" he thundered. "I thought we'd gotten rid of his constant inquiries and interference years ago."

"I'll find out," Cassius replied. "But don't jump to conclusions. It's probably a coincidence."

Milton scoffed. "You know what they say. In life, nothing is a coincidence." He looked around the table with a stern expression on his face. "This meeting is closed."

Chairs scraped against the tiled floor, and everybody rushed out the door.

Fleur placed her hand on Cassius's arm. "Is that man a threat?"

Cassius's Adam's apple bobbed three times, as if he was trying to compose himself. Then he glanced at her with unease.

"I pray to God he's not."

Chapter 13

"DID YOU HAVE A GOOD NAP?" Cassius asked, helping Fleur into the passenger seat of his car and showing her how to buckle the seatbelt.

After the morning's meeting, she'd rested on the couch until Emmett joined her for lunch, bringing a muffin with sausage and eggs. She'd questioned him about the man who'd interrupted the meeting. He'd only shrugged. "I don't know anything about that."

His response had tempted her to call him a liar, but she let it go. It wasn't worth it to fight over. Next week, she would be gone and would never see him again.

"Not really," she replied to Cassius, the soft leather seat of his two-door Tesla super comfortable, the smell inside strong but not unpleasant. "I don't like doctors, so I'm a bit nervous."

Throughout her teenage years, she'd gone to many doctors in the hope they could help with what was ailing her. Not even one had an answer, solution, or medication. It wouldn't be different now.

He started the engine and pulled out of the parking lot. "Don't be, Fleur. It's just a routine physical evaluation. It'll be fine."

Glued to the window, she watched the landscape fly by, the electric car floating silently over the pavement. "It's busy. Look at all the automobiles and houses," she commented. The changes over the last two centuries were hard to take in.

"The invention of the car has transformed the way people live," Cassius explained, giving her an encouraging smile. "All I can recommend is to let it wash over you, like a dream. Do you think you can do that?"

Having to comprehend everything that changed since her time in only a week would be too much for anyone, and she knew what he meant. "I'll try."

As they approached Heemstead, it got busier and busier. Despite her efforts to stay relaxed, the ocean of cars, traffic lights, motorcycles, bicycle riders, and buildings had overpowered her senses. When they arrived at the hospital and Cassius opened her door, she felt like hiding and covering her ears, afraid to leave the comforting safety of the car.

"Nobody's out to hurt you, and everything will be fine," he assured her, offering his hand to help her step out.

The hospital seemed to be made of dark glass and towered over them. She felt dizzy looking up. As they neared the entrance, the glass doors automatically opened, like magic, and she slowed her pace.

"You don't have to be scared, Fleur," Cassius reassured her. "The doors have motion-detecting sensors that activate a motor. A lot of things work automatically now. It's what we call technology."

Technology brought her here, she thought. She didn't like, trust, or appreciate it.

Cassius opened the folder he carried under his arm and studied a piece of paper inside. "We have to be on the second floor. Let's take the stairs instead of the elevators."

The entrance hall, with tall windows and vibrant colors, was bright and inviting, the stairwell to the second floor wide and open. Several women worked behind a reception desk in a large waiting area. One of them nodded in their direction when they approached. "Good afternoon. Do you have an appointment?"

"We're here to see Dr. Lara Tubbing."

She started typing. "Are you Fleur Keizer?"

Cassius pulled several printed sheets from his folder and handed them to her. "Yes, this is Fleur, and these are her insurance papers."

The nurse took the papers and handed Fleur a clipboard. "While you wait, could you please fill out this questionnaire?"

They sat down in the corner of the waiting room, the first question on the paperwork asking for her name, address, and date of birth. "I couldn't possibly tell them I'm born in 1841," Fleur said, fighting the heavy fatigue that crept in.

Cassius took the clipboard from her. "You don't have to worry about this. Dr. Tubbing is aware of the unusual situation, and she'll take care of this."

A few minutes later, a door opened, and a man dressed in a loose-fitting blue outfit called her name. They followed him into an examination room. "I see you're here for a complete wellness exam. Could you step on the scale, please?" Next, he asked her to sit down on a tall bed covered with paper. "Let's take your blood pressure." He placed a cuff around her upper arm and pumped it up. "One hundred twenty-nine over eighty-six," he said when he was done. "Have you had trouble with high blood pressure before?"

Fleur shrugged with dazed puzzlement. "I don't know what that means."

His eyes reflected understanding. "You must be nervous." He took the clipboard from Cassius, and when he noticed the empty pages, he raised his eyebrows but said nothing. "While I get Dr. Tubbing, could you please undress." He handed Fleur a gown before closing the door behind him.

"I'll give you some privacy," Cassius said and followed him out.

"You can't leave me," Fleur cried out after him, her eyes huge in her pale face.

"Don't worry. I'll guard your room and won't let anyone else in besides the doctor."

Left alone, she let her head hang forward, her energy depleted, her brain muddled. What if they figured out something was seriously wrong with her, and they wouldn't allow her to go home?

Someone knocked and a woman in a white coat entered, her long dark hair tied in a ponytail, her black shoes similar to the ugly clogs she wore herself. The doctor eyed her curiously. "Nice to meet you, Fleur. I'm Dr. Tubbing and would like to examine you if that's okay."

Fleur had seen many doctors but never one that was female. "Are you an actual doctor?"

"I am," Dr. Tubbing smiled, and placed a white device on the tip of Fleur's index finger. "I understand you've been through a lot and that there's concern about your health. Can you tell me about that?"

People always expected her to be strong. Used to lying, instead of admitting how broken she felt, Fleur straightened her back. "I'm often tired, but it's been like that for years, and I'm not worried about it." Her voice sounded strangled, and she shivered.

The doctor removed the device from her finger. "I see that see the oxygen level in your blood is far below it should be. Your blood pressure is elevated, and you're underweight. Do you eat properly? Are you in any pain?"

She'd eaten all kinds of new food since she was here. Most of it seemed healthy, and the doctor wouldn't be interested to hear about the discomfort from the occasional swelling in her joints. "I'm used to eating healthy and I'm not in pain," she said.

The doctor removed the device hanging around her neck. "With this stethoscope, I can listen to your heart," she explained.

She placed the round end above Fleur's left breast, telling her to breathe slowly. From there, she moved the device to her back. Next, she examined her nose and mouth, checked her eyes, and touched her neck with her cool fingers.

"Fleur," she said at the end of her exam. "Your irregular and chaotic heartbeat is very concerning and severe enough to alert a cardiologist. Let me see if there's one available. In the meantime, a nurse will draw your blood and take you to radiology for an x-ray."

After she left, Cassius came back in. "How are you doing, Fleur?" he asked.

Confused and afraid, she gazed at him. "The doctor is concerned about my heart and wants to take me to another room. I don't understand."

"Don't worry," Cassius said. "An x-ray doesn't hurt. All they do is make you lie on a metal table while a machine takes pictures of the inside of your body. And if you're scared when they draw your blood, you can look the other way."

Shortly after Fleur had come back, a polite knock on the door announced the arrival of Dr. Stevenson, a balding man with a ring of gray hair, his coat sparkling white.

"I'm a cardiologist, Miss Keizer," he introduced himself, his examination almost the same as Dr. Tubbing's. "Are your feet and ankles often this swollen?" He pressed his fingertips into her skin, leaving indentations.

"Are they swollen?" she asked, wondering what her feet had to do with her heart.

Dr. Stevenson typed on the keyboard of a workstation they had wheeled in. "Based on your heart arrhythmias and other symptoms, we believe you have a heart defect or suffer from heart disease. How long have you experienced heart palpitations, Fleur?"

Fleur shriveled within herself, her fingers cold as ice. "There's nothing wrong with my heart. I'm healthy and fully capable to travel." She swallowed her tears and bit her lip to stop it from trembling, hanging onto the lie she so desperately wanted him to believe.

"I see." The doctor's sharp, yet compassionate eyes looked down at her. "Maybe you have a family member who died of a heart attack, stroke, or other heart problems?"

When she didn't answer, he turned to Cassius. "I assume you are her stepfather or guardian?"

"I'm her guardian," Cassius replied, recognizing that the doctor wasn't aware of Fleur's unique and classified situation.

"I'm very concerned and want to set up appointments for an MRI, chest x-rays, and an electro and echocardiogram. We also need full blood work and a urinalysis."

Chapter 14

Forrest and Cassius

"MY NAME IS FORREST OVERTON. I'm here to see Cassius Rewick."

The security guard checked Forrest's identification and waved him through, the tall metal gates closing behind him. He parked his car in front of the building and stepped out.

"Mr. Rewick is waiting for you in his office," the purple-haired secretary greeted him politely. "Please, follow me."

"That's not necessary. I remember where it is," he replied, recalling the last time he'd been in this building. It had been with Detective Jaeger, right before the officer retired. The door to Rewick's office stood open and he entered.

Cassius Rewick sat behind his desk and Milton Thornton stood at the window.

"Mr. Overton," Cassius said, waving at the chair in front of his desk. "Please, take a seat."

Forrest sat down, barely recognizing the unhealthy-looking man with sad brown eyes and worry lines etched deep in his face.

His gray suit jacket hung loosely around his stooped shoulders. The years hadn't been kind to him.

"Coffee, tea, anything else?" Cassius asked.

Forrest forced the nervous lump in his throat down. "Water would be nice."

"Milton, you want anything?"

"I'm good," Milton replied, his voice stiff and impatient.

Cassius pressed a button on his phone, his hand shaking. "Darlene, could you bring two bottles of water?"

A few seconds later, Darlene walked in with the requested water and closed the door behind her.

To compose himself, Forrest took a welcome swig of the ice-cold liquid. Although he had convinced himself he'd seen his daughter on the security footage, doubts assailed him from the moment he entered through the gates, the entire property breathing government, military, and secrecy. His fingers nervously drummed the arm of his chair. They would consider him a lunatic, when he unfoundedly accused them of transporting Fleur into the future. He crossed and uncrossed his legs. He hadn't even told Kara about his suspicions. *What was he doing here?*

Cassius shifted in his chair. His head pounded and stomach acid burned its way into his esophagus. He hadn't been able to eat since Forrest had come unannounced the day before, the disturbing news about Fleur's health adding to his distress. He took a deep, long breath. Guilt and remorse drained him, robbing him of sleep and his ability to work and concentrate. Nothing productive had come out of his hands since Fleur's arrival and he felt like a failure. The only accomplishment of his career had been ruining Forrest Overton's and the Keizer family's lives. With tired, worn-out eyes, he leaned back in his chair, readying himself for what was to come.

"Thanks for seeing me," Forrest said, wondering if Cassius was sick. Parkinsons maybe, or something worse? He waited while Cassius adjusted his tie, shifted in his chair for the third time, and leaned back with an anxious expression on his face. It seemed they were both nervous. That feeling strengthened his resolve.

"As I explained over the phone, I'm here to talk about my missing daughter," he said. His gaze shifted between Cassius and Milton. The commander stood with straight shoulders and his hands folded behind his back, observing him with his sharp gray eyes. It added to his discomfort.

Cassius picked up a folder on his desk, glanced at it, and threw it back down. "Yes, of course, and thank you for coming in to see me."

Forrest frowned at the odd remark. He was the one who had requested the meeting and who should be thankful.

"Look, this conversation is very difficult for me," Cassius continued, a sheen of sweat on his brow. He folded his hands in front of him, evading eye contact.

Something was definitely wrong with the man, Forrest decided, and raised an impatient eyebrow.

"As you know, the Abernathey Research Center has always denied involvement in the disappearance of Annet Sherman. There was no evidence or reason to believe our research could have been the cause."

Until Fleur had appeared out of nowhere, Cassius had

trusted the theory that there hadn't been a connection between Abernathey and Annet's disappearance, hanging on to the belief that SMITS couldn't possibly transport people through time travel. But instead of sounding sincere, he realized he appeared defensive, the guilt ripping his insides apart. His eyes roamed around the office until he met Forrest's penetrating gaze.

"Mr. Overton, what I'm going to tell you is highly confidential and when word gets out, the consequences for anyone involved could be severe."

To hide the turmoil he felt inside, Forrest laughed without mirth. He wasn't here to solve riddles or promise secrecy. Whatever was going on, he wanted the truth. "Stop beating around the bush," he said, his resentment for the man and his damn research strengthening.

Cassius realized Forrest had changed since he'd seen him last. He exuded confidence in his charcoal suit and looked distinguished. The fact that his blond hair and blue eyes had the exact same color as Fleur's didn't go unnoticed either.

Why didn't the man speak up? Forrest grumbled inside, ready to pull Cassius over his desk, demanding answers. "After all these years, are you admitting you're responsible for Annet's disappearance?" he said, raising his voice.

Cassius rubbed his chin. It had become clear Fleur had heart problems, and although she pretended nothing was wrong, he knew better. It was time to be frank.

When Cassius still didn't respond, Forrest got up from his chair and placed his hands on Cassius's desk. "I demand to know!"

At his loud voice, Milton Thornton turned away from the

window and walked up to him. "Please, calm down, Mr. Overton," he said, stretching his arms in front of him, making a calming gesture with his hands.

Forrest turned around to face him. "If it turns out you're involved, I'll sue both your asses for destroying my life," he yelled, pointing with his finger in the direction of each man. "Any lawyer will be eager to take the case."

"We didn't know," Milton replied.

"Yes, you did. Only you tried to cover it up." He was so angry he could barely think straight. Then he paled. "You're admitting it?"

The three men looked from one to the other.

"It appears so," Milton acknowledged.

All the fight went out of him and, deflated, Forrest sunk down in his chair. "Is Fleur here?"

"Yes, your daughter is here," Milton said, his voice stern, his expression grim.

For the second time, Forrest bolted upright, gasping for breath. "I want to see her."

Cassius pulled out a handkerchief and wiped the sheen of perspiration from his forehead. "No, you can't," he said, then sighed.

Relief, exhilaration, and anger fought for control as Forrest tried to wrap his mind around what he'd just heard. "You can't keep me from seeing my daughter. Where is she? Here on the property?" Wild-eyed, he peered around, ready to start searching.

Milton blocked his exit. "If you want to continue this conversation, you really need to calm down, Mr. Overton," he said, his arms stretched out in front of him, keeping him at a distance. "For your own and your daughter's sake."

Forrest inhaled through his nostrils. They were playing games with him. He reached for his phone, ready to call Geoff. "My brother-in-law is a lawyer. I want him here."

"Please, don't, Mr. Overton," Milton said with a cold stare. "That would be a grave mistake."

Forrest scoffed. "I'm calling him, unless you give me one good reason not to."

Cassius raised himself from behind his desk and leaned forward with a wild look, breathing forcefully. "You can't see her, because Fleur doesn't know you're her father." His voice bounced off the wall and he fell back down in his chair. "Sorry. I didn't mean to raise my voice."

Dumbstruck, Forrest glared at him. "She doesn't? Why the hell not?" And then he knew. Annet had written she'd never told Fleur anything about him, believing it would only create problems for all parties involved. When he'd first read it, he'd been hurt, but then he understood. Fleur would never have been able to meet him, and the knowledge would have only made her doubt who she was and her rightful position within the family.

"Then why did you agree to see me today?" He raked his hair from his forehead, still angry and confused.

"If you sit down, I'll explain," Cassius said, his eyes holding a deep sadness.

Once Forrest had put his phone back in his pocket and calmed down enough to listen, he sat down, as did Milton.

"Eight days ago, Fleur arrived here out of nowhere," Cassius began. "She was confused, afraid, weak, and tired. The first several days, all she did was sleep. We assumed the time travel had caused her exhaustion, and that she needed time to heal. But instead of getting better, her condition seemed to worsen. Yesterday, I took her to Heemstead General for a complete physical examination. Her physician called in a cardiologist, who ordered more tests. The cardiologist, Dr. Stevenson, called me this morning, telling me Fleur is very ill. She suffers from heart disease. Is there anyone in your family who has heart trouble?"

Forrest stared at both men, shock and concern reverberating through him. "Heart disease?" He thought about his parents, now in their mid-eighties, still active and healthy. And about Annet's mother Barbara, who still resided at the White Castle apartment where he'd lived with Annet, wheeling her husband Chuck around since his stroke. He shook his head. "I don't believe anyone in my family was diagnosed with heart disease, and Annet's mother is still alive, but I know little about Annet's grandparents." He stared out the window, letting the troubling news sink in. "What's her prognosis?"

"All they know for certain is that her mitral valve is damaged, resulting in fatigue, shortness of breath, and heart palpitations," Cassius informed him. "They want her to come in for further testing, and we're waiting to hear from their scheduling department. In the meantime, Fleur needs to rest and avoid stress, and that's the other reason you can't see her."

Chapter 15

Forrest

FIFTEEN MINUTES LATER, Forrest walked out of Cassius's office. He glanced around the hall and at Darlene. *Did she know where they kept Fleur?* Tempted to ask, he stopped at the reception desk.

"Have a good day, Mr. Overton," Darlene smiled. The phone rang and she picked it up. "Abernathey Research Center, how may I direct your call?"

Forrest raised his hand in a goodbye and left the building. Overwhelmed by the idea his oldest daughter was so close but still beyond his reach, he peered around. The parking lot was half full and he noticed six armed soldiers who stood between two Humvees. The green military vehicles had two doors and a soft top and looked intimidating. He also noticed a row of small homes along the parking lot, all four the exact same size, the siding off-white. He wondered if they kept Fleur in one of them, and what those soldiers would do if he started snooping around.

Instead of searching for Fleur, he climbed in his car,

clutching the paperwork they'd asked him to fill out about Fleur's family's medical history. He put the wrinkled pages on the passenger seat and stared out in front of him. All he wanted to do was find Fleur, hug her, and assure her everything would be okay. That he would be there for her. The thought that she had landed among strangers and had to process everything that happened on her own was unbearable.

Then he thought about her heart problems and how alone she must have felt, in the car on the way to the hospital through busy traffic, with cars, motorcycles, bicycles, buses, and semi-trucks all around her. In the exam room with doctors prodding her and asking questions she couldn't answer, and having to undergo procedures she couldn't understand. It had to have been awful and nerve-wracking.

They should have contacted him right away, he thought, so he could have been the one to comfort her and help her through it all.

Tears sprung in his eyes. "Annet, my dear," he whispered. "Fleur is here, with us, and I'll do whatever I can to help her."

He started the engine. Milton and Cassius had assured him Fleur was safe and well taken care of, and he had agreed with the need for complete confidentiality. He remembered clearly how difficult it had been to deal with the public after word got out over Annet's letters. Fortunately, interest had died down after several months, and the story was shelved as negative propaganda and false information. But he knew all that curiosity would be rekindled when they found out about Fleur, the news spreading like wildfire with no one able to extinguish it. He slammed his fist against the steering wheel. He understood their need for discretion and secrecy, but he would never agree to stay away from Fleur. Although she didn't realize it, his daughter needed him.

He pulled his phone from his pocket and called his wife. "Kara," he said, batting the tears from his eyes with an angry swipe. "I need to talk to you."

Chapter 16

Fleur

"THIS IS A TACO," Emmett explained several days later opening a white container with four circular pieces of bread, filled with meat and topped with chopped onions, tomatoes and cheese. "It's Mexican food and very popular." He put one taco on her plate. "You have to try it."

Emmett was on a quest to introduce her to lots of different cuisines.

"Food all the way from Mexico?" Fleur asked, looking with suspicion at the green substance in a separate container.

"That's guacamole," Emmett explained. "It's made from avocadoes."

They both glanced up when the door opened, and Cassius walked in. "Fleur, there's someone I would like you to meet," he said. "Is that okay?"

Casually dressed in one of Cassius's shirts and a pair of blue jeans, Fleur hesitated. Cassius seemed tense, maybe even nervous, the two parallel frown lines above his nose pronounced. "Who is it?"

"His name is Forrest Overton. He used to be a very good friend of your mother's and he's waiting outside."

She got up and straightened out her clothes. It had to be someone Cassius trusted, otherwise he wouldn't have allowed him to meet her. But it was obvious he wasn't pleased with the situation. "Should I be concerned?" she asked, glancing between Cassius and Emmett.

Both men evaded her uneasy stare and a minute later, a tall and slender man with blond curly hair entered the living room.

Fleur curtsied politely, used to always being respectful to strangers, especially if they were invited into your home. "Nice to make your acquaintance, Mr. Overton," she mumbled.

Instead of answering, the stranger just stood there, studying her, a perturbed expression on his face.

"Would you care for a cato?" she asked, tensing up even more under his penetrating blue stare.

As if her words shook him out of his reverie, he blinked several times and his eyes cleared with understanding. "Do you mean a taco? No, thank you, although they smell delicious."

"Sit down, Forrest," Cassius directed him, waving in the direction of the chair at the head of the table. "I'll make a pot of coffee. You all want one?"

Instead, Forrest sat down next to Fleur, making her as inconspicuously as possible shift away from him.

"Don't let your food get cold," he said.

Wary and self-consciously, Fleur took a bite, her visitor's

eyes watching her every move. To hide her discomfort, she wiped her mouth and glanced at Emmett, hoping he would finally say or do something to defuse the tension. Instead of helping, he stared down at his food and didn't say anything.

Their guest shifted in his chair. "That's a beautiful dress," he commented, his eyes on the yellow dress hanging over the back of a chair. Emmett had picked it up at the dry-cleaner that morning and she hadn't taken the time to hang it in her room, yet.

"It's mine," Fleur said, glad to see the intrusive man shift his attention away from her, even if it was to something that belonged to her. "It was torn and dirty, and they fixed it."

Cassius returned from the kitchen with four steaming mugs. "Do you use cream and sugar, Forrest?" He put the tray on the table.

"Black is fine," Forrest answered, and reached for a mug. "Did they already introduce you to Chinese food, Fleur? The curry chicken with white rice from Sue Ling's Chinese Cuisine used to be your mother's favorite meal."

Fleur peeked at Cassius for help. She had no idea how she was supposed to react.

"It's alright, Fleur," he assured her, some of his initial tension easing up. "Mr. Overton knows what happened to your mother, and after a lot of pressure from him, Milton and I read him in, and told him about you."

Almost every day, Cassius had warned her not to tell anyone who she was, and now he was spreading the word himself. It only made her more confused. *How could someone pressure Cassius into seeing her when this person couldn't even know about her existence?*

"Did your mother never mention my name?" Forrest asked.

He inhaled a deep breath, his jaw tense, and Fleur wondered why he was acting so peculiarly. It had been twenty years or more since he'd seen her mother, and it couldn't be that important.

"My mother may have mentioned your name several times when I was younger, but I don't really recall," she said, getting prickly under the increased tenseness and unanswered questions spinning through her head.

Forrest shook his head, his eyes filled with sadness. "I used to love her very much, and it broke my heart when she disappeared."

Oh, dear, Fleur thought, unprepared to meet one of her mother's former love interests. This was getting worse. Why hadn't Cassius warned her?

"Fortunately, I found another woman I fell deeply in love with," Forrest continued. "Her name is Kara, and we have two gorgeous daughters, Josie and Caro. I'm sure they would love to meet you. Especially Caro. She looks so much like you. Don't you agree, Emmett?"

Emmett hadn't spoken a word since Forrest appeared, his food still untouched in front of him.

"Do you know Mr. Overton?" she asked him, her suspicion that something was completely wrong increasing.

Emmett nodded. "Forrest is my neighbor."

Bewildered, Fleur drew away. She hadn't rested all morning, and a debilitating fatigue took hold of every cell in her body and started to pull her down, her brain muddling over.

As if he could read her mind, Cassius finished his coffee and got up. "Emmet, Forrest, it's time to go and let Fleur rest."

Emmett gathered the leftovers, put them in the paper bag, and hurried out the door. Forrest got up too.

"I can't tell you how wonderful it has been to meet you, Fleur," he said, taking her hand in warm grip. "I look forward to seeing you again soon."

Cassius guided him out, gathered the empty mugs, and took them to the kitchen. When he returned, Fleur had pulled his oversized sweater over her head, and sat on the couch, ready to demand answers. But too fatigued to think, she shivered.

He draped the quilt over her shoulders, and when she was settled, he handed her a cellphone. "This is for you," he said.

Through a weary fog, she stared at the device in her hand. "You bought me a phone?"

He sat down next to her on the couch. "I want you to have a way to contact the people you know," he said.

Who in the world could he think of? Everyone she knew lived or worked on ARC's compound. "You seemed uncomfortable with Mr. Overton's visit, and I can't help but wonder if this has anything to do with him."

He viewed her with a combination of hesitance, solemness, and awe before releasing a long deep breath. "Yes and no," he replied, settling deeper into the couch, and taking his time, as if he was trying to form the right words in his head. Then he reached out to her, but right before he could touch her arm, he pulled his hand back and dropped it in his lap.

"I recognize you're in a fragile mental and physical state, and the last thing you need is more negativity or stress, but there's some news I can't keep from you, Fleur."

Immediate fear settled in her stomach, her grip around the phone so tight that her knuckles turned white. "What is it?" she cried out, bracing herself for bad news.

"You need to stay here a while longer than you'd hoped for."

Fleur shook her head in denial. "Why?"

Cassius's features were drawn with sorrow. "Dr. Stevenson called this morning. You're very ill, Fleur, and we can't send you back in the condition you're in. There's a high probability you wouldn't survive."

Despair settled over her like a dark cloud, suffocating her. "What's wrong with me?" she whispered, drawing in a shuddering breath.

"The cardiologist discovered damage to your heart that interferes with its ability to pump blood through your body," Cassius explained, repeating what the doctor had told him. "That's why you're so tired all the time."

Tears rolled down her face as his words sunk in.

"But don't despair. He's optimistic he can fix your heart."

Fleur squeezed her eyes shut, trying to accept the fact that they knew her health was compromised, and that she would be trapped here, just as she'd been so afraid of.

"I've been sick for very long," she admitted. "But I survived the first time, coming over here. Why would it be any different the second time?"

"Because the risk is too great, Fleur," Cassius replied.

She raised her head and gazed at him through her tears. "My parents dragged me from one doctor to the other as I struggled to make it through another day. Do you really believe Dr. Stevenson can help me?"

Chapter 17

Forrest

FORREST HURRIED AFTER EMMETT. "How long did you know?" he asked when he caught up with him.

Emmett shrugged. "Only a week or so." Then he sighed. "I'm sorry I couldn't tell you."

"You don't have to apologize, and I'm sorry I pestered you so much. Before they allowed me to see her, I had to sign papers too, promising I wouldn't tell her I'm her father. I'm not happy about it. I believe she has the right to know, but I want you to know I understand completely you couldn't say anything, and again I'm sorry."

"Don't worry about it," Emmett smiled with a cheeky grin. "I'm glad they told you. It makes life much easier for me."

He disappeared into the building and Forrest stepped into his car. He couldn't wait to talk to Kara about Fleur when he got home. The moment he saw his wife, he took her in his arms.

"Fleur looked so fragile, small and pale," he sighed in her hair, finding the support he needed in her quiet presence and comforting embrace. "I'm so worried about her."

Kara guided him to the love seat next to the fireplace and sat beside him, stroking his arm.

He batted a few tears away. "Do you realize that in her time, people still travel primarily by horseback? She shouldn't have to be dealing with heart disease. Isn't it enough she has to get used to our modern technology, busy traffic, and fast pace of living? And how about computers and the social media advances that even affect the physical and mental health of people born in this century?"

"I can't imagine," Kara agreed softly.

Forrest grabbed her hand, his mind overrun with everything that could go wrong. "Heart disease is life-threatening, and I wonder why Annet didn't mention it in her letters." A deep frown creased his forehead. "I do remember she wrote about Fleur and Frank contracting scarlet fever and that it took her a long time to recover. But other than that..."

"Why are you talking about scarlet fever?" Caro asked, coming down the stairs. It didn't happen often that she found her parents clinging to each other in the uncomfortable loveseat, especially not in the early afternoon. She rushed over. "Why are you both home? What's going on?"

Forrest and Kara had always talked openly to their daughters about Annet's disappearance through time and their older sister, Fleur. For both girls, her name was an enigma, someone from the past, like all their forefathers.

"Everything is fine," Kara said, reassuring her daughter. "We're talking about Fleur and Frank, who both contracted scarlet fever, just like you and Josie did when you were little. It's a mild bacterial infection and after the doctor prescribed an antibiotic, all your symptoms disappeared in a few days. Do you remember that?"

"Oh, yes," Caro replied, rolling her eyes. She sat down in a chair and pulled out her phone. "That pain in my throat was the worst."

"Fleur wasn't so lucky since they didn't have antibiotics yet, and she stayed sick for a long time," Kara continued, still holding on to Forrest's arm.

Caro typed on her phone and read out loud. "Scarlet fever is caused by an infection with the streptococcus bacteria. When not treated properly, rheumatic fever can develop. Do you think that's what she had?"

"What else does it say, Caro?" Forrest asked, his interest piqued.

His daughter's fingers rapidly clicked on the small keyboard. "Rheumatic fever is an inflammatory disease that most often affected children between the ages of five and fifteen and can cause permanent heart damage if not treated properly."

"Heart damage?" Forrest repeated.

"Yes, this article talks about damaged heart valves and heart failure that usually occur ten to twelve years after the original illness. That's scary."

Forrest pulled his phone from his pocket. "I have to call Rewick."

Chapter 18

Fleur

FLEUR WATCHED THE NUMBERS on the digital alarm clock next to her bed change from 8:59 to 9:00 am. The only clocks she'd been familiar with were the clocks with pendulums that needed to be wound up or had weights you had to pull down each day. Now, she could also look at her new phone to find out what time it was. She turned it on and clicked on the contacts. Cassius had entered his and Emmett's phone numbers in there, along with Forrest Overton's. The man had seemed nice enough, but that didn't mean she was interested in talking to him.

She clicked on Emmett's name. Below his number were three icons. Emmett had explained how to call and send a message, but she didn't know what the other icon meant.

She pressed on the blue icon, and a bubble appeared with a keyboard below it. *Good morning,* she typed. *This is Fleur.*

His response was immediate. *You have a phone?*

They texted a few times back and forth, ending with the

promise that he would order chicken curry for lunch.

She fell back on her pillow and stared at the ceiling. Cassius had told her last night how proud he was that she adjusted so well. She didn't feel proud or well-adjusted at all, with panicked thoughts racing through her mind, and the constant dread in her body so heavy she could barely function. Each minute of the day, she missed her family and longed to tell them about the doctor who wanted to fix her heart. They would be so relieved and overjoyed. And even Jeremiah would be pleased, her lack of energy often disappointing him. If she got better, she could go on long walks to the ocean, tend to the rose and vegetable garden with the gardener, help Henry Jonkers, their coachman, with the horses, go to university, and do all the things she hadn't been able to. Yesterday, the hope for a full recovery from her debilitating disease had taken root and overnight, it sprouted. If they really could help her, everything that had happened to her was so worth it.

The alarm clock read 9:32. It was time to get up. She put on Javina's bathrobe and headed to the kitchen. "You're not at work?" she asked Cassius, finding him behind the computer in the living room.

"I was just about to knock on your door, sleepyhead," he chuckled. "How are you?"

"Hopeful," she replied. "I want to make toast and coffee. Can I get you anything?"

"I'll join you for a cup," he replied, following her into the kitchen. "I just got off the phone with the hospital. They scheduled you for an MRI tomorrow morning at ten, to get images of your chest and heart, followed by an electrocardiogram and an echocardiogram. It will be a busy morning, and I recommend taking it easy today, with lots of rest."

The idea of spending the entire day inside didn't appeal to her.

"You could play on your phone," he said, noticing her displeasure. "And I'm sure Emmett will come and see you."

She opened and closed several cabinets. "There's only one slice of bread left. Do you have flour and yeast?"

"I guess it's time to go to the grocery store," Cassius replied. Then he looked at her with hesitation. "I don't know if it's wise, but what do you think about going with me?"

Fleur's eyes lit up. "Are you sure?"

Half an hour later, they drove into Dunedam.

"The Safeway at the edge of town offers everything we may need," Cassius said.

"Everything in one store?" Fleur asked. "Even bread and meat?"

"You probably had to go to the bakery and the butcher, I assume?" Cassius grinned and pulled into a huge parking lot.

Fleur stayed close to Cassius as he pushed their shopping cart through the aisles. The number of items for sale in the huge store was mindboggling. Rice crackers, broccoli, hotdogs, Jell-O, chips, barbeque sauce. So many things she'd never heard of.

"See anything you like, Fleur?" he asked, putting a jar of strawberry jam in their cart, joining the two loaves of bread and chocolate chip cookies. "How about peanut butter, crackers, ice cream?"

He added a gallon of milk, a tub of spreadable butter, and a tray with eggs to their growing supply of groceries.

"We have a milkman who stops by every morning," Fleur told him, grateful she was wearing a button up blouse with long sleeves, the coolers in the dairy department blowing cold air. "The milk has cream on top and is much more delicious than the thin milk you buy."

"I'm sure it is," Cassius laughed. "Come, let's go to the produce department." He pushed the cart between rows of fresh vegetables and fruits, the variety extraordinary. Fresh apples and pears available in the spring! She was used to only being able to eat those fruits if they had canned them in the fall. Lettuce, radishes, sprouts, cabbage, and tomatoes. How could they sell them fresh this time of the year, while they always had to wait the entire summer before they became available? She picked up an avocado and wondered what it could be.

"Do you like bananas?" Cassius asked.

Fleur had never seen a yellow banana before. "I don't know."

"How about oranges?"

She was familiar with those. "They're delicious."

Cassius put four oranges in a plastic bag and put them in the cart, along with several bananas and a bag of red grapes. At the cash register, he threw in several candy bars. "I can't wait for you to try these," he said.

Fleur tagged along, grateful for their outing, the store beyond anything she'd ever seen. Back at home, she helped Cassius carry it all inside and by the time everything was put away, she was exhausted.

"You should text Emmett to tell him to save that chicken

curry for another day," Cassius suggested. "I'll make us fresh turkey sandwiches with tomato, onion, lettuce and avocado instead."

The next morning at ten, Cassius and Fleur arrived at the hospital. Everything seemed a lot less scary than the first time.

"This is the third day I've kept you from your work," she said to Cassius while they sat in the waiting room. A woman on the television talked about yesterday's mass shooting in a church. She turned her back to the screen, the news of someone randomly killing strangers too disturbing.

"You're much more important to me than SMITS," he assured her.

They were called back in by the same nurse from last time, and followed him into the elevator. "Hold on to the bar," Cassius warned her when it felt as if the world dropped out from under her.

The elevator doors opened into the basement, where the hospital did imaging. Faced with her own mortality, Fleur tried not to think and passively submitted herself through the motions. She undressed, put on a gown and hospital socks, believing the best course of action was to remain quiet, as if nothing affected her, while inside she battled a deep fear.

"I'm here to take you in for your MRI," a nurse told her. "Have you ever had one before?"

Fleur shook her head, the stress exhausting her energy, leaving her devoid of any interest to interact. "We use an MRI machine to produce high-resolution images of the inside of your body which will help Dr. Stevenson diagnose what's wrong with your heart and other organs. I read in your file that you had scarlet fever when you were a child. Fortunately, that's much less common than it used to be, although I heard about a recent outbreak in Scotland," the nurse chattered on, trying to make her feel comfortable. "Do you have any metal in or on your body, like jewelry, piercings?"

The rhythmic pounding inside the machine made me fall asleep, she texted Emmett, sitting comfortably on the couch in the living room, the afternoon sun warming the house.

I wish I could have been there for you, he texted back. *Can I stop by after work? I missed our lunch date.*

Yes, please, she replied, already looking forward to his visit.

He sent her a red heart emoji, and she sent one back, for the first time since her arrival feeling young and slightly brazen, the prospect of getting better boosting her confidence.

She closed her eyes for a few minutes. Emmett was always so understanding, kind, and enthusiastic, while Jeremiah was ambitious and demanding. He had often pushed her beyond her capabilities. At the time, she'd appreciated it, because no one challenged her; her family always worried about her health, unknowingly excluding her from activities she gladly would have undertaken. But now she understood why her parents had been so concerned.

Voices outside took her back to the moment and she sat up.

"Fleur?" Cassius asked, walking inside. "Are you feeling good enough to receive visitors?"

She recognized Forrest Overton, who followed him in. He was accompanied by two women. The older, oddly dressed woman immediately pushed everybody aside and hurried toward her, wrapping her arms around her middle. She barely reached her chin.

"Fleur, my baby," she exclaimed between her breasts. "I can't believe I finally get to meet you." The woman took a step back, the multitude of necklaces dangling from her neck clattering against each other. "I'm your grandmother, Barbara!"

Fleur stared down at the wrinkled face of the tiny woman, astonished by her bright red mouth and the longest black eyelashes she'd ever seen. "My grandmother?"

Barbara pulled a handkerchief from a bright yellow purse, which was decorated with colorful beads, tassels, and fringes. She pressed the hankie underneath her eyes, drying a few tears. "I sure hope my daughter, your mother, told you about me?"

"I asked you not to get overexcited, Barbara," Forrest said.

"Nonsense," Barbara replied, pushing a strand of dark red hair from her forehead. "I'm sure Fleur is very relieved to see a family member. Aren't you honey?"

Fleur couldn't help but smile. She'd never had a grandmother before, and although she didn't understand why the woman was dressed like somebody from the circus, it was wonderful to meet her.

"Look at that gorgeous smile," Barbara laughed, claiming victory.

Cassius watched from the sideline, carefully monitoring Fleur's reaction. "Let me know if it gets too much for you," he said.

"Don't worry, I can handle myself," Fleur replied, glad about the distraction. "Please, take a seat. Do you care for any refreshments?"

"A glass of red wine would be nice," Barbara immediately responded.

Forrest shook his head. "No, thank you, Fleur. We won't take up much of your time. I hoped realizing you have family here would make you feel more secure and welcome. Therefore, I wanted you to meet Barbara and my wife."

The second woman extended her hand, her lovely face devoid of makeup, her long hair tied together in a loose ponytail. "Hi, Fleur. My name is Kara Overton. Alex Keizer was one of my ancestors, and that makes me one of your family members, too."

Kindness radiated from her eyes, her grip full of warmth. "I heard about your health problems, and we all want you to know we're here for you during this stressful time."

"Whatever you need," Barbara added. "Although my car croaked again the other day. I think it's the battery. Forrest, when you take me home, can you buy me a new battery at the auto parts store?"

"We'll see," Forrest replied, shaking his head. "How did it go at the hospital this morning, Fleur?"

Fleur sat down on the couch, and Barbara immediately joined her. "Those MRI machines can be so claustrophobic," she said, patting Fleur's knee. "Chuck always freaks out, but he's a sissy, so don't mind him." She stared into Fleur's face, taking in every detail. "You're so beautiful," she continued, the quivering of her bottom lip softening her harsh features. "Exactly like you are in the paintings."

When Forrest had become a parent, he'd realized how much

Barbara must have missed her only daughter. At Christmas, he'd started sending her two free entry tickets for Keizer Manor. Each year, she'd used them to see the paintings of Annet and the three grandchildren she would never meet.

"We could hear from Fleur's cardiologist by Friday, but for certain no later than Monday," Cassius informed them. "Based on their findings, she could have surgery a few days later."

"I understand scarlet fever caused the damage to your heart," Barbara said. "You poor girl. All that suffering. You must be so relieved doctors in our time can fix almost anything."

"How did you know I had scarlet fever, grandmother?" she asked.

"Well, from Annet's letters, of course," Barbara replied, glancing at Forrest with a huge smile on her face. "Did you hear her call me grandmother?" She pulled out her handkerchief for the second time to bat her eyes, careful not to smudge her makeup.

Emmett had told Fleur about the letters her mother had left inside *Lost in the Storm*. "Are you talking about the letters inside the painting?"

Forrest got up from his chair. "Barbara, it's time to go." He helped her up from the couch and ushered her out, while Barbara blew kisses in Fleur's direction and waved. "Come and visit me some day, dear."

Kara gave Fleur a warm hug. "We would love to welcome you to our house for a family dinner this coming weekend, so you can meet our daughters, Josie and Caro. If you want, we can invite Emmett, too."

Chapter 19

"TWO GOATS will be delivered this morning," Cassius told her over breakfast the next morning. "Before we perform our first test, the army will send an additional division to set up and maintain a secure perimeter, because we need to make certain there won't be anyone within a two-mile radius of the research facility. Everybody else must be in the basement. We can't be safe enough."

Fleur's pulse raced with excitement, the idea of this first test possibly making progress toward her return home. "How can we let my parents know we sent the goat?"

"Each goat will wear a collar with your parents' names on it," Cassius explained. "And we will attach a waterproof container to the collar, just big enough to hold a small letter. You have the entire morning to think about what you want to write them."

Grateful tears welled up in her eyes. "You're doing so much for me, Cassius."

"It's the least I can do, kiddo," he said, gathering the empty plates.

Another note landed in the garbage can, on top of all the

others. She had so much to tell her parents. About SMITS, Cassius, her upcoming heart surgery, Barbara, and Emmett. Heat crawled up the back of her neck as she thought about the previous evening. Emmett had finally brought the promised delicious chicken curry, and they had spent the evening on the couch, playing on her phone, listening to music, and talking for hours.

It had surprised her to find out he lived in the coach house on the Keizer Estate, and she'd enjoyed talking to him about the house and the grounds, and about Kara and her daughters. Knowing she had family here warmed her ailing heart.

"Do you forgive me for not telling you?" he'd asked, holding her hand. "I don't want to keep anything from you, but we were sworn to secrecy about everything that involves you."

For the first time since she'd met him, he'd opened up about himself, his younger brother Finn, who had a secret crush on Caro Overton, and his parents, who played in a band.

She'd readily accepted his apology and looked forward to seeing him during his lunch break.

Dear Mom and Dad, she wrote for the sixth time. *I'm so sorry I went out in the storm and caused you so much grief.*

A hand on her shoulder woke her up.

"It's time for the first test, Fleur. We need to head over to the main building," Cassius said.

She pushed the quilt back, got up, and straightened out her new outfit. Emmett had brought her a bag of clothes from Josie and Caro. She'd tried them on and after Emmett left, she'd been too tired to take the last outfit off.

"I don't believe I've seen that top before," Cassius remarked. "That blue compliments your eyes."

"Emmett dropped off a bag full of clothes from Josie and Caro, and a pair of sandals," Fleur said. "At first, I didn't understand why you introduced me to Forrest. Now that I realize he married into the Keizer family, I do, and want to thank you for allowing him, his wife, and my grandmother on the property. It's wonderful to know I have family here." She rushed to the door, super excited to send a message to her parents. "It's also such a coincidence that Emmett is Forrest's neighbor. Did he give you my note?"

"Yes, we made a copy and secured it safely inside the container of each goat's collar," he replied, guiding her inside the research center.

"Are we able to see the goat disappear?"

"Multiple cameras, set up in various angles, will capture every single second," he said, relieved to see Fleur so happy.

They joined all the employees in the basement, the atmosphere charged with tension and expectation. Emmett waved at her from the adjacent workshop. She waved back.

"You can sit here, Fleur," Cassius said. He rolled a chair in front of six monitors, all directed at the fence. "From here, you'll have a first-row seat."

Commander Thornton joined them at five minutes to three. Everyone got quiet. "The only people allowed to move around are Cassius, Adam, Ramon, and Emmett," his voice thundered. "The rest of you, find a place along the walls to make sure you're out of their way. Cassius, you're in command."

At three o'clock sharp, Cassius pushed the red button and

SMITS's engine turned on. At the noise, Fleur covered her ears.

"How is it looking, guys?" Cassius yelled over the grinding and clatter of the machine. All three men gave him a thumbs up.

"Increase to fifty... sixty... seventy." Cassius leaned over and yelled in Fleur's ear. "You appeared at a reading between one hundred and one hundred and ten, but we can't be certain because of the faulty sensor. Keep your eyes on the screens."

The goat stood on the pavement, eating from the fresh hay they had put down to keep it from wandering off. Like Cassius had predicted, as soon as the machine hit one hundred, the goat disappeared in the blink of an eye.

Everyone applauded and several guys stamped their feet on the concrete floor, yelling hooray. "Congratulations, Cassius," Milton said, slapping him on his shoulder and smiling enthusiastically. "This is groundbreaking!"

"Revolutionary!" another man yelled.

"Watch out Marty McFly and Doc Brown, here we come," another guy laughed, referring to the *Back to the Future* trilogy.

Half an hour later, the second goat had disappeared, and everyone went back upstairs, ready to start their weekend after a sensational and memorable day.

"How does it feel to travel through time, Fleur?" a young man in a green uniform asked, joining her in the hallway outside the control room.

Nobody had asked her this before. "I really can't tell you. That storm knocked me unconscious," she replied. "But I can share that waking up was the worst experience in my entire life. I was in so much pain."

"Was it like getting hit by lightning?" he asked curiously,

following her to the bottom of the stairs.

"You know you're not supposed to talk to the lady, Hamilton," another army-clad man yelled from up ahead. "Leave her alone."

"Mind your own business, Jones!" he yelled back before returning his attention to Fleur. "Sorry for disturbing you, Miss. I just wanted to tell you we're happy they made good progress today towards securing your swift return, and that you, at least, got to meet your real father, Mr. Overton." He touched his military cap and ran up the stairs with two steps at a time, following his fellow recruits.

Fleur leaned against the whitewashed wall, afraid she would fall, her knees weak and her heart rate erratic, making her dizzy.

"Forrest Overton is not my father," she yelled after him, with no one around to listen. "Why would you say that?"

Chapter 20

THE GLORIOUS DAY, filled with sunshine and promise, had turned ugly by the casual remark of a young soldier. Fighting the urge to lie down and cry, she chewed on the inside of her cheek until it hurt. Sometimes it helped. Sometimes it didn't.

Instead of taking refuge in her bedroom, she sunk down in Cassius's recliner and stared straight in front of her, arms folded in front of her chest, her mouth set in a straight line. *Forrest Overton wasn't her father. He couldn't be.* Angry at the entire world for bringing her here, forcing her to live on some compound, and keeping her away from her loved ones and everything she held dear, she moped at its injustice.

Or could he be?

No, Cassius would have told her. He knew she wasn't a child needing protection.

Ten minutes later, Cassius walked in. "You left so suddenly. Are you okay?"

Always the same question, she thought, fighting against the small voice in her head, telling her she was being unreasonable. "Yes, I'm fine."

He walked over, studying her. "I can tell something is bothering you. Would you care to tell me what it is?"

"Why should I?" she replied, stubbornly resisting looking at him.

Cassius put his hands in the pockets of his slacks and swayed lightly from left to right, tapping his foot on the vinyl floor.

The irritating sound unraveled her, and she cast a quick glance in his direction. "Could you please stop that!"

"Sure." He sat down on her favorite corner of the couch, grabbed a magazine from the end table, and took out his glasses before he started reading.

With a miserable shrug, she turned away from him, indecisive to demand answers or ignore her anxious inner doubts.

The minutes ticked by, the only sound the rustling of the magazine when Cassius turned a page.

The least he could do was show concern, she sulked. Or try to make her feel better, instead of calmly leafing through a magazine without a care in the world.

"I think I want to know the truth about the letters," she blurted out, her voice shaking.

He studied her over his glasses. "What letters?"

"Don't play dumb," she said in a huff. "The letters my mother left inside *Lost in the Storm*. Who were they for?"

With a deep sigh, Cassius lowered his magazine and took off his glasses. "They were for Forrest Overton."

The ground beneath her feet started to shake. "Why?"

"Listen," Cassius began, both hands making a calming motion. "I don't know if this is the right time to talk about this.

The doctor...."

"I know what the doctor said." Her voice quivered and she furiously batted her tears away. "What I don't know is why my mother wrote letters to her former lover while she was married to my father!"

"All right, all right," Cassius said, rubbing his eyes. "But only if you calm down first."

Unable to stay in her seat any longer, Fleur got up and started pacing the room. When he stayed silent, she stopped in front of him, placing a hand on each hip. "Is Forrest Overton my father?"

She gazed into his soulful, dark eyes and read the answer. A whimpering cry escaped her lips. "You're lying!"

Cassius grabbed her icy hand, fondly pulled her down on the couch next to him and wrapped his arm around her shivering body.

"No, it can't be," she cried. Choking sobs poured from her quivering mouth as she broke down into a million pieces.

"Let it all out, sweetheart," he whispered in her hair, his warm hand calmly rubbing her arm. "I haven't seen you cry once."

"It's all your fault," she cried against his shoulder, the tightening in her chest making it difficult to breathe. "Why did you do it?"

He pulled her even closer. "It is my fault, and I can't tell you how sorry I am."

Drained of her last drop of energy, her sobs subsided. Cassius slid away from under her and went in search of a box of tissues, her pillow and blanket. Like a loving parent, he tucked her in and disappeared into the kitchen to make a pot of chamomile tea.

Fleur blew her nose and pulled her knees into her chest, grieving over the loss of the naïve young woman she used to be. Over the father, who was no longer hers. "I was always so proud to be your daughter, Father," she wailed. Images of her father in front of his easel seeped into her mind, his strong hands bringing the delicate anthers of a flower to life, the featherlight eyelashes of a baby, or the drop of morning dew on a leaf. She remembered how he'd comforted her when she was sad, had made her feel safe when she was scared, and how easily he could calm her down when she was angry. Alex Keizer had been her hero, her role model, her father, and after everything else being stolen from her, they had taken him away too.

The tightening in her chest intensified and, lost in her own heartbreak, she faded away.

Chapter 21

Forrest

THE DOORS OF KEIZER MANOR closed at five and the last visitors left the museum forty-five minutes later. It was time to go home.

Want me to stop at the take-and-bake for pizza? he texted Kara, knowing Fridays were always busy at the Orange Fine Art Studio and Gallery where she'd worked for the last twenty-five years.

She responded with three heart emojis and a thumbs up followed by, *I should be home around seven.*

He shut down his computer and headed to the side exit, wishing the security guard he passed on his way out a good evening. *How many pizzas should I order?* he thought. Finn spent more and more evenings at their house, and so did Josie's new boyfriend, Arlo. The family was getting bigger. If only Fleur would have been able to join them, everything would be perfect.

"One family size pepperoni and a Thai Chicken with extra onions," he ordered and sat down on the hard wooden bench to wait when his phone buzzed in his pocket.

He glanced at the screen. *Cassius Rewick?* "This is Forrest," he said.

"Forrest, I'm on my way to the hospital with Fleur in the backseat. She's barely conscious but breathing."

"You're driving her to the hospital?" he gasped. "Why didn't you call 911?"

"I panicked," Cassius replied, expelling loud bursts of breath into the phone. "And all I could think of was picking her up, and rushing her to the emergency room. I'm already halfway."

"I'll meet you there," he immediately replied and yelled at one of the pizza artists. "Sorry, I gotta go."

Despite his haste, he kept a close eye on the speed limits, the red lights staying red forever, the roads packed with commuters wanting to get home. He parked as close to the emergency entrance as possible and rushed inside.

"My daughter, Fleur Keizer, did someone bring her in?" he asked the nurse manning the reception desk.

"Not within the last fifteen minutes," she replied from behind the glass partition wall.

"Then he's still on his way with my daughter," he told her, both hands on the counter. "She's barely breathing, and they could be here any minute."

The nurse pressed a button on a desk phone. "Charles, you there? We have an incoming driver with a possible unconscious woman," she spoke close to a microphone, before sending Forrest a reassuring smile. "We'll be ready for her, sir."

Screeching tires outside made him look towards the entrance. He immediately recognized Cassius, flying out of the driver's seat and rounding the car so he could open the back door. Two men dressed in scrubs appeared with a gurney and lifted Fleur from the backseat, wheeling her away. Forrest and Cassius saw the doors of the emergency room close behind them.

"Can we go in?" Forrest yelled, attracting the attention of the receptionist.

She shook her head. "For now, you'll need to wait until they've had the chance to assess her condition. When they find out more, only one of you will be allowed to see her."

Cassius looked at Forrest, beads of sweat rolling down from his hairline and glistening on his forehead. "I'll move my car and be right back."

Forrest glanced around the waiting room, anxiety written on the faces of everyone there.

"So sorry," a man his age mumbled. "My wife is inside with my sixteen-year-old son. He fell from a tree trying to save our neighbor's kitten. I think he broke his arm."

The two chairs kitty-corner from the man were empty, and Forrest sagged down, resting his elbows on his knees, his hands buried in his blond curls.

Cassius returned several minutes later and handed the receptionist some paperwork before joining Forrest, a red handkerchief in his hand. "I can't believe I didn't call 911," he muttered, guilt written all over his face. He blew his nose and wiped his forehead. "Any word yet?"

"No, nothing," Forrest replied, shifting in his chair. "What happened to her? Do you know?"

The doors of the emergency room opened, and a nurse

walked out. "Suzanne Parker?"

A woman grabbed her purse and disappeared down a hallway, following the nurse.

Obviously distraught, Cassius hung his head, shaking it back and forth. "We tested SMITS this afternoon and everything went well, but shortly after we finished, Fleur disappeared." He looked up, a sorrowful grin lifting one corner of his mouth. "I found her at home, extremely upset. Somehow, she must have figured out who you are, Forrest, and she wasn't happy when I told her she was right."

Forrest's breath stuck in his throat. "She knows I'm her father?"

Cassius let out a deep sigh. "Yes, she does and after she calmed down enough, I brought her a pillow and blanket, and left to make tea. When I returned, she was gasping for air. I immediately realized something was wrong." A tear welled up in the corner of his eye. "All I could think of was getting her here as soon as possible." His voice cracked. "I'm so sorry I panicked and pray I didn't make matters worse."

"I would be lying if I told you I'm not glad she found out," Forrest admitted, letting out a deep sigh. "But sometimes the truth comes at too big of a cost."

They sat silently next to each other, each absorbed by his own worries and thoughts. The television in the far corner predicted sunny skies with the chance of showers for the next several days. Each time the doors opened, they sprung up. The third person to get called was the man sitting close to them. "Good luck with your daughter," he said.

"And you with your son," Forrest replied. He threw an

impatient glance at the clock. They had been here close to half an hour, and still no word.

The doors opened again, and a nurse walked out. "Mr. Rewick?"

They both stood and headed in his direction. "Fleur is doing much better and is asking for you," he said to Forrest.

"I'm Rewick, her guardian," Cassius said.

The nurse quickly recovered from his surprise. "If you want to follow me."

"I'll text you," Cassius said, before he hurried through the doors.

Left alone, Forrest sat back down in the plastic chair and called Kara. "You have to pick up the pizzas," he explained. "I'm at the hospital and don't know when I'll be home."

They chatted for a few minutes until a text from Cassius came in.

They put her on oxygen and she's doing good, but she doesn't want to see you. Let's ask her again tomorrow.

Chapter 22

Fleur

"FLEUR, CAN YOU HEAR ME?" a loud voice asked with urgency. She felt someone pull up her eyelid and a bright light caused her to flinch. "There you are," the voice said.

Something covered her mouth, and she tried to lift her hand to remove it, but her muscles were barely strong enough to lift one finger. "Where am I?" She opened her eyes and stared into the eyes of a woman in light-blue scrubs.

"You're in the hospital," she answered, listening to Fleur's heart with a stethoscope. Another nurse stood at the foot of her bed with a clipboard in her hands.

The curtain around her bed opened and a man in a white coat wearing a mask and a close-fitted cap entered. He studied the clipboard and conferred with the nurses. "Can you contact the cardiac unit to let them know we'll be sending a patient there in about a half hour."

He looked at Fleur, his eyes kind and reassuring. "Were you under a lot of stress when you started to have trouble breathing?"

Fleur nodded, remembering exactly how she'd felt, the pain in her heart still there.

He checked the readings on the heart monitor next to her bed. "Your oxygen level has improved, and so has your blood pressure and heart rate. Keep that oxygen mask on, and I'll be back to check on you in fifteen minutes before you're transferred, to make sure you're set to go."

Before he walked out, he turned to the nurse with the stethoscope. "Can you put her in a gown?"

The nurse helped Fleur change and reapplied the heart pads onto her chest. "Do you want to call any next of kin?"

Fleur closed her eyes and an escaped tear rolled down her cheek. "I don't have next of kin."

Cassius had joined her before they wheeled her bed into the elevator that took her to the cardiac care unit, where they treated people with serious or acute heart problems. He had stayed with her until she began to doze off.

Overnight, beeps, clicks, whooshing sounds, and light coming from the hallway into her room kept her restless, making it impossible to sleep. She was frightened of what was going on with her heart, and what they were going to do. The nurse who checked on her several times during the night couldn't give her any answers. All she said was that she had to wait for the cardiologist.

"Remember to press the call button on your bed in case you need help," another nurse said when she woke up the next morning, checking the IV attached to her underarm. She had just helped Fleur to the bathroom and back into bed.

All the nurses were kind and attentive and reassured her she was in good hands. Their compassion helped ease some of her anxiety.

The egg white omelet with spinach, bell pepper, mushroom, and onion they served her half an hour later on a breakfast tray smelled delicious. Her hand shook lightly as she lifted the fork to her mouth.

She finished her omelet and reached for the cup of mixed fruit when Cassius walked in. He looked tired and old, a strained expression on his face. He sat down in the chair next to her bed. "You look much better without that oxygen mask," he said, attempting a joke to hide his concern.

She looked right through it. "I feel much better, so you can let go of that frown," she replied and smiled, glad to see him.

Cassius relaxed his shoulders, some of his tension defused.

"I'm sorry for what I said yesterday, Cassius," she whispered. Her fingers played nervously with the narrow hose attached to the tube beneath her nose to give her extra oxygen. "I realize you didn't want anything like this to happen either, and you've been nothing but kind, by opening your home to me and paying for all my expenses, without asking for anything in return."

He shook his head, his eyes reflecting sadness and remorse. "I deserved everything you said."

"No, you didn't. And I want you to know how grateful I am for everything you did, including rushing me to the hospital last night. You saved my life."

"Now don't make me out like a hero," he laughed. He handed her the fruit that she'd put down after he'd sat in the chair and watched her eat. "Emmett can't wait to visit, but they only allow immediate family into the cardiac care unit, unless you make him a designated visitor."

"Tell me where I need to sign," she laughed.

Half an hour later, Dr. Stevenson walked in and shook Cassius's hand before he addressed Fleur. "All your test results are in, Fleur, and we scheduled you for surgery on Monday."

"Can you give us a bit more information about what's going on with Fleur, doctor?" Cassius asked.

Dr. Stevenson dragged a chair over and sat down next to him. "If not treated properly, scarlet fever can develop into rheumatic fever. We believe this happened to Fleur."

"I was ill for a long time," Fleur said, remembering the sore throat and pain in her chest, the fever, headache, and nausea.

The doctor nodded. "Rheumatic fever is an inflammatory disease that can cause permanent damage to the heart. This is called rheumatic heart disease, and usually occurs ten to sometimes twenty years after the original illness. In your case, it resulted in narrowing and damaging of the mitral valve, decreasing your blood flow. Your tricuspid valve is affected, too. During surgery, I will either repair or replace both valves."

Cassius grabbed Fleur's fidgeting hand. "What's her outlook, doctor?"

"We believe Fleur's heart failure is progressing rapidly from stage three to stage four," he replied. "Without surgery, her life expectancy is less than one year. Fortunately, Fleur is a young and strong woman who must have taken very good care of her health. She's otherwise in excellent condition. If we can repair her valves, she probably won't need another surgery for many years and should be able to live a full and healthy life."

It was hard to grasp all the information. The words heart disease, valves, and surgery frightened her more than she wanted to admit. "How long will it take for me to recover?" she asked, her voice strangled.

Suddenly, the monitor next to her bed beeped an alarm signal. Dr. Stevenson jumped up to check her oxygen flow and straightened out the kink in the tube. The beeping stopped.

"The oxygen saturation in your blood fell below ninety," he explained, keeping his eye on the monitor. Then he glanced at his watch. "Sorry, I must go. Any more questions before I hurry out of here?"

"Recovery time?" Cassius reminded him.

"Oh, yes. Fleur, we hope to use a minimally invasive method, involving only small incisions in your chest. After surgery, patients stay in the hospital for three to four days. But it will take up to a month or two to get your energy back and up to three months before you feel your old self again."

Chapter 23

Annet, 1864

ANNET WATCHED DARK CLOUDS roll in over the snow-covered dunes, the temperatures inside Keizer Manor barely over fifty degrees. It was the first time they were still here in December, the wicked winds and merciless winter storms making it impossible to keep the house warm. But Annet refused to leave. She had to be there when Fleur came home.

Despite her multiple pairs of long stockings, extra petticoat, heavy gown, boots, hat, and gloves, she shivered. "Here comes another storm." Her eyes misted over. "Maybe this one will bring her back to us."

Over the last eight weeks, they had scoured the dunes and plowed through a foot of snow until their toes, fingers, and noses nearly froze off.

Alex tightened his grip around her shoulders, pulling her close. "It's too cold to go out," he said, watching heavy snow starting to fall. "We won't survive the rage of this storm, and neither will the men."

After Fleur disappeared, they had employed four extra men to help keep the fires going in every room and search every inch of the dunes. With visibility close to zero, and snow flying horizontally, piling up against the manor, she knew it would be too risky. "Yes, we have to wait until it clears."

The door behind them opened and Gloria, the housekeeper in their employ for twenty-five years, walked in. She had Violette by the hand, dressed in multiple layers of clothes, like everybody else.

Annett barely noticed. Since Fleur's disappearance, nothing penetrated the heavy despair that had settled over her like a dark cloak, not even the sight of her youngest daughter.

"I hope you're not going out today," Gloria said, her breath visible in the cold room. "It's too dangerous."

"No, we're not," Alex replied. "Instead, we're heading to Heemstead as soon as the storm dies down. Can you start preparations?"

Gloria curtsied and disappeared. As soon as the door closed behind her, Annet became unglued. "Don't you dare give up on our daughter," she yelled, stamping with her right foot on the carpet. "I'm staying here until she's found, do you hear me!" She hissed several swear words. Unable to find or help Fleur infuriated her to no avail, the idea she had traveled through time and could be lost forever, unacceptable.

"Stop your tantrum immediately," Alex shot back at her. "Look at what it does to Violette and the rest of us. You must snap out of your selfish stupor and accept the facts."

Violette had fled to a corner of the room and covered her

ears. Alex rushed over and took her in his arms. "Mama is not mad at you," he whispered, hugging her close.

Led by fear and anxiety, Annet crossed her arms and turned her back against them. Fleur was out there, and all she needed to do was stay here, search, and wait until she found her way home. Unrelenting snow covered the windows, blocking her view, and all she saw was her own reflection and the dark room behind her. A desperate sense of loneliness enveloped her, the emptiness in her heart a deep ache. She wrung her gloved hands, the muscles in her neck tense and painful. Darn! Wasn't there anything more she could do?

Gradually, her tattered emotions calmed, only to be replaced by shame over her outburst. Her agitated behavior was irrefutable evidence of how much her life had spun out of control. Besides, her anguish wore on her marriage, and it equally wore on the children, the employees, and the business, her long absence causing problems at the factory and the shipping yard. But, against her own better judgement, she strengthened her resolve. She could never give up on Fleur. Ever. Angry, she wiped her tears away. "No matter what you say, I'm staying."

She heard the door close. Without a word, Alex and Violette had walked out.

Still brooding over all the injustices in the world, Annet noticed a lonely rider hunched over his horse, battling his way through the snow to the front door. He dismounted and tied his horse to a post. Before he could knock, Annet opened the door to let him in.

"Let's get you out of this dreadful weather," she cried out, wondering what had brought their coachman and Scott and Trudy Jonkers' boy out under these horrendous conditions.

Henry stamped his feet on the mat and shook the snow off his coat, like a dog, wet flakes flying around and landing on the tiled floor.

"Warm up by the fire in the drawing room while I ask Gloria to make a hot toddy," Annet said. In the kitchen, she found her husband and Violette, enjoying a hot cocoa. "Henry Jonkers just arrived," she told him. "I don't know yet what brought him here."

Alex followed her into the drawing room, finding Henry in front of the hearth warming his hands, the red flames flickering brightly.

"Sorry to disturb you both," he said.

"No concern, Son," Alex replied. "I'm sure what brought you is of importance."

Henry nodded. "Yesterday, my parents sent word that they received three passengers. They need to be delivered from their farm to the Keizer Estate in Heemstead no later than tomorrow."

A passenger was the code name used for a slave who'd escaped their white owner in the South. Together with the Jonkers' family, Alex and Annet had been part of the Underground Railroad for several years, risking their own freedom by harboring slaves in their home, on their way to safety in Canada. Annet and Alex exchanged worried glances, the stakes high and the danger great.

"We already planned to leave the manor and go home to the

Keizer Estate in Heemstead as soon as the weather breaks today. How does it look out there?"

"Grandmother says it will clear before sunset," Henry said, his grandmother Amelia famous for her inaccurate weather predictions. He rolled his eyes and laughed.

"Let's hope she's right." Alex grinned and added more wood to the fire to crank it up. He'd aged over the last few months, and Annet knew she had too. Their sleepless nights were impossible to count, the heartache etched in their faces.

Gloria arrived with three hot drinks, and they sat down in the hardback chairs closest to the fire. While the men talked, Annet stared into the flames, thinking about the slaves they'd sheltered throughout the years, most of them ripped away from their homes and families, arriving with scars on their backs, burns or cuts on their faces, and sometimes with missing fingers and hands, or with their teeth knocked out. Shame welled inside her at her own self-pitying behavior while there were people who had lost so much more than her. Resolutely, she shot to her feet. "I'll go home as well."

"But Ma'am, your husband just told me you wanted to stay here in case Fleur comes home?"

"Receiving those passengers is more important right now," she said, straightening her back.

At sunset, warmer air moved in and snow changed into drizzle. By morning, it was far above freezing, some of the thick layer of snow already beginning to melt.

Henry Jonkers had spent the night, and helped one of the stable boys hitch the two horses to the carriage.

"I'm so grateful you want to stay at the Manor to keep searching for Fleur, Henry," Annet told him, giving him an appreciative hug.

The Jonkers had been her best friends since she'd landed in 1840, all forlorn and terrified, and she'd seen all their children grow up. They were like family to her. "On our way home, we'll inform your parents of your whereabouts and we'll ask your wife to come and join you."

Henry and his wife lived at the coach house at the Keizer Estate in Heemstead, the young couple barely married for one year.

"That would be wonderful, ma'am," he replied.

Gloria and Violette joined Alex and Annet outside, and the four of them climbed into the carriage, all bundled up, ready to leave.

"Let's go," the coachman said. The two robust workhorses pulled the wheels through the slushy snow, the sand underneath still frozen.

Annet turned around in her seat and gazed at Keizer Manor until it was out of sight.

"I look forward to seeing Frank," Alex said when they reached the main road.

Their son was studying at Heemstead University to become an industrial engineer. He'd reluctantly left their summer home to return to classes shortly after Fleur's disappearance.

"Me too," Violette said, her hand in Alex's.

Annet stayed quiet, her mind with Fleur, the passengers who were due to arrive around midnight, and all the work she'd neglected over the last two months.

"I just realized it will be Christmas in four days," she said. They all knew nobody would celebrate this year.

Chapter 24

Annet

DURING THEIR FIRST NIGHT back at the Keizer Estate in Heemstead, Annet and Alex slid out of bed and got dressed in the dark. It was close to midnight, and without lighting a single candle, they headed down the stairs and into the kitchen. They'd made sure it would be warm, and the coal bed in the furnace glowed bright red. Alex added more coal while Annet rekindled the cast iron cookstove to reheat the vegetable soup, her stomach clenched into a tight knot. She knew how much there was at stake, each time feeling more scared than before. Tonight, it almost became too much, her nerves jangled, her unlimited well of courage almost dried up.

They didn't have to wait long for the four sharp knocks on the kitchen door, the signal that the passengers had arrived. Alex hurried to let them in, only three women standing there, the driver who'd delivered them long gone. They stumbled in, hunched over and shaking like leaves. In the fire's glow, Annet could tell they were exhausted, barely able to stay upright.

"Please, take a seat at the table," she said, welcoming them inside. "I have soup and bread."

Annet looked them over, noticing their clothes were in good condition and their coats and woolen scarves around their heads and necks seemed warm; somebody else along the way had already clothed them.

"Thank you, ma'am," one of them said, her large brown eyes flitting back and forth, skittish and afraid.

Annet filled three bowls while Alex cut and buttered the bread, wrapping the rest in a linen rag for them to eat later. They ate in silence, sending their hosts grateful glances. As soon as they were done, Annet lit a candle, opened the cellar door, and motioned them to follow her down the stairs. Alex stayed behind, standing guard in case one of the kitchen maids wandered in.

"Hold on to the railing," Annet warned the women and lit another candle when she reached the dirt floor. She handed the candle to one of them. Without speaking, she guided them past the bags of potatoes, cases of wine, and crates filled with turnips, beets, carrots, and other root vegetables. The shelves against the back wall of the cellar were filled with metal containers used for canning. Annet waved them to the darkest corner and opened a partition of the shelves, like a door, the hidden hinges oiled and quiet. One of the women peered into the dark hole behind it, accidentally knocking one of the cans off the shelf. It landed on the ground with a loud thud and rolled away. Annet pressed a finger against her mouth, their scared faces lit by the light of the flickering candle. "Shhh. Come, quickly."

The women scurried after Annet into the dark and

uninviting hole. It resembled a prison cell, with two bunks on either side and a bucket in the middle. The smell of mildew clung to the stained brick walls, the air oppressive.

"Each bunk has enough blankets to keep you warm and there are candles, plenty of water, and food in this crate," Annet explained. "The secret door remains unlocked, but don't open it, because you might stumble into someone on the other side. Your next transport will be here within forty-eight hours, and I'll check on you in twenty-four. Please, stay as quiet as a mouse, for everyone's safety."

Annet wanted to comfort the women with words of encouragement. They were so scared and leaving them in a dark hole without windows had to be terrifying. But the fewer words that were exchanged, the less the runaways could recall in case they were captured and possibly tortured to reveal information about the safe houses.

"Thank you, ma'am. We'll be eternally grateful," one of them said.

"Farewell," Annet replied.

Alex waited for her at the top of the stairs. One look at her face was enough for him to open his arms and pull her into a comforting embrace.

The next day dragged on, the knowledge of the poor women in the cellar and the longing for Fleur crushing her normally positive and fiery spirit. She barely recognized herself.

"Fortunately, we don't have young ones we need to hide right now," Alex said.

Fleur was the only one of their children who knew about

their dangerous work. On occasion, she would sneak into the cellar at night to play cards, checkers, or another board game with the escapees. Especially when they brought children, to keep them occupied and distracted during the long hours.

Just after midnight, Annet went down to the cellar. At the sound of the opening door, the three women huddled together in the farthest corner of their cell, relief evident on their faces when they recognized her.

"Is everything going well?" she asked, the stench of human feces almost making her vomit. "Let me empty the bucket."

When she returned, one of the women lay on her bunk.

"Ma'am," one of the other two said. "Perlie's running a fever and in a lot of pain. She can barely stand and doesn't want to eat."

Annet touched the young woman's forehead. She was burning up. "I'll get my husband," she said and hurried to get Alex.

Half an hour later, they undressed the young woman in their bedroom upstairs and lowered her into the bathtub, the water cold. "We have to bring your fever down, and wash out your wounds," Annet explained, the infected lacerations on the poor girl's back oozing pus. She'd been beaten severely, the bright red gashes angry and jagged.

Or should she let Perlie's body temperature help kill the infections? She questioned her own actions. They lifted the moaning girl out of the bathtub and onto the floor, where they'd made a makeshift bed. Calling a doctor was a risk they couldn't take and Annet dried and dressed her wounds to the best of her ability, her only knowledge the few specifics she remembered from her past.

"I don't know what else to do, Alex," she exclaimed, close to tears. "What if she doesn't make it?"

Chapter 25

Fleur

HOOKED UP TO TUBES and with a mask for oxygen covering her nose and mouth, Fleur opened her eyes. Compression boots on her lower legs gently inflated and deflated, to help the blood flow in her legs. A nurse checked her breathing, blood pressure, heart rate, temperature, and oxygen level. She smiled and unhooked her. "Hi Fleur. Your surgery went well, and we're ready to move you to the intensive care unit."

A tear escaped from the corner of Fleur's eye and dripped onto the soft linen of her pillow, followed by a second and a third.

"No need to cry, Hon," the nurse said. "You're doing great."

They rolled her bed from the recovery room to the ICU. The white ceilings of the hospital flew by in a blur, the elevator ride, the nurse's words, and the arrival in her room like a dream.

"Rest and save your strength," the nurse said. She hooked Fleur back up to the monitors, checked the readings, and patted her arm. "Dr. Stevenson will come and see you soon."

Groggy and slightly sick to her stomach, Fleur nodded and closed her eyes. The relief of having survived surgery made her head spin.

When she opened her eyes, Emmett sat next to her bed, holding her hand. "Did I fall asleep?" she croaked, her throat painful and her voice hoarse.

He pressed his lips into her palm and kissed it several times, his face drawn, his eyes large and filled with concern. "How do you feel?"

"Thirsty," she replied, fighting to stay awake.

He picked up the cup of water from the nightstand, lifted her mask, and placed the straw between her lips. "The nurse told me you would be, so I came prepared."

She took a sip and swallowed hard, the cool water soothing her throat. "I'm alive," she whispered. She took another sip and closed her eyes, the desire to fall back asleep overwhelming. She shivered underneath the blankets and dozed off.

"Are you cold? Do you want another blanket?"

Emmett's concerned voice penetrated the fog in her brain and a lump formed in her sore throat, making it impossible to speak.

He placed her palm against his cheek. "It'll be all right," he whispered hoarsely. "I know it will."

His skin felt warm, his stubble soft yet bristly, his grip strong and reassuring. *Don't leave,* she thought while she drifted off.

How long she'd slept, she didn't know, but when she opened her eyes, Emmett was still there.

Overcome by emotions, all she could do was stare at his

handsome face, warm feelings for him rising inside her. *For heaven's sake,* Fleur, she thought. *You can't allow yourself to fall in love with him.* They had no future together, and the potential consequences of a romance between them would only cause unwanted pain and complications.

Unaware she'd woken up, Emmett put his teeth into a donut, one booted foot resting on his knee, the chair slightly tipped backwards.

"Did you save one for me?" she whispered.

He dropped his chair back on all fours and wiped the powdered sugar off his mouth with a sheepish grin. "I got so hungry. How are you feeling?" His eyes searched hers, his brows knitted in concern.

"Tired and a bit emotional," she whispered.

"You've been through a lot."

He helped her take another sip of water, the pain in her throat less severe and the nausea in her stomach dissipated. She shifted in her bed to ease the discomfort in her upper body.

"Do you have a lot of pain?" Emmett asked, noticing her grimace. "Is there anything I can do for you?"

At the sound of approaching footsteps, he turned around in his chair and watched Cassius walk in, a bouquet in his hand.

"Fleur, you're awake." A huge grin illuminated his face. "How are you, my dear?" He approached the bed and hugged her gently, ignoring the oxygen mask, tubes, and other hospital equipment. "I better be careful before everything starts to beep in protest." He put the flowers on the table below the television, next to several other bouquets, balloons, and get-well cards. Cassius read the cards. "All well wishes from Forrest and Kara,

Josie and Caro, and your grandmother Barbara."

Anger simmered inside her. Why did these strangers intrude on her life? She pressed her lips together, biting away her irrational feelings of resentment against them.

Someone knocked on the door, and Dr. Stevenson walked in. "Good afternoon," he said.

Emmett moved away from her bed to make room for him.

The cardiologist checked the readings on the monitors and the dressing that covered her surgical incisions. He nodded his approval. "That looks good. Now, can you cough for me several times to clear your lungs?"

Fleur breathed in with difficulty and coughed, ready to rip her mask off.

"You need to do this every hour while you're awake, and you need to take long and deep breaths, to lower your risk of pneumonia." He gave her an encouraging smile. "Trust me, it'll get easier. And I'll ask a nurse to replace your mask with an oxygen tube under your nose. That will be much more comfortable."

"How did the surgery go, Doctor?" Cassius asked.

Dr. Stevenson removed his surgical cap and stuffed it in the pocket of his blue scrubs. "I have good news. We repaired Fleur's tricuspid valve, and although the damage to her mitral valve was severe, we decided a repair was the better option, considering her age."

He seemed pleased with the outcome, and Fleur let out a teary gasp of relief. "Does that mean my heart is fixed and I'll be healthy again?"

The surgeon nodded. "We're going to monitor you closely

over the next several years, but for now, you're on the road to a full recovery."

"Oh my God, this is amazing," Emmett jubilated and planted a joyful kiss on her forehead, the tension on his face lifted. "I'm so happy!"

"Thank you so much, Doctor," Cassius said with a grateful smile. He grabbed Fleur's hand and squeezed it, the positive outcome taking a huge load off his mind. "Congratulations, Honey."

"How long does she need to stay in the hospital, Dr. Stevenson?" Emmett asked quickly before the surgeon walked out.

Dr. Stevenson stopped at the foot of Fleur's bed. "For tonight, we'll keep her in the ICU, and tomorrow she'll be moved to a regular room in the Cardiac Care Unit where she'll stay for about three days."

Fleur watched the three men move around in the room. Much of what they said went by her.

"She'll be tired and sore during that time, and may experience some brief, sharp pains on either side of her chest. Her chest, shoulders, and upper back may ache also, and she could show signs of depression, anxiety, and anger. But she'll improve each day, and after she's home for three to five weeks, she should be able to do many of her usual activities. Of course, we want to monitor her closely and check her incisions. After that, we suggest an echocardiogram six months from now, followed by yearly check-ups to assess her valve function."

Bright rays of sunlight beamed into her room, waking her

up. For the third night in a row, it felt like she'd barely slept, with hospital personnel constantly walking in and out, and the arrival of another patient in the empty bed next to her.

"We're having another glorious spring day," a nurse chitchatted while she checked her incision sites. "My six-year-old is on the school bus for a field trip at the petting zoo. I'm so glad it's not raining."

Fleur had no idea what a field trip, a petting zoo, or a school bus was. She still had a lot to learn and discover about this new world. "Can you tell me more about that?"

The nurse chattered on while she helped Fleur to the bathroom and back, checked all her vitals, and filled her glass with water. Everybody had been friendly and caring, the room sparkling clean, the sheets and blankets immaculately white, and the offered variety of food offered was remarkable.

"Yogurt with granola and fresh fruit sounds wonderful," she replied, when they came to ask what she wanted for breakfast.

Fruits and vegetables seemed to be available year-round. Room temperature was regulated by the touch of a button, machines did your laundry, and cellphones kept you in touch with the outside world. Gradually, she began to get used to, and even appreciate, this intriguing, luxurious and noisy world, especially the doctors giving her a second chance at life. She couldn't be more grateful.

After a visit from Dr. Stevenson, the chatty nurse came to get her. "Ready to move to a room in the Cardiac Care Unit?" she asked and helped her into a wheelchair.

Tired and still sore, Fleur winced at the pain in various

muscles. With her brain still in a fog and her emotions in disarray, she was relieved to follow orders and that she didn't have to make any decisions. Soon, she was settled in, her bed next to a window overlooking the city. One of the nurse's aides rolled in a cart with all the flowers and get-well cards she'd received, including the one from Gerhard and Andrea Overton, and Jackie, Geoff, Stephanie, and Marcus. She didn't recall who these people were and dozed off until a nurse brought in her lunch.

"Why do they constantly have to wake me?" she grumbled to herself, ill-tempered and drained. With Emmett and Cassius at work, the afternoon stretched out in front of her, and all she wanted to do was sleep. She took a bite of the turkey sandwich. It was dry and tasteless and nothing like the fresh baked bread from home.

She grabbed her phone and texted Emmett in the hope he would reply. He didn't. The only other numbers in her phone were for Cassius and Forrest, both not an option, and the puzzle game Emmett had installed was a complete waste of time. A sullen mood settled over her, and she stared at the ceiling, unhappy with the world.

Voices at the door made her glance up.

"Hi, Fleur," Kara Overton said as she walked in. Forrest's wife was accompanied by two young women, one dark-haired and one blonde. "We heard your surgery was a success and wanted to see how you're doing." Kara carried a huge bouquet of yellow flowers and put it at the foot of the bed before awkwardly giving her a half-hug. "I hope it's okay I brought Josie and Caro. They were so eager to meet you."

"Oh, my word, Fleur," Josie cried out, her brown eyes sparkling and her smile radiant. "I can't believe how much you look like Caro." She pulled her younger sister closer to the bed. "Look, what do you think?"

Caro sent her sister a warning glare. "Please, Josie. You promised to tone it down." Then she turned her attention to Fleur. "We're so happy you're doing better. Are you in any pain?" She tucked her long blonde curls behind her ear, her warm smile shy and a bit nervous.

"To tell you the truth," Fleur said, concentrating on her steady heartbeat. "I'm feeling better. It's hard to explain. Although I'm very tired, it seems my mind is clearer."

"That's so wonderful to hear," Kara said, her expression shifting from concern to relief. "Congratulations."

Caro stood next to Fleur's bed and clapped her hands together. "I'm so happy for you that the surgery went well. It must have been very difficult and scary to realize your heart wasn't working well." Her soft blue eyes misted over. "I read up on it online, and from what I understand, the repair on your heart will improve the oxygen supply to your brain. It could very well be that you already notice an improvement."

Fleur didn't understand what Caro was saying, but she recognized her concern was genuine and appreciated her kind words.

"While you're getting acquainted, I'll find a vase for the flowers," Kara said while Josie busied herself with the plastic chairs, dragging them closer to Fleur's bed.

"I'm very happy too, and so excited to finally meet you." Josie's brown eyes sparkled with delight. "Growing up, Dad talked about you all the time, and I can't wait to hear all your stories about the time when you grew up." Her excited, joyful laughter filled the room. "I have another sister! This is so dope. I can hardly believe it's for real." She sat down in one of the chairs and leaned with her elbows on Fleur's bed. "It must have been so hard for you in the beginning, after you arrived, Fleur. How were you able to adjust?"

Thinking back to her first week here, Fleur realized most of it had gone by in a big blur. She'd been so tired and overwhelmed with all the new impressions. Instead, she told them how Emmett had scared her with his motorcycle, and they all laughed.

"I saw you at the Keizer Museum with Emmet," Josie said with interest. "You sat next to my grandmother, and you looked so familiar, but I couldn't place you."

Fleur remembered the girl who'd asked if Emmett was going to attend a party. "Was that you?"

"Yes, I was so curious who you were."

Kara walked back into the room. "Please, Josie. Fleur is recovering from heart surgery." She placed the flowers next to the other vases, checking their water and pulling a few dead leaves.

The unexpected arrival of the three women had come as a welcome surprise, and Fleur appreciated the distraction. Their friendly, caring voices and their strange familiarity twisted her scarred heart and warmed her insides. Tears gathered in her eyes, and she pressed her hand to her mouth to keep from crying, her somber mood forgotten. "Sorry for being so emotional," she smiled through her tears. "I felt a little lost and hopeless and am so delighted you came to brighten my day."

Kara pulled a small pack of tissues from her purse. "Who else needs one?" she asked, patting her own eyes dry.

Chapter 26

FLEUR PLACED HER HAND under her breast and felt her heartbeat, strong and steady.

"Can I really go home already, Dr. Stevenson?" It had only been three days since her surgery, and she'd expected to stay much longer.

"Yes, you can, Fleur," Dr. Stevenson said. "Everything has gone well, and I don't see any reason to keep you here."

Cassius stood next to her bed and placed his hand on her arm, a huge grin on his face. "Wonderful news."

The doctor returned his smile. "Fleur, you'll still be tired for several weeks, but with each passing day, you'll feel more energized. I would like to see you again in two weeks, with another follow-up at two months. Hopefully by then, I can give you a clean bill of health."

A nurse helped her get dressed and into the wheelchair, rolling her outside while Cassius got the car. On the way home, Fleur glanced through all the papers the doctor had given her concerning suggested activities, diet, medication, and incision care.

"Do you think I need to stay here for more than two months before I can go home?" she asked Cassius. "That's such a long time."

"All I know is that the Department of Defense won't authorize your return until Dr. Stevenson assures us you're in good health."

Fleur stared out the passenger window at the busy city traffic. They passed a bus full of people that came to a halt at a bus stop, and Cassius changed lanes. "Don't you think I'll be healthy enough in two weeks?"

"It's not up to me, Fleur. I know flying after surgery can sometimes increase the risk of blood clots and what you'll be put through is probably even more strenuous on your body than what astronauts endure when they're shot into space in a rocket."

Fleur touched the bandage covering her scar with her fingertips. She couldn't wait to go home, but blood clots sounded scary.

They soon drove through Dunedam and passed Keizer Manor. Cassius slowed down and came to a halt at a gate. It was set up at the beginning of the road towards the Research Center. *Had they built that in the seven days she'd been at the hospital?* It seemed impossible.

Cassius showed his driver license and security pass to one of the soldiers guarding the gate before they were allowed to go through.

Inside the new perimeter, Fleur noticed four tents and several green vehicles with huge tires.

"Those are army tents and vehicles, Fleur," Cassius

explained, clutching the steering wheel in a tight grip. "People talk, and the government is afraid the public will realize what's happening here, so they increased security."

She could tell from his tense shoulders and brooding expression that he wasn't happy about the changes. "Can I still go in and out?"

"Of course you can," he reassured her. "But from now on, you also need to show identification. I have a card for you at home."

By the time they reached Cassius's house, Fleur was exhausted.

Cassius rounded the car and helped her get out. "I went grocery shopping earlier today," he told her, the bag with her personal belonging hanging from his shoulder. "I bought the yogurt and oatmeal cookies you really like. Lots of bananas and apples, grapes, bread, salad, carrots. You name it."

The door of the house opened, and Emmett came running out, picking her up as if she weighed nothing. "I'll carry you inside," he said and kissed her cheek.

She winced in pain, and he loosened his grip. "Sorry, I don't want to hurt you."

Fleur wrapped her arms around his neck and kissed him back, excited to see him. "How did you find out I was coming home today?"

He carried her over the threshold into the living room and carefully sat her down on the couch, the room decorated with paper garlands and a big sign that read *Welcome Home*.

"Did you do that for me?" she asked, cheerfully clapping her hands.

"Lucia from next door brought the garlands," Emmett replied with a gleeful grin. "I made the sign."

"And Forrest and Kara ordered a cake," Cassius said, carrying in a beautifully decorated chocolate cake.

After Emmett and Cassius went back to work, Fleur dozed on the couch and thought about Forrest. He desperately wanted to see her and had reached out to her through Cassius, Emmett, and multiple text messages she had ignored.

Emmett had put a good word in for him. He'd known him his entire life and told her he was a good man, and a caring husband and father. But seeing him was still too much to ask. Her life was in such turmoil, with her heart surgery, her developing feelings for Emmett, and all the adjustments she constantly had to make.

"I understand you miss your family terribly," Emmett had said. "But you have another family here, with grandparents, uncles and aunts who are all eager to meet you."

She knew he was right, and only wanted to help, but she needed more time, the idea of Alex Keizer not being her biological father still too devastating to accept.

Her phone pinged, and she found several messages from Josie, Caro, and Kara, welcoming her home. It still surprised her how easy it was to stay in touch compared to sending letters by mail that took days to arrive.

At a knock on the door, she pushed the blanket away and sat up. "Come on in," she yelled, expecting Lucia, who'd promised to stop by. Instead of the neighbor girl, Forrest walked in, a large bouquet in his hand. "Hi, Fleur," he said. Under his arm, he carried a thick manila envelope. "Can I come in for five minutes?"

She sagged back down on the couch. He was the last person she wanted to see.

Forrest looked at the decorations, and the chocolate cake and dirty saucers that were still on the coffee table. "It's so festive in here." He took several steps in her direction. "Rightfully so. Recovering from heart surgery is a big deal, and I'm so grateful the doctors could help you. How are you feeling, honey?"

For no apparent reason, tears stung behind her eyes. "Still tired," she said and straightened out her wrinkled blouse. "But I'm grateful to be home."

Forrest studied her. "You have more color in your cheeks and look wonderful. Are you still in pain?"

"Just a little." To avoid his gaze, she examined her fingernails. "The doctor said I'll have good days and bad days, but that I should be back to normal in several weeks." She made a funny face and laughed. "To be honest, I don't even know what that would feel like. I'm so used to being sick, miserable, and worthless." Despite her bravado, her own words made her feel hollow, sad, and vulnerable, and she didn't understand why.

He sat down in Cassius's recliner and placed the flowers on the coffee table. "I'm sure the good days will quickly outnumber the bad, and soon you'll feel better than ever." His blond curls fell over his forehead, his grin warm and reassuring. "Look, I realize you're not ready to see me." He paused and tapped with his fingers on the envelope in his lap. "And I totally understand if you never are, but I believe that if you're back home in several months, there's a chance you may come to regret not getting to know me."

He held up the thick envelope. "These are copies of the letters your mother wrote me, and you can do with them whatever you want. Just understand that I always wanted to be a father and that I've loved you from the moment your mother told me she was pregnant. Finally getting to meet you is one of the greatest joys of my life."

After he left, she lay back down and stared at the ceiling, the envelope Forrest had given her still on the table next to the flowers. Scared to find out what was inside, she burrowed a little deeper under the warm quilt, her already shaky world wobbling precariously. Ten minutes later, she changed position, the outline of a yellow rectangular envelope imprinted on her brain. She tossed and turned for a little while longer. Then gave up. She wasn't tired enough to sleep, her mind buzzing with energy. It was a sensation she wasn't used to.

Around four o'clock, Emmett walked in. She'd just washed the three dirty saucers, put the leftover cake in the fridge, and settled back on the couch with a book. "You're off early?" she asked. One look at him was enough for her to recognize that something was bothering him.

He shrugged. "They just told me my internship will end in four weeks. I expected to be here for another two months."

Fleur closed her book. "Why?"

"They didn't say, and Cassius has no idea either." He scowled. "Since the military took over, everything's changed." He took a deep breath and sat down next to her. "Did you see all the army barracks they set up?" He lifted her legs, scooted underneath them and winked at her. "This is cozy."

Instead of protesting at the intimacy, like she knew she was supposed to, she enjoyed feeling his hand on her knee, and his muscular legs warm beneath hers. In a very short time, he'd become far more important to her than she wanted, and a tingle moved up into her stomach. He was so handsome, charming, and kind, and she longed to slide her fingers through his wavy brown hair.

"Earlier today, I had a meeting with Cassius, Ramon and Adam," Emmett said, interrupting her thoughts. "We talked about the impact SMITS's forces have on people and various objects."

"What do you mean?" Fleur asked.

"It's kinda complicated," he replied. "Your mother traveled two-hundred years into the past, while you traveled less than two-hundred years into the future. In what year the goats have landed, we can only imagine. Our plan is to experiment with smaller objects that we want to send to the past and the future."

Subconsciously, Fleur rubbed the strips of tape covering her incision. It still hurt a little. "Do you think it has something to do with weight?"

"Yes, we do," he replied. "We believe that if we use a couch, for example, it might either travel farther in time, or just the opposite. We just don't know and need to start experimenting."

The idea of a flying couch made her laugh. "As long as it doesn't land on someone's head, it could be amusing."

"That's one reason the military is here, to make sure nobody will get hurt or get accidentally sucked up."

Fleur laughed even louder. "Sucking up like a big vacuum cleaner!" When Emmett didn't reply, she examined his face. "Did I say something wrong?"

"Not at all," he quickly reassured her. "It's just that.... this is the first time I heard you laugh so free from restraint, and the sound is music to my ears."

It was hard to believe she'd only been here a month. So much had happened in the few short weeks. "It seems my mind is already sharper than before surgery," she said, smiling happily. "As if a fog has lifted."

Emmett grabbed her hands and pulled her closer until she sat in his lap. "I love seeing you so cheerful," he whispered against her mouth, his arms strong around her back.

With her fingertips, she brushed a strand of hair behind his ear and leaned in closer. Jeremiah had only kissed her a few times, and they'd been awkward and reserved. She'd dreamed of being in Emmett's arms, hoping it would feel different, better. She planted a hesitant kiss on his lips to encourage him, immediately shocked at her wanton behavior. Before she could pull back, his lips parted slightly, the tip of his tongue probing tenderly against hers as he gazed into her eyes.

Unable to resist, she opened her mouth, allowing him access, his breath warm and sweet on her skin. She wrapped her arms around his neck as he gently deepened his kiss, seeking and exploring, warming her insides. It had never been like this with Jeremiah, his ungainly advances only tolerated, her replies cool and distant.

"Is it okay that I kiss you?" he asked, raining tender kisses on her cheeks, nose, and lips.

A heady sensation made her head spin, and she buried her hand into his hair, pulling him closer. "Yes," she sighed breathlessly.

They kissed long and tender, caressing, and hugging for the first time, getting to know each other's taste and smell, their powerful sensations new and mysterious.

At the sound of the door opening, they moved away from each other, but not in time for Cassius to notice. "Don't mind me," he said, and hurried to the kitchen.

Chapter 27

"THIS MORNING, we'll send blue plastic storage bins to the past and the future," Cassius said over breakfast the next day.

Fleur didn't reply. With her elbow on the table, her chin resting in her palm, she stared straight ahead, her mind on the magical moment when Emmett had kissed her. She could still feel the touch of his warm lips, his loving embrace, and the soft stubble on his cheeks. "I'm sorry?"

Cassius finished his coffee and wiped his mouth with a paper towel. "I put a letter inside each bin, addressed to the Abernathey Research Center, asking the finder to drop it in the mail to receive a reward."

"That's a smart idea," Fleur agreed.

"Promise you stay inside until you hear from me that it's safe," he warned her for the third time. He put on his suit jacket and cast a wary glance toward her. "Fleur, did you hear me?"

"Yes, yes," she quickly answered and took the last bite of her cold eggs. "Good luck this morning."

After Cassius left, she cleaned off the breakfast table and did the dishes. She'd slept like a baby and felt energetic and full of hope. With her surgery behind her, her health wouldn't be an issue much longer, and with SMITS starting up and the men preparing for her safe return, everything was back on track.

Until thoughts of Emmett and the memory of being in his arms whirled through her mind, forcing her to take inventory of her growing feelings for him. "Not smart, Fleur," she said to herself, aware it would hurt to bid him farewell when the time came around. She sat down on the couch and clutched her elbows. The only choice she had was to harden her heart and suppress her feelings. Because, God forbid, she really shouldn't fall in love with him, like her mother had fallen in love with her father, giving up on Forrest. She shivered. Or had their love been a lie and had she, unbeknownst to her father, written letters to the former lover she had lost?

She gazed at the thick envelope that lay untouched on the coffee table. There was only one way to find out. Her hand trembled when she pulled out the stack of papers. Her mother's handwriting immediately jumped right out.

"January 3, 1851," she read out loud.

My dearest Forrest,

How hard it must be to believe what happened to me, I can only imagine. It took me years to come to terms with it myself. All I can hope is that my letters will somehow reach you soon after my disappearance, so you will get closure, making it possible for you to move on with your life, like I did.

Immediate relief washed over her. This wasn't a love letter. On the contrary. "Forgive me for doubting you, Mother," she mumbled, and continued reading.

Today is Fleur's tenth birthday. She's my daughter, and I realize this must come as another shock to you, she is your daughter too. Unfortunately, photography is still in its early stages, but a few days ago I recruited a photographer who took a beautiful black-and-white photo of her. I will include it with this letter.

She lowered her hands and closed her eyes to will the pain away, tears leaving wet spots on the paper. Although she'd still hoped Forrest wasn't her real father, with the evidence right in front of her, she couldn't deny it any longer.

After sitting like that for several minutes, she put the letters back inside. For now, she had enough to process. Her life was a mess. To distract herself, she turned on the television and watched men in colored shirts run across a green field, kicking a ball. When the game was over, a man talked about kick-off, top league, and World Cup. He might as well have spoken Spanish. She didn't understand any of it. It didn't matter. All she wanted was to relieve the tension and bury her feelings, her teeth clenched so tight that it hurt.

Suddenly, she noticed how dark it had gotten, and when rain clattered against the window, she jumped up to look outside. They had fired SMITS back up. She stared at the pelting rain on the pavement and the green clouds forming overhead. This was exciting and promising, but at the same time terrifying. The tumult went on for five minutes and she stayed at the window until the clouds disappeared, the rain stopped, and the sun came out. A minute later, her phone rang. It was Cassius.

"Everything went according to plan, and it's safe," he said.

"That's wonderful," she replied, and glanced at the clock. It was almost noon. Until today, she would have been exhausted by this time and in need of rest. Instead, she felt well enough to go outside. She put on her borrowed sandals and opened the door. Clean ocean air filled her lungs, the fresh smell of the recent storm all around. She folded her hands and gazed up at the sky. "Thank you, Lord, for bringing me here and healing my damaged heart. Thank you."

Emmett left the research center and noticed her wandering around aimlessly in the parking lot "Is everything okay?" he asked, examining her face. "You seem upset."

Immediately worried about her looks, she touched her hair. "It's just those letters," she admitted and turned away to hide her tear-stricken face.

"You shouldn't read those by yourself, baby," he said, and slipped his arm around her waist. "How about we read them together later tonight? Because while I'm on my lunch break, I'd much rather hold you in my arms and cuddle.

Chapter 28

AFTER EMMETT WENT BACK TO WORK, Fleur did a few breathing exercises, took a nap, and prepared one of her father's favorite meals for dinner. Potatoes, carrots, and onions, all mashed together, and served with sausage and gravy.

"Look at you," Emmett said when he joined her after work. "All busy in the kitchen."

She added water to the pan and placed it on the stove. "We had a cook, and I've never done this before. Does this seem right to you?"

He pretended to inspect her work. "Looks mighty damn fine to me, ma'am." He took her in his arms and his mouth searched for hers, kissing her ravenously when he found it.

For several seconds, she clung to his shoulders and kissed him back, wanting more. Instead, she drew away with a smile. "You're such a distraction. I need to finish making dinner before Cassius gets home."

He kissed the tip of her nose and let her go. "Can I help?"

After dinner, Cassius disappeared into the kitchen to clean

up, while Fleur and Emmett migrated to the couch.

"You still want to read those letters, right?" he asked, and picked the envelope off the floor.

Fleur gazed around the cozy room and reflected on her friendship with Cassius and Emmet. They made her feel welcome and at home in this strange world. Without them, she would have been lost, the letters never to be read and ending in the garbage. "Why don't you read them to me?" she asked, her voice pleading.

"Of course," Emmett replied and pulled out the entire stack. "January 3rd," he began, with Fleur next to him, her head resting against his shoulder. He soon finished the first letter.

"I want to see those pictures of you."

She was relieved he didn't comment on Forrest being her biological father. Something he'd known his entire life, but that she still struggled to accept. He continued reading about Annet's difficulties adjusting to her new environment, the numerous confrontations she had with her father and brother-in-law, problems at the shipping yard, and her desire to expand the clothing factory.

"It reads more like a diary than personal letters," he concluded after he finished the seventh letter. "As if your mother wants to vent frustrations and concerns, going over her problems while writing them down. Don't you agree?"

With each letter, Fleur had become more and more enthralled, remembering several heated conversations around the dining room table, broken off by her father, who always tried to keep the peace. She also recalled the horrible fire at the shipyard that caused the death of two dock workers. It had devastated her mother, believing as owners, it was all their fault, and that they should compensate the workers' families.

"I was so worried they were love letters for Forrest," she admitted.

"Oh, no, on the contrary," Emmett agreed full heartedly. "Here, listen to this. I don't know what I would do without Alex. His comforting presence is the only reason I don't throw in the towel."

Fleur nodded. She couldn't be prouder of her mother's accomplishments and distinction. "My mother is the strongest and smartest woman I know." She placed her hand on Emmett's knee, the material of his work pants hard and coarse. "Someday soon, I'm going to tell her that."

Emmett took a gulp from his water bottle and coughed a few times to clear his throat. "Sorry," he apologized. "I choked."

Fleur looked at the next letter. "This one is about scarlet fever." She took the letter and started reading herself.

Hundreds of children in Heemstead are ill with scarlet fever, and the mortality rate is high. Fleur and Frank are ill too. To keep Violette safe, Alex took her to Keizer Manor, and I'm staying home to take care of Fleur and Frank. We have to keep them isolated and burn their clothes and bedding to prevent contagion. I wash my hands a hundred times a day, clean doorknobs, surfaces, and everything they touch. I also give them as much fresh fruit and vegetables as possible. It's a constant fight to make them eat and drink.

She didn't remember that her father had left for the coast

with Violette. Maybe she'd been too sick to notice.

It's been several days without change. Tragically, one of Frank's friends lost his battle against this horrible disease. He was only ten years old. It's a full-blown epidemic and there's so much heartbreak. The entire family is on edge, and my father-in-law walks around the house like a ghost. He cares much more for the children than he likes to let on.

Fortunately, it looks like Frank's fever is subsiding, and his throat is less painful, but Fleur is still fighting. The poor little thing. Her tongue is red and bumpy, she has a terrible skin rash and the glands in her neck are swollen. She's so ill, and I don't know what to do. I'm so scared.

Another ten days have gone by, and Fleur is finally showing signs of improvement. I don't dare to say it out loud, but I believe she's going to pull through. We are so incredibly fortunate to still have our three children with us, while other parents have lost more than one, including Trudy and Scott Jonkers who lost two of their six children. We will try to comfort them in their grief and pay for the funeral expenses.

The last three weeks have been the hardest of my life, and I'm completely exhausted, but also grateful I didn't get sick myself. Or is scarlet fever mainly a childhood illness, like the measles, chicken pox, and mumps? I never had those and wish I remembered more.

Alex sent word that he and Violette will come home tomorrow. The house feels empty without them, and I've missed them so much. I can't wait to see them.

"I'm so grateful you pulled through," Emmett whispered in her hair, hugging her tight. "Otherwise, I never would have met you."

Chapter 29

EVERYTHING FLEUR HAD LEARNED about her mother kept her awake. She felt guilty for not understanding her better, listening to her more, and being kinder. Instead, she had judged her hardworking, smart, and caring mother while she struggled to adjust to a different world, a completely different lifestyle, and a time where women weren't treated equally. She remembered how often her mother had complained about that. "Ignorant bullheads, narcissistic assholes, conceited jerks." All kinds of words only her mother used. She laughed softly at the memory, the love she felt for her mother stronger than ever before.

Reading the letters had also brought back memories of Fleur's and the Jonkers's illness, her parents' friends who had the dairy farm along the Dune Road. Each time her family vacationed at Keizer Manor, they'd stopped there to buy eggs, fresh milk, cheese, and vegetables they grew in their garden. Russell Jr. was her age, and their second son and now their coachman, Henry, was the same age as Frank. She had loved to visit and hang out with the chickens, their dog, and the cows. It was a completely different world than her life in the city.

At the crack of dawn, she got dressed and climbed behind the computer. So much had changed in the last two centuries. Homesick, she typed in Jonkers Dairy Farm in Dunedam with one finger. If it still existed, it would be less than two miles from the research center, and she could ask Emmett to take her there on his motorcycle. The search results yielded nothing.

A door opened and Cassius appeared from his bedroom in his blue and white plaid pajamas. "Why are you up so early?"

She turned around in her chair. "I understand you're experimenting with SMITS. Is it possible to send another letter to my parents? There's so much I want to tell them."

The morning flew by with her required breathing exercises and walk along the perimeter of the research center, followed by a warm shower. As instructed, she let the soapy water run over the incision and carefully patted it dry with a clean towel. With a cup of tea, she finally sat down to write, the words flowing easily after going over them in her head.

At lunch time, she sat down behind the computer with Emmett. "Cassius asked me to look into metal containers so we can securely send off your letter," he explained. He had brought a salad loaded with chicken and croutons, and two forks. "Since we don't know how long they will be exposed to the elements, they need to be strong and made from aluminum or brass, because those metals don't rust."

He typed in "round metal container" and images of cannisters, pots, and vases appeared, none of them suitable for what they had in mind, until one image caught his attention. "Maybe this is an idea?" he said and clicked on it.

A picture of a shiny metal pipe with a lid on each side appeared.

"A time capsule? What's that?" Fleur asked.

He enlarged the image. "When I was a senior in high school, we left trinkets in them that were important to us. The plan is to open them on our twenty-fifth high school reunion, I believe." He grinned at the memory. "But time capsules are mainly intended to leave information for the future, to help them understand the past, and they should be able to withstand centuries."

"Just like my mother's letters," Fleur nodded.

On Saturday, she woke up to bright sunlight, nervous about the upcoming visit to the coach house at the Keizer Estate, where Emmett lived with his parents. He wanted her to meet them and his brother Finn. She stared at her meager wardrobe. Emmett had assured her nobody dressed up for lunch and that she should wear whatever she wanted. "But if you want, I can take you shopping."

That didn't help much, and she settled on Lucia's red dress. With the crochet lace, round neck, and short sleeves, it was less casual than pants and a top, and would make her feel better. Then she decided against it. Wearing a dress on a motorcycle would be difficult, and she slipped into a pair of jeans and a shirt instead.

Around ten, Emmett knocked on the door. "You look gorgeous," he said, his eyes filled with admiration.

All she had done differently was her hair, and she smiled. "Thanks."

On the way out, she grabbed her light jacket, but instead of bringing his motorcycle, Emmett walked to the shiny red four-door hatchback parked in front of the house.

"Oh, you're taking me in a car?"

"It's my mother's." He opened the passenger door to let her step in.

Fleur's heart thudded steadily and strong, and her mind was clear. "I feel much better now than I have in years."

Emmett climbed in on the driver's side and leaned over to give her a quick kiss. "I'm so happy to hear it. But my mother insisted it wouldn't be safe for you on the back of my motorcycle yet. I hope you're not mad."

"No, it's very considerate of her," Fleur said, appreciating the gesture.

Emmet started the engine and they drove off. "My parents really look forward to meeting you, and don't be surprised if there's food up the wazoo. They like to go overboard."

Fleur's shoulders tensed at the idea of what lay ahead. *What if they didn't like her?*

On the way to Heemstead, Emmett turned onto the service road. Their internet search for the name Jonkers had brought up a company in an industrial area, and the small screen on the dashboard told them they had reached their destination.

"The farm used to be here somewhere," Fleur said, but all they saw was a huge metal building with tall glass windows, covering at least two acres, and a parking lot with white vans, the words Jonkers Solar and Electric Company in black lettering on the sides.

"This can't be it," Fleur whispered, shaking her head in denial. Subdued, she took in the drastic changes— the dirt road, pastures, cows, farmhouse, and barn all gone.

"Do you want me to go in and ask?" Emmett asked.

She expelled a long sigh. "No, there's no point." To conceal her disappointment, she put on a brave face.

"Since there's nothing here and you don't want me to go in, do you want to shop for clothes?" Emmett suggested. "There's a boutique in Heemstead that Josie and Caro talk about all the time."

"Sure," she replied, preparing herself for anything. "Throwing in a trip to a store could be fun."

Emmett helped her navigate through the boutique. The selection was huge, and she had no idea what to look for. They even sold a variety of shoes in a corner.

"They only sell name brands," Emmett told her.

Fleur shrugged helplessly. "You have to pick out for me what you like," she told him, and took the garments he chose into the dressing room.

An hour later, they left the store, and dressed in a new short-sleeved blouse, capris, and elegant strap sandals, she stepped out of the car at the coach house. From where she stood, she used to be able to see the main house. Now, it was hidden behind tall oak and fir trees and a row of dense shrubs. The coach house itself hadn't changed much. The sturdy stone walls looked brand-new, the bricks a deep color red, and the wooden garage doors were painted in a fresh green coat.

"Two years ago, we had the entire building sandblasted and regrouted," Emmett explained. "The garage doors are new. The old ones were too far gone."

The front door opened, and a man and a woman rushed out. "I'm so delighted to meet you, Fleur. I'm Skye, Emmett's mother. And this is my husband, Rix."

Fleur let herself get hugged and welcomed in, their excited voices and friendly chatter crashing over her like a warm wave.

Unable to speak from nerves, she followed them through the kitchen into a bright and cluttered living room. Bookshelves and paintings covered the walls, there were two desks with computers, and an array of chairs, pillows, and plants. An easel with an unfinished painting stood next to the tall windows, and two orange cats slept on the couch, a forgotten toy mouse next to them.

She recalled entering through the scullery into the kitchen where the huge black kitchen range fueled by coal had dominated the space. Cold water was piped in from the main house to a zinc basin in the scullery, for handwashing, cleaning food, and washing dishes and pots. All the wooden floors had been worn. It had been dark inside, with only two small windows, and nothing here now was remotely close to what it used to look like. The Castella's had made it into a warm and comfortable home, with lots of light, and she felt herself relax.

"I dabble a bit with paint, just like your famous father," Skye winked. "I hope you're hungry. Lunch is ready."

Fleur noticed the dining table was set for eight, the chairs surrounding it a mix and match of colors. She wondered if she could eat, her stomach tight in a nervous knot.

"Finn just left to pick up Caro and Josie," Skye continued. "They should be here soon."

Excited voices announced their arrival.

"Fleur, you look so much better," Caro cried out, hugging her close. Then she examined her clothes and smiled. "Your outfit. I love it. Where did you find these fancy clothes?"

The young man next to her extended his hand. "Hi, Fleur," he said.

"Oh, this is Arlo, my boyfriend," Josie said, introducing him. The tall man had long black hair tied in a ponytail, high cheekbones, and a stunning reddish-brown skin tone. Only used to seeing men with their hair cut to ear level, his hairstyle took her by surprise, and she wondered if he came from a different country.

"Arlo is Native American," Josie explained. "Isn't he cute?"

Cute wasn't a word Fleur would have used to describe the extremely handsome man. "Nice to meet you, Arlo," she said.

"Hi, I'm Finn," Emmett's brother introduced himself, shaking her hand and looking her over. "Sorry, if I stare," he laughed. "But Emmett is my brother you know, and I have to look out for him."

"Stop it," Emmett growled, hitting him playfully on his shoulder.

Just like Emmett, Finn's dark-blond hair was a curly mess,

and he had the same smile.

The next one to greet her was Josie, who hugged her. "Caro was right. You look fantastic," she said. "And I love what you did to your hair." Fleur had braided it in a stylish crown on top of her head. "You need to show me how you did that."

They all sat down, the conversation casual and uplifting throughout the meal, and Fleur forgot her initial anxiety. Everyone was kind and attentive and nobody asked uncomfortable questions. Underneath the table, Emmett's hand rested on her knee.

"It's almost like I've known you forever, Fleur," Josie commented at the end of the meal.

Arlo leaned forward. "Where are you from, Fleur?" he asked. "I think I detect an unusual accent."

During her hospital stay, people had constantly asked her questions she couldn't answer. She would never see those people again, and it had been fun to come up with random answers. This time, it was different.

Josie quickly came to her rescue. "She doesn't have an accent," she laughed, waving him off. "Fleur grew up in Heemstead."

Skye cleared the table, and Fleur got up to help. "We've got this, Fleur," Skye smiled. "Thanks for offering."

Emmett took her hand. "Come, I want to show you my parents' practice room before we head to the main house."

She followed him through the kitchen to what used to be the space where they stored her grandfather's shiny black carriage and her parents' smaller wagon. Just like the rest of the house, it had changed considerably. The wooden walls were sheet rocked, and the floor concrete instead of packed dirt. Only the ceiling remained recognizable to her, with the exposed beams and the loft, accessible with a wooden ladder. "I used to hide up there when I wanted to be alone," Fleur told him.

"So did I when I was younger." Emmett beamed. He sat down behind the drumkit set up in the corner and banged with two sticks on the hi-hats, toms, and snare in rapid succession. The noise was awful, and Fleur covered her ears.

"It can't be that bad," Emmett yelled over the banging.

To her relief, he stopped the loud racket. "Those are guitars," he explained, pointing at several other instruments. "And these are keyboards. They're like a piano, but different. Do you play an instrument, or sing?"

Other than her aunt Elise who played the harp, nobody she knew played music. "No, but I know how to dance the polka and the waltz." She pretended to pick up a corner of her long skirt and swirled around the room, avoiding microphone stands and cords laying crisscross over the floor.

Emmett took her in his arms. "I'm glad you're relaxing a little. You were so tense."

For a moment she'd forgotten they would head over to the main house, where Forrest lived, and her nerves multiplied. She had no doubt it had changed immensely, like everything else, and didn't look forward to it.

The door cracked open, and one of the orange cats appeared. He rubbed against her leg.

"This is Kenny," Emmett told her and petted the friendly animal until Josie, Arlo, Caro, and Finn joined them.

"Are you ready?" Caro asked.

Fleur's heart raced out of control and her legs felt weak, but instead of initiating fatigue, it felt like an adrenaline rush, and she beamed. "I'm ready!"

The six of them left the coach house, rounded a row of tall hedges, and followed the road until they had a good look at the house. Fleur slowed down to take in the familiar and cherished building. Other than the paved driveway, different flowerpots, and unfamiliar curtains behind the windows, it looked the same – the sky a brilliant blue behind it, the green of the trees lush and vibrant. Even the light scent of roses and fresh cut grass wafting in the air was identical.

Finally, I'm home, she thought for a moment, until she realized it wouldn't be her family waiting behind the closed door.

Caro caught her distress and read her mind. "We're your family, too, Fleur." She tucked an arm in hers as they walked up the steps onto the terrace. "And we're so happy to welcome you home."

Chapter 30

GRATEFUL FOR THE DISTRACTION Josie and Caro offered, Fleur entered the hallway. To find it in almost the exact same state as she was used to, emotions overcame her, and her face crumbled. This was the house where she was born and raised. The home where she'd lived for twenty-three years, and she loved everything about it. To keep from crying she pressed her lips together.

Forrest and Kara appeared and hugged her, giving her time to compose herself. Josie, Caro, and Finn disappeared into the kitchen, and they followed them.

Emmett took her hand in his. "Did it change much?" he asked.

Although the entire kitchen was modernized, the floorplan was the same, with the cookstove, counters, and sink where they used to be. The larder, where they stored food was a pantry now, the scullery more like a mudroom, and the dining nook where the servants used to sit was still there too. "It's the same, but also very different," she said, taking it all in.

"I'm sure it must be difficult for you to see the changes," Forrest said.

Kara wrung her hands and grinned apologetic. "When I moved in, my grandmother Catherine had already rented out part of the house, to help cover the expenses," she said. "In order to keep the house, we had to make some tough decisions. We decided to remodel the attic and the upstairs wings and turn them into apartments for extra income. I'm so sorry."

Their bedrooms used to be in the left wing upstairs, and the entire right wing had belonged to Uncle Leo and Aunt Elise. It was difficult to comprehend, and Fleur gazed around, avoiding eye-contact.

"But the downstairs is all ours," Forrest smiled. "And you and Emmett can look around wherever you want."

Fleur didn't answer. It had been a mistake to come here.

"Fleur, honey, I realize you've had a long day, and you seem a bit tired. We don't want you to overexert yourself.

It was something her mother used to tell her all the time. Usually it irritated her, because she was always the only one who became tired, but she *was* exhausted, all the impressions leaving her worn-out. She nodded. "Yes, I think it's best to leave."

She said goodbye to everyone while Emmett got the car. Kara and Forrest walked her out and when Emmett pulled up, Forrest opened the passenger door for her.

"I heard that Cassius sent a time capsule to the past," he inquired.

Emmett sat inside with the engine running. "Stainless steel, waterproof, with a guaranteed lifetime of two hundred years and Fleur's parents' names and address engraved on the side," he said, helping Fleur buckle up.

"I wrote my mother a letter," Fleur added. "I also placed a brochure of the Keizer Manor's Museum inside, and a picture of myself in my hospital bed."

"That's very exciting," Forrest said before he kissed her on the cheek and closed the door.

On the way home, Fleur thought about the plastic containers Cassius had sent off to the past and the future. There hadn't been a single reply to any of the letters inside. Cassius theorized they probably traveled further in time than expected, and that heavier items would travel less far. He'd made a graph, based on Fleur's and Annet's weight, and filled the two-foot-long capsule up with lead, in the hope it would land in the exact year they wanted. For now, they didn't know anything, and only further experimenting could possibly substantiate his theory. Thinking about it made her squeamish and uncertain of the outcome, and all she could do was close off her mind and hope for some kind of proof that Cassius was on the right track.

Chapter 31

BACK AT ABERNATHEY, two soldiers stopped them at the gate. Emmett showed them his employee card and driver's license.

"Can we see your entry pass and identification too, Miss?"

Fleur paled. "Where did I put them?" Then she remembered. "I handed them to you when I tried on my new clothes."

"Yes, of course," Emmett apologized. He pulled the two cards from his back pocket and gave them to the guard.

The young soldier looked them over and nudged his partner. "Look man, this is Fleur Keizer," he said, dividing a curious glance between her and Emmett.

The second soldier came closer and peeked inside. "For real?"

Emmett fired an impatient glance at both men. "Can you please let us through?"

They took a step back and opened the gate, still gawking at her as they drove off.

"Their eyes almost dropped out of their sockets when they realized who you are," Emmett muttered. "Damn idiots."

Fleur stared at her hands. "Do you think they heard about me?"

Emmett scoffed. "You better believe it." He parked the car and followed her inside.

Worried about the implications of news about her existence spreading, she sat down on the couch. "I'm glad Caro's boyfriend left after lunch. His constant questions made me very uncomfortable, and I didn't know what to say." She leaned her head against the back of the couch and closed her eyes, exhausted from the stressful day.

"We have to come up with a plausible story," Emmett said. He sat down next to her and drew her close. She placed her hand on his chest and snuggled against his long, lean body. "Thank you for introducing me to your parents. You look so much like your father. Did you know that?"

He slowly opened her fingers and laced them between his. "They always say my father is super handsome."

She felt his soft chuckle against her cheek. "They are right," she mused and turned her head to look at him. He sat so close that she could see every detail of his hazel eyes and dark lashes, his mouth barely an inch away from hers. "You obviously inherited your good looks from your handsome dad."

Before she ended her sentence, he captured her lips in a tender kiss, his tongue gently probing until she softened against him, allowing him full access. It was all the encouragement he needed, and his lips grew hard, seeking and demanding, as their mouths dissolved together, until she gasped for air. His kiss awakened feelings within her she'd never experienced before. Shocked at her own eager response, she groaned deep in her throat, the sound like a purring cat longing to be petted, the warm, heady sensation making her dizzy.

With his arms around her, he shifted position until she lay down on the couch, his mouth never leaving hers, nibbling and kissing. Blanketed by his weight, she returned his kisses, the feeling of the hardness of his loins against her hips releasing a storm of emotions. She wrapped her arms around his waist and pressed her fingers into the solid muscles of his back, the desire pulsing through her terrifying.

As if he felt her sudden hesitance, he raised himself up on his elbow, his eyes searching hers. "You should rest." He brushed a few loose strands of long hair off her face, his touch tender and featherlight. "I better go."

Another exciting week went by, filled with many activities and tasks. It started with Forrest taking her for lunch to meet his parents.

"I'm so grateful your mother named you after me," her grandmother Andrea Overton had said with tears in her eyes while her husband patted her hand.

Forrest had also insisted on taking her to the hospital for her first checkup. Dr. Stevenson listened to her heart, took her blood pressure, and let his assistant draw blood. "Everything looks good, but you have to come back in four weeks for another chest X-ray and echocardiogram," he concluded.

Four weeks? That was so far out.

After Cassius and his team sent off the third capsule, with another letter and several pictures inside, Commander

Thornton invited her into his office. "I was called by the head of the Department of Defense," he said. "They're disgruntled with the slow process. The constant army presence is very costly, and they want us to send you back and wrap it up as soon as you're cleared by your cardiologist."

"Don't wait on my account," she answered. "I'm ready now."

"I'll reach out to your doctor," the Commander promised.

She told no one about the meeting. Not even Emmett.

Chapter 32

ON SATURDAY AFTERNOON, Emmett came to pick her up on his motorcycle. Feeling heavy-hearted that their budding relationship was doomed from the start, Fleur had spent the early part of the week keeping her distance, to protect herself from the inevitable heartbreak, trying to close herself off, and not give in to the temptation of his addictive kisses. But she was fighting a losing battle. The harder she tried to pull away, the more he tried to please her, and despite her efforts, they grew closer each day. The thought of having to say goodbye and never being able to see him again weighed heavily on her heart. She would miss him so much. And not only him. She also had to say farewell to Cassius, who had been like a grandfather to her. And to Forrest, Kara, Josie, and Caro, her second family. The longer she stayed here, the harder it would be.

When Emmett arrived, he took her in his arms, and immediate electricity skittered across her back. She clung to his shoulders and kissed him, her love for him gushing like a fountain. Knowing it would all end soon, her feelings bordered on desperation.

"You must be really happy to see me," he grinned. "Are you

ready to go?"

She put on her helmet and hopped on his motorcycle. The plan was to visit her grandmother Barbara, and to join Emmett's parents at a brewpub where they played with their band.

Ten minutes later, they pulled up in front of the White Castle Apartment Complex where Forrest and Annet had lived for seven years before Annet had disappeared in time. The old and run-down building was nothing like she'd expected – the siding dilapidated, and windows of several apartments were boarded up. The door of apartment #14 opened and Barbara stepped out, her long hair colored raven black, her lips bright red. She stretched her arms out in front of her and wiggled her skinny jeans-clad hips. "Oh, sweetheart, so nice of you to visit!"

A tiny dog came running out of the apartment after her, yapping furiously. Barbara picked her up. "Hush, Violette!"

Afraid the feisty dog might bite, Fleur gave her grandmother only a half-hug. "Did you name your dog after my sister?"

"I named my first pooch Fleur, and my second one Frank," Barbara smiled, her powdered face deeply wrinkled. "Since I had to go without, I made my dogs into my grandbabies." She touched Fleur's cheek affectionately. "Fleur is the French word for flower. I have no clue how Annet came up with that. She doesn't have a French bone in her body."

Emmett locked his motorcycle, and with their helmets in hand, they followed Barbara inside her apartment. A man with disheveled, gray hair sat in a wheelchair in the living room, his bulging stomach stretching the front of his stained gray shirt.

"This is Chuck, my husband of twenty-two years," Barbara introduced him.

"Well, I'll be darned," Chuck laughed, shaking their hands. "I thought Barb here was pulling my leg about all that time travel shit, but here you are. Come, sit. I was just about to crack open a cold one. You want to join me?" He bobbed his bushy eyebrows, his cheerful demeanor surprising considering his physical state.

"Chuck had a stroke several years back and his left side has given him trouble ever since," Barbara explained. She stood in front of the refrigerator. "Beer, coke or wine?"

"Coke, please," Emmett replied.

While Barbara poured herself a glass of red wine, Fleur took in the threadbare carpet, water-stained ceiling, missing pieces of trim, and damaged kitchen cabinets.

"It ain't much, is it?" Chuck commented with a wry smirk. "Within several weeks, they're going to tear the entire rathole down and replace it with condos. They don't give a crap about us poor folk, not caring that nobody wants to rent to a cripple on social security. Having a yapper like Violette don't help either."

"Doesn't your father have an apartment for rent, Fleur?" Barbara asked from the kitchen. She joined them with a bowl in each hand, one filled with peanuts, the other with pieces of cheese.

"Your grandma likes cheese with her wine," Chuck joked, and slapped himself on the leg. At the noise, Violette immediately barked.

"Aren't we funny?" Barbara replied and kissed him on his bald spot before she picked up the excited dog and sat down.

It was obvious the odd couple loved each other, the entire

visit full of jokes, funny stories, and small talk.

"I like them," Emmett commented after they said their goodbyes.

He drove to the Market Square, where he parked at the brewpub. Forrest and Kara were already there, watching Rix, Skye, and the rest of the band set up their equipment.

"Back in the day, this was Gloria's diner," Forrest told Fleur. "Your mother and I used to eat here regularly. The food was decent and inexpensive, and we enjoyed the view of the Old Historic Pump and the surrounding stores. Has it changed much?"

Fleur glanced outside. "The pump looks so new. How's that possible?"

Forrest nodded. "Through the centuries, the pump has been restored several times because of its cultural and historic value," he explained. "But it hasn't functioned in decades."

The arrival of Josie and Caro with Finn and Arlo distracted them. They all grouped around a large table set up close to the stage. A waitress appeared at their table, leaving menus, and taking drink orders.

"What do you like to eat, Fleur?" Josie asked.

Fleur glanced at the menu. "They don't even serve eel pie, or terrapin stew. What a terrible restaurant." She grinned mischievously. "Only joking."

Chapter 33

Forrest

"DIDN'T FLEUR LOOK FANTASTIC last night?" Forrest said, with unconcealed pride. Having Fleur in his life had lifted a weight off his shoulders and he couldn't be happier. "I think she's gained a little weight since her surgery. Her skin glows, and she has a sparkle in her eyes."

Kara buttered her toast, her plate loaded with scrambled eggs and sausages for their usual Sunday morning breakfast. "She does look much better compared to the pale, underweight girl we first met."

"Did you see her dancing?" Forrest continued. "She was bubbly and cheerful, and it was fun to see her personality come out."

"It was so cool hanging out with Fleur," Caro agreed. "Several people asked me if we were twins, but other than the same hair, I don't think we look alike."

Kara smiled. "I'm sure there are similarities because she's your half-sister."

"That's what I told them. Or shouldn't I have said that, Dad?"

Forrest didn't reply and stared out in front of him, in deep concentration, his brow furrowed.

"Dad," Caro said, shaking his arm. "You're not listening. What's going on?"

With a long sigh, Forrest leaned back in his chair. "In hindsight, I believe it was a risk to take Fleur out in public. What if people figure out who she is? With the internet and social media, that news could spread like wildfire and cause major problems."

Kara placed her hand on his. "Honey, you know that it's only a matter of weeks before they're going to send her back. Let her have some fun in the meantime, don't you agree?"

Forrest pushed his eggs around on his plate, a sad expression on his face. "From the family tree your father made of the Keizer Family, we know there's only a birthdate for Fleur. I talked to your father the other day, and he assured me no matter how hard he looks in all the available resources and archives, he can't find anything about her death. What if she never goes back and ends up staying here? What will her life be like when everyone knows she traveled through time?"

Josie said nothing during the entire conversation, her food still untouched in front of her. "Dad," she said. "Arlo told me last night he talked to one of the soldiers manning the gate at Abernathey. The guy thought he recognized Fleur and asked him if Fleur was the girl they're protecting. I didn't know what to say but I believe Arlo put two and two together and figured out who Fleur is. What should I do?"

Forrest slammed his fist on the table. "Darn, I knew it." He rubbed his chin, trying to come up with an answer, a solution, but he didn't have one. "Call him," he ended up saying. "Ask him to come over so we can talk. Maybe it's not too late."

An hour later, Forrest retreated to the bedroom and pulled out his cellphone.

"Barbara, it's Forrest. I heard Fleur and Emmett visited with you yesterday. I'm only calling to remind you not to talk to anyone about her."

"I know you think I'm crazy," she replied, her voice shrill. "But I would never risk my granddaughter's safety."

The feisty old lady would never change. "I love you, too." He grinned and disconnected.

Next, he called his own parents, Kara's parents, his sister Jackie, and Rix. He needed to make sure everyone was on board, telling people the story he'd just come up with. That he had fathered a child in his early twenties during a one-night fling, that the baby was given up for adoption by her teenage mother, and that they were reunited when Fleur started to search for her biological parents. It sounded plausible.

The last one he reached out to was Fleur, to share his concern and what she should say in case someone questioned her.

Guilt overtook him while they talked. Since her arrival, all she talked about was her wish to return to 1864, and to be reunited with her family and friends back home. Because of her fragile state and surgery, he'd kept the family tree's information from her. He'd also decided to only share Annet's letters up to the time of Fleur's disappearance. She needed hope to cling to, but he was convinced she would never go back.

Chapter 34

Annet, 1875

"YES, RIGHT THERE," Annet yelled at the workers who hung *Lost in the Storm* in its rightful place on the far wall, with all the letters she'd written for Forrest through the years safely secured inside. "Perfect! Thank you so much."

Sunlight filtered through the stained-glass windows onto the walls, the scraping of the ladders and footsteps of the men gathering their tools loud on the rust-colored tiled floor.

"My husband will pay you," she told them before they headed out.

"Thank you, ma'am," the man in charge said, his loud voice echoing off the bare stone walls.

When the door closed behind them, an oppressive silence fell in the tall and empty space, all of the furniture gone, the carpets rolled up and hauled off.

She took several steps back to take a last look at the painting, the desperation of the slender young woman in the long white dress and the little girl whose dress matched her own, the desolate landscape, the threatening clouds and lightning flashes haunting her each day. She wrapped her arms around her middle and shivered. With nothing left but loss, heartache, and despair, the time had come to close Keizer Manor and say goodbye, all her dreams from the past lost the moment her daughter disappeared. It had been eleven years and every detail was etched in her very being.

Unwanted tears rolled down her cheeks, and she tore her eyes away from the haunting scene. The painting had overshadowed her life, and she couldn't allow it to dominate the rest of her days. At sixty, she wasn't old, just tired and dejected, her feisty stubbornness beaten down and her optimism disintegrated. She couldn't live her life in a dark cloud any longer, dragging everybody with her into this morass of gloom and doom. People needed her. Frank and his wife Isabelle were expecting their second child, her sister-in-law, Elise, struggled with her health, and Alex still blamed himself for Fleur's disappearance, the recent loss of his father adding to his despondency.

By closing Keizer Manor, she hoped to rekindle her energy, let go of the grief, and revive what was lost. They all deserved it.

At the door, she turned around one last time. "Now don't think I'll ever forget you, my sweet girl," she whispered. "I love you forever."

Henry Jonkers, gathered the last personal items from the house and helped Annet climb into the waiting carriage, her pale face drawn, her expression tense.

"Thank you for everything, Henry," she acknowledged him

before closing the door.

The ride home was long and difficult, and filled with doubt. She'd closed the door on Keizer Manor, the fantastic summers they'd spent there as a family now part of history. *Had she made the right decision?*

At the Keizer Estate, a young butler appeared and escorted her inside. "Mrs. Leo Keizer is asking for you," he informed her.

Annet hurried upstairs to the right wing, where her brother- and sister-in-law still lived after all these years. "Elise? You were asking for me?"

Elise sat on the couch with a small puppy in her lap. "I did." She caressed the dog's soft white coat, delight radiating from her eyes. "Look at this little guy. Leo found him abandoned in the street. We don't know what kind of dog he is, but I don't care. I love him already so much already."

Annet joined her on the couch and petted the dog's little head. *Maybe we should get a dog too,* she thought. They could be great companions and often help people suffering from depression and anxiety, making them feel less lonely. Something they all needed help with.

"Mrs. Keizer?" somebody hollered at the bottom of the stairs.

"Stay with your puppy, Elise," Annet said. "I'll check what's going on."

At the bottom of the stairs, she found her husband with Henry Jonkers, their coachman, and his older brother, Russell Jr.

Russell Jr. lifted his head. "Ma'am," he said. "Sorry to disturb you."

"There's nothing wrong with your parents, I hope?" she asked with immediate concern.

"No, not all," he replied. "We found a goat wandering down the road, and I brought it here."

Annet started to laugh. "I just contemplated getting a dog, but a goat could be fun too."

She smiled at Alex and kissed him. "It's wonderful to be home."

He returned her kiss and gave her a warm hug before he turned his attention back to the Jonkers' boys. "What's so special about this goat?"

"It's huge, clean, and well fed," Russell Jr. told them while they followed him to the stables. "And it's domesticated, with a bright red collar made of the strangest material I've ever seen."

"A goat with a collar?"

"Yes, that's why I brought it here, because both your names are printed on it."

They entered the stable, the smell of fresh hay and manure one she'd come to appreciate. Annet knelt next to the goat, their names on the collar printed in bright white letters. She reached for the buckle and noticed a round container attached to the metal ring. "Look at this," she said.

Alex removed the goat's collar and examined it. "Such craftmanship." Then he turned to Henry. "Henry, do we have small pliers? I want to find out if there's something inside that small cylinder."

Annet looked at Russell. "We're grateful that you drove all the way out here. Make sure you get something to eat before you head home."

"Thank you, Mrs. Keizer," he said. "I'll stay with my brother Henry. His wife made sauerkraut."

"Give my love to your parents."

Alex had taken off the cylinder and Annet pushed him out of the stable.

"Hey, what's going on?" he asked, examining her excited face.

"That goat came from the future, Alex," she whispered.

He frowned. "How? What?"

Anticipation made her quiver. "That collar was made of nylon, and I've seen pendant cases like that before on dogs. They usually contain the dog-owner's name and phone number, but what if...." She almost didn't dare to say the words out loud. "What if Fleur left a message in there?"

"Then what are we lingering here for?" Alex replied and grabbed her by the hand. Together, they ran towards the library, where they knew they wouldn't be disturbed.

Alex's fingers trembled when he pried the pendant open and used his fingernails to pull out a rolled-up piece of paper. He spread the three-by-five-inch note on the table and began to decipher the small scribbles.

Dear Mom and Dad,

In her eagerness, Annet pushed Alex aside. "Is it from Fleur?" she shrieked, struggling to believe her own eyes.

"Yes, it is," Alex replied and made a fist, hitting the table in a rapid crescendo, his face flushed with excitement. "I can't believe it."

They stared at each other, the news too good to be true. "Let's sit, let's sit!" Annet cried out and reached for the note.

I'm in the future because a man named Cassius invented a machine that caused the powerful storm that swept me away and transported me across time. He's kind and helpful, and I'm doing fine.

"A man-made machine caused all this! How dare he!" Annet fumed. "If I ever get my hands on him, I'll strangle him."

"Keep reading," Alex said, with tears in his eyes.

I met my grandmother Barbara, your old friend Forrest and his wife Kara, and a nice young man named Emmett Castella. I've been in a car, on the back of a motorcycle, and at Keizer Manor that's now a museum. It's exciting, but I miss you all so much.

Annet had trouble staying quiet, her daughter's words pulling her emotions through the wringer, her next words almost turning her into a puddle.

I'm so sorry I never believed your stories about the future, Mother. Please forgive me. And Father, please forgive me for sneaking out against your wishes. I shouldn't have.

There's nothing to forgive, Annet's heart cried out. Absolutely nothing.

Cassius promised to send me back, but first, I need to have surgery on my heart. I hope you're not missing me too much. Give my love to Frank and Violette. They're never going to believe it. All my love, Fleur.

The small note held so much information, Annet had a hard time wrapping her mind around it. She flew up from her chair and started running. "Frank! Violette! Fleur is alive!"

Chapter 35

Fleur

DRESSED IN A SUIT AND TIE, Cassius appeared from his bedroom. He had a small black suitcase in his hand and pulled another one behind him that rolled on small wheels. "I hope you didn't forget I'm flying to Washington D.C. with Milton. We leave in about an hour and won't be back until Wednesday."

"You'll be gone for two nights, am I right?" she asked, surprised how fast the days had flown by.

"Yes, but there's plenty of food in the refrigerator. And you can call me anytime. You know that, right?"

"Don't worry. I'll be fine," she said. "Do you have time for breakfast before you go? I made coffee."

He shook his head. "Sorry, I don't. I'll eat something at the airport."

Cassius hadn't told her the reason he was leaving, and she wondered if it had anything to do with SMITS or her. "What are your meetings about?" she asked.

Cassius adjusted his tie. "There will be several meetings about SMITS, the lack of any promising results after all the tests, and on how to proceed. Several high-ranking officials also voiced their concern over the risks involved, saying that experimenting with time is unethical and dangerous. That it could cause complications we can't predict and that the consequences are incalculable. To be honest, I must agree with them." The deep resonance of his voice vibrated, and he gave her a soulful stare. "Look what it did to you."

Fleur stood, wrapped her arms around his middle and put her cheek against his chest. "Without you and SMITS, I wouldn't have had surgery and would have been dead soon. Tell them that."

He pulled her close for a few seconds and then kissed the top of her head. "This afternoon, Emmett and Adam will oversee the sendoff of the fourth capsule. Is your letter ready?"

She walked him out. "It will be. Emmett is picking it up at lunch time. I'll miss you. Be careful."

With Cassius gone, the house felt empty, the idea of being alone for two nights unsettling. Her phone rang, and she glanced at the screen. *Why would Forrest call her again?*

"There's something important I want to talk to you about, and I hope you and Emmett can come over for dinner tonight," he said. "Kara's parents will be there, too."

He sounded distant and unhappy. Different than the joyful, energetic Forrest she'd come to know. Something important had to be going on, and she had the premonition that whatever it was he wanted to tell her, she wouldn't enjoy hearing it.

"We will be there," she said and then texted Emmet. "Forrest wants us to come over for dinner."

"Do you think we can leave early and still meet up with John and Titus at seven?" he texted back.

Emmett had wanted to introduce her to his best friends tonight and she'd completely forgotten.

"We can try."

Mad at herself for forgetting about Emmett's friends and worried over tonight's dinner, Fleur stared at the blank page in her notebook and started writing to her parents, grandfather, and siblings back home.

Last Saturday, Emmett and I visited Barbara and Chuck.

She told them about the names of her grandmother's dogs, the night out with the band, and Forrest's strange story about an adoption.

I feel so much better since my surgery and like to dance all the time. When I'm back, I want to attend university, work, travel, and ride horseback. The currents of energy coursing through my veins are making me unable to sit still. I had no idea it would feel so liberating to be free of the constant fatigue and muddled brain. Modern medicine has given me my life back and I couldn't be more thankful.

While she wrote, her mind kept wandering back to Forrest's phone call. With an exasperated sigh, she finished the letter and made copies. She also copied her previous letters and stuffed them in the envelope, together with the picture Emmett had printed off the computer of her with Josie and Caro at the bar, their arms around each other's shoulders, smiling at the camera, and all the other pictures.

With an hour to spare before lunch, Fleur headed outside and walked the perimeter, a light spring wind rustling the dune grasses and the sun warm on her face.

"Good morning, Fleur," one of the soldiers guarding the gate said, ogling her. "How's your day going?"

Emmett had told her she shouldn't talk to the soldiers. He had sounded jealous, and she didn't understand why. Heavens, what reason could she possibly have to want to meet another man? Having him in her life was complicated enough.

"I'm doing very well. Thank you," she replied, and wanted to walk further to finish her round.

"Did you have fun at the bar last Saturday? I saw you dancing," the young soldier continued.

She immediately remembered Forrest's story. "I was adopted and was there meeting with my father and half-sisters."

"Great story," the second soldier joined in, his voice mocking. He was older, with deep-set eyes, the scowl on his round face one of resentment.

What an unpleasant man, she thought, and hurried off. *No wonder Emmett hadn't wanted her to talk to them.*

Over lunch, she told Emmett about her encounter.

"Didn't Cassius and I warn you not to talk to anyone, including the soldiers, Fleur. The fewer people that know about your existence, the better," he replied, his eyes full of concern.

What kind of life is that, she thought, his answer fueling her desire to leave. Instead of sharing her opinion, she stayed quiet, her pending departure only causing tension between them.

Around five, Emmet picked her up and drove to his parents' house. They said a quick hello before heading to the main house. Kara's parents were already there, and after a bit of small talk, they gathered around the dining table.

Forrest sat across from her. He stayed quiet throughout the meal, occasionally glancing at her with either sadness, fear, or doubt. She didn't know which, and her hand shook a little while she ate the lasagna, a sense of foreboding causing her to tense up. Uneasily, she shifted in her chair. Until today, she'd tried to enjoy her life here as much as she could. But the constant effort of adjusting, learning new habits, eating strange food, and the concern over her health mixed in with her love for Emmett and the uncertainty of her future pulled her downward into a spiral of gloom.

Italian food, she thought irritably. *What's wrong with potatoes, beans and pork?*

Finally, the meal was over. Caro and Josie gathered the dirty dishes and followed Kara to the kitchen. When Fleur tried to get up too, Forrest stopped her.

"I wanted to talk to you about the Keizer family tree Kara's father put together," he said. "Do you know what a family tree is?"

Of course, she didn't. "Must be another one of your alien habits," she grumbled. Dr. Stevenson had told her to expect possible mood swings after her heart surgery, including depression, fear, anxiety, helplessness, and anger. She doubted if she could contribute her bitterness to that, the dark mood that had settled over her earlier in the day firmly in place.

"Let me explain," Kara's father said. He sat down next to her with a notepad and wrote her grandfather and grandmother's names on the top, with Leo and Alex Keizer below theirs. Next to Leo, he made an X and added Elise's name. And next to Alex, he made an X and added her mother's name. "The X means they're married," he said. Then he added Frank, Violette and her own name below the ones from her parents.

"I made a tree of the entire Keizer family to discover more about my ancestors," Kara's father continued. "With each person, I added their birth, death, and marriage date, and when available, a picture. According to the tree, our family lineage comes from Frank, who married Isabelle Winthrop. They had four children, and Violette and her husband had two." He added several lines on the paper, creating a chart that illustrated the people in her family and the relationships between them.

"What about me?" Fleur asked, her interest peaked.

In the ominous silence that fell, Kara's father's gaze shifted between her and Forrest. "I hate to be a harbinger of bad news, Fleur, I really do," he said, his fingers playing with the pen in his hand. "Besides your birthdate, there's nothing about your existence available in any of the archives."

Emmett's hand found hers under the table and squeezed her fingers in a tight grip.

"What does that mean?" she cried out, barely able to comprehend the implications of the bizarre information. "That I never married? That I never had children, or that I didn't even exist?"

Then it dawned on her. They were trying to tell her she would never go back and had to live her life out in the twenty-first century. She rose from her chair and planted her hands on the table.

"Why are you saying that?" she fumed in disbelief. "Are you saying this because you want to keep me here? Trapped in your crazy world where people pollute the world and live in tents on the street. In a time with droughts, heatwaves, floods, and wildfires? No, thank you. That's not for me!"

"Fleur, sweetheart," Forrest said to calm her down. "We understand how difficult this must be, and that's why I didn't tell you before. You were too ill, too fragile."

His words fueled her anger. "Don't pity me with your so-called compassion and well-meaning fatherly nonsense. You should have told me the truth instead of keeping this information from me. I had the right to know!"

With guilt written all over his face, Forrest came to his feet and grabbed an envelope from the cupboard behind him. "These are the rest of your mother's letters. Sorry I kept them from you." He slid the envelope across the table with a heavy sigh.

Filled with bitterness and frustration, Fleur gulped her despair down. "My mother changed history, and so will I. You'll see."

Chapter 36

ON THE WAY HOME, bitter tears streamed down her face and into her mouth, the helmet making it impossible to wipe them away. When they arrived, she quickly jumped off, handed her helmet to Emmett, and hurried to the door.

Inside, she threw off her coat, kicked off her shoes and dove into bed. She pulled the blanket up to her chin and closed her eyes, to shut out the world and put a stop to the troubled thoughts that rambled through her exhausted brain.

The mattress sagged next to her, and two caring arms pulled her up to a comforting body, Emmett's breath warm in her neck. "We'll find a solution," he whispered in a husky and soothing voice. "We'll make it work." He rhythmically stroked her arm and murmured reassurances in her ear until her tension defused, his presence calming and his words comforting, throwing a lifeline to the other world where she belonged.

When he moved to create a little distance between them, she panicked. "Can't you stay a while longer?"

He chuckled. "I shouldn't lay on your bed in these pants. It rained earlier this afternoon, and I splashed mud all over them on the way here."

"Please, don't go," she pleaded. "I don't want to be alone."

When he saw her frightened face, he took off his pants, joined her under the covers, and propped himself up against the headboard.

With a grateful sigh, she curled up against him, craving his consoling presence and the contact with someone who truly cared for her. "Thank you for being here," she said and placed her hand on his chest.

"I'll stay for a little while, until you feel more comfortable," he replied.

With her eyes closed, she listened to Emmett's heart and felt the pounding through his shirt, the strong rhythmic beating matching her own. Her fingertips played with one of his buttons until it came undone. She let her hand slide through the opening to feel his bare skin underneath her palm, the hair on his chest curly and soft.

His breathing shuttered, and he placed his hand on hers. "I don't think this is a good idea."

She felt the hard muscles of his thigh move against her leg as he changed position, his hand squeezing hers so hard that it hurt. "I better go."

He moved away from her, his body rigid, his entire demeanor suddenly standoffish.

Fleur got up on one elbow to look at him. "Did I do something wrong?"

With one leg hanging over the edge of the bed, he stared at the ceiling, as if he could find an answer to her question there. Then he sighed. "With Cassius gone, I don't think..." He was searching for words. "You know, about chaperones and stuff like that."

She grabbed his arm before he could slip away. "You're saying that we shouldn't be alone, together, in a bed."

He pulled his eyes from the ceiling and stared at her. "Fleur, I really tried hard to fight my feelings for you, but the harder I fought, the stronger they became. If we stay here, I'm afraid I'll give in to everything that I've locked up inside since the day we met." His eyes misted over; his expression guarded. "I can't allow that to happen because once you're gone, after sharing something that I know will be the best thing ever, I'll be devastated, heartbroken... lost."

His strangled words found their way straight into her soul, her feelings for him having grown stronger each day, no matter how hard she'd tried to bury them, to ignore them. She inched closer to him and reached out to his face. "One of my father's favorites poets is Alfred, Lord Tennyson. He wrote *"It's better to have loved and lost than never to have loved at all."* I never understood what those words meant." She gave him a quivering smile. "Now I do." Her hand shook as she traced his handsome features with her fingertips, the thought of losing him too unbearable to consider. "Please, take me in your arms and love me. It's what I've been dreaming of for weeks."

"Oh, Fleur," he said in a voice that was something between a whimper and a growl. "Don't say that unless you mean it."

Without hesitation, she wrapped her hand around his neck and pulled him down. "I am sure," she vowed in a fervent whisper, and looked at him directly. "I love you, Emmett Castella, with all my heart."

Their breath intermingled as he lowered his face. "I love you too," he spoke against her lips, his arms wrapping around her like a warm blanket. "So, so much." Emotion darkened his eyes as he took possession of her mouth with a scorching kiss, barely allowing her to breathe for a long time. She tasted the salt of one of his tears on her tongue and ached to tell him how marvelous she thought he was. How considerate, kind, and beautiful.

Her body came alive under his touch and her breathing quickened, the sensations surging through her, electrifying. Full of longing, she pulled her shirt over her head, threw it on the floor, and moved closer. The unbridled admiration and desire on his face almost made her cry.

He cupped her bottom with both hands and grounded his hips against her. "I hope I don't scare you," he sighed. "Please, tell me if I do."

She'd never felt male hardness before. Instead of being afraid, it heightened her desire, and she pushed herself closer against his chest, returning his kisses hungrily. "I'm not scared," she urged him on. "I want this."

They kissed endlessly until her body throbbed with longing from the touch of his hands in places where no one had ever been before. "I'll always be yours," she swore and disappeared into his embrace.

At the crack of dawn, she opened her eyes and stared straight into Emmett's warm hazel eyes. "Good morning, sunshine," he smiled from his pillow. "How did you sleep?" He reached out to stroke a strand of hair off her forehead. She grabbed his hand and pressed it against her mouth.

"Wonderful and filled with dreams," she replied, and rolled

over to look at the clock. The sheet slipped from her shoulder and Emmett drew a sharp intake of breath at the sight of her milky skin, the swelling of her breast, and the imperfections of her surgical incisions. His fingers traced the red narrow lines. "Does it still hurt?"

She shook her head. "Do they make me ugly?"

He pushed himself up on one elbow and placed his warm lips on the scars. "They're a beautiful reminder of your healthy heart, and I love them." His mouth left a trail of kisses on her skin, his feather light touches rekindling the fire that had scorched through her body the night before.

Instead of continuing his path, he laid back down and pulled her close, their faces only inches apart. She noticed a sudden vulnerability and nervousness in his eyes.

"I wanted to tell you it was my first time, with you, last night, and I felt so clumsy," he whispered. "Was I too forceful? Did I cause you any discomfort or pain?"

Emmett had been her first one too, and yes, it had hurt a little, but he'd been gentle and caring, and the initial sharp twinges had soon disappeared and were forgotten in the throes of their lovemaking.

"My discomfort was insignificant compared to what you gave me," she admitted, her fingers timidly smoothing down the curly hair on his chest, his skin burning underneath her palm.

Under her reassuring words, his muscles relaxed and the crease between his eyes smoothed.

He let his hand inquisitively slide down over her arm until it settled lightly on the curve of her hip. "And you still love me?" he asked, his warm smell mingled with the faint scent of sex and fabric softener.

She breathed in the intoxicating aroma, the sensual sensations coursing through her veins still new and uncharted. A sudden touch of melancholy caught her by surprise. In a matter of months, Emmett had changed her life completely and become so important to her. She couldn't imagine a life without him. He'd become her home, her safe haven, her future. "In your arms, I feel like the most treasured woman on earth," she smiled. "I love you with everything inside me. Forever."

His strong white teeth flashed, and the loving expression on his devastatingly handsome face almost brought her to tears.

"Then kiss me," he whispered.

Chapter 37

WITH ONLY TEN MINUTES to make it to work on time, Emmett took a hasty shower, threw on his clothes and hurried out the door after a quick kiss, his hair only toweled dry, a plain slice of bread his breakfast.

Still in the afterglow of their lovemaking, Fleur took a long, leisurely shower, the places where he'd been still sensitive. Dressed in Javina's bathrobe, she made a pot of tea and enjoyed a slice of toast with raspberry jam. Overnight, she'd become a woman, her virginity lost to a man from the future, her life surreal and her future unpredictable. Only time would tell what would happen. She began cleaning off the table and grabbed the vacuum cleaner when she noticed the manila envelope on the coffee table. Those had to be the missing letters Forrest had talked about, and he must have handed them to Emmett after she'd rushed out of the house.

She opened the envelope and began to read. The first letter was filled with heartache and hopelessness over Fleur's disappearance. The pain her family had felt like her own, all-encompassing, and entombing her heart. Each word hardened Fleur's resolve to go home. All she had to do was convince

Emmett to go with her.

The vacuum cleaner forgotten, she sunk down on the couch to read the next four letters, all written in intervals of one year. Annet wrote about her grief and how difficult it was for all of them to adjust to a life without Fleur. But not a single mention of the goats or the time capsules they had sent into the frenzy of the storm. *What had happened to them? Why hadn't they arrived?* All kinds of different scenarios forged through her head, one more bizarre than the other, until she felt a leaden fear steal upon her. *If the goat and capsules never made it, would she be able to make her way home, or would she be lost too?* She rubbed her forehead where a headache loomed, the muscles in her shoulders and neck stiff with tension.

Filled with unease and doubt, she read the last letter, dated March 10, 1875.

Dear Forrest,

It's been over ten years since Fleur's disappearance. We've grieved so long, and Keizer Manor has become an empty shell, a mausoleum, a place we dread to visit. Therefore, we decided to donate the property to the state on the condition that it will always be a museum, dedicated to Alex's work.

Over the coming months, we will transport all his paintings and hang them in their rightful place, with Fleur's bedroom solely dedicated to her. Violette painted the watercolor of Fleur in the garden. She has Alex's talent and lives in a dreamworld, with fairies, pixies, and princes. I worry about her. Losing her big sister has made such an enormous impact on her kind soul. Fortunately, we have Frank's two toddlers to distract us all.

When we hand over the keys of Keizer Manor, I will place my letters inside Lost in the Storm. I feel tired and old, and plan to enjoy the rest of my years with Alex. He's complaining about stiffness in his joints, and it wouldn't surprise me if he suffers from arthritis.

If there's anything important I want to share after transferring ownership, I'll write again and leave my letters in a safe place for someone to find.

Please, Forrest, keep on praying for good news about Fleur, like we all do. Our sweet, sweet girl.

Her hands dropped in her lap, her thoughts disorganized, the sensation that she was trapped in a life where she didn't belong becoming too real. On stress overload, her mind searched for a solution, for a way out of the uncertain mess her life had become. To push her anxiety down, she slowly breathed in and out as her heart rate gradually slowed and the fog in her mind lifted. Her mother mentioned more letters. If she actually wrote them, Fleur had to find them. Determined and with purpose, she got dressed, washed her face, and checked her appearance in the bathroom mirror, the blush on her cheeks and the tenacious sparkle in her eyes mirroring her feelings.

On the way out the door, she heard strange tinkly sounds coming from the house next door, the car parked out front telling her Lucia was home. She knocked and Lucia yelled from inside. "Come on in."

Fleur opened the door and found Lucia on the floor, her

body all twisted up. "What are you doing?" she smiled.

Lucia laughed and sagged down in a big blob. "I'm trying to conquer this eight-angle yoga pose. Glad you came. That gives me a reason to quit."

"What's yoga?"

"Well, my Victorian friend, they say yoga is good for you." Lucia got off the floor and stretched her arms above her head. "Self-reflection, stress relief, flexibility. You should try it. It might help you cope with all your weird stuff."

If only curling herself up in a ball could help in her situation, Fleur thought. "I need a favor. Could you drive me to Keizer Manor? I need to talk to Forrest."

Lucia disappeared into her bedroom to change and returned a few minutes later, asking her a million questions along the way. "You should text him, so we can go in for free. I would love to walk around the museum while you talk to him."

When they arrived, Forrest was waiting for her at the entrance. He gave her a brief hug. "Let's talk in my office." He guided the two young women inside.

"Text me when you're ready to go home," Lucia said and headed off.

At the end of the hallway, Forrest opened a door. "Please, sit," he said, and rounded his cluttered desk, the pictures of his family covered with sticky notes.

"I just read the last of my mother's letters," she said, jumping right in. "She mentions there could be more. When you built the apartments at the Keizer Estate, did you find any?"

Forrest sank down into his chair and formed a steeple with his fingers beneath his chin. He regarded her attentively with a sad look. "I'd hoped to find more letters myself and when we remodeled your old bedroom, we almost completely tore it apart. There was nothing."

Disappointed, Fleur bit her lip, her bedroom the first place where she would have looked. "How about the library, the kitchen?"

The sorrowful expression on Forrest's face intensified. "Fleur, sweetheart, trust me. We remodeled extensively and searched everywhere, and I wracked my brain over it for years."

Not ready to give up, she nearly flew off her chair. "Well, they must be there. Try harder!"

Forrest hadn't seen that feisty spirit in his daughter yet. "You take after your mother, after all," he chuckled. "Listen, sweetheart. They're not inside any of the paintings or here at Keizer Manor. And if there are any letters, I don't know where they could be."

Fleur paced the floor with impatient steps. "They could be in the coach house."

"It's unlikely," Forrest said. "You have to remember your mother never knew I would marry Kara and move there. Therefore, I highly doubted from day one that she would have left letters anywhere on the estate."

"Then they have to be in Grandmother Barbara's apartment!" Fleur decided, remembering that's where Forrest and Annet had lived together for many years.

Forrest shook his head. "The apartment building was constructed around 1950, and that was long after your mother passed away."

"But what if she instructed Frank or Violette to hide them

there?"

A knock on the door disrupted their heated conversation. Forrest got up and opened it. "Sorry, I need a few more minutes," he told his secretary. Then he gazed at Fleur. "They're going to demolish the apartment complex soon. Do you want me to find out when?"

Fleur didn't have to think twice. "Of course!"

Ten minutes later, she texted Lucia that she was ready to go.

"Those paintings of you upstairs are amazing," Lucia chattered when she joined her, the other visitors fortunately not paying attention to what she said. "Hey, I need to pick up a few groceries and wanted to check out that new shoe store on Second. You want to join me?"

Fleur had always tried to keep the adventurous side of her nature hidden beneath a sweet, polite smile and demure attitude. Even her mother had encouraged her to live by the standards of the time, assuring her it would only make life easier. She had rebelled against it until her health declined, depleting her energy, the restrictive clothing exhausting and the four layers heavy on her thin frame. She looked at her jean-clad legs and blouse. Not having to spend hours to get strapped into a corset was liberating and one of the biggest advantages of today. "I would love to," she grinned and followed her friend outside.

"It must have taken forever to go from one place to the next with a horse and carriage," Lucia commented on the way to Dunedam.

"Yes, life was quite different then," Fleur agreed, holding on to her seat as Lucia raced to catch the yellow light.

At the last second, she hit the brakes and came to a stop. "Sorry," she laughed, tapping her fingers on the steering wheel. "What I wanted to ask is, since you were raised all prudish and Victorian style, how do you deal with your sudden freedom?"

People in the twenty-first century spoke much more frankly than she was used to. "What do you mean?"

"Well, that gorgeous, proper and prim yellow dress, for example," Lucia chuckled and hit the gas when the light turned green. "It's all hoops, petticoats, and corsety like, with lots of lace and stuff. And I'm sure you couldn't hang out with your boyfriend without a, how do you call it, a guard or an escort? No, that's not the right word. A chaperone! That's it."

Fleur remembered how much Frank had disliked chaperoning when Jeremiah came to visit, especially since the lovebirds had often tried to sneak off together. "We have our ways to get together," she said. "But you can't be older than twenty-one. What do your parents think about you living with your brother and not with them?"

Lucia shrugged. "At eighteen, I moved in with my boyfriend. When we broke up, my parents were relieved that I moved in with Adam instead of coming home."

Fleur couldn't imagine that her parents wouldn't welcome their daughter back after a failed relationship. Quietly, she peered out the window. Like her mother and Forrest, Lucia had lived together with a man without the protection and security of a proper marriage. It seemed wrong and improper.

At the grocery store, Lucia filled her basket with the strangest food, like quinoa, eggplant, tofu, and tahini. "I'm vegan," she explained, and put coconut water into her cart.

Fleur didn't ask what that meant. Lucia's uncomplicated company was a needed and welcome distraction, and Fleur simply followed her around, watching her read product labels and checking the grocery list on her phone. At the self-checkout, the girls bagged the groceries and carried them to the car. The next stop was the new shoe store. Like a pair of young teenagers, they tried on various sandals, giggling and talking, until her phone pinged.

"Hi Fleur, where are you?" Emmett texted with several question marks.

"Shopping with Lucia," she texted back.

"Have fun," he replied with a smiley face and a heart.

Fleur had always been there when Emmett came over for lunch and although he didn't seem to mind, she felt bad.

Lucia cut into her somber musings by elbowing her arm. "You suddenly look down in the dumps," she stated. "Chin up, girl. You and Emmett have been glued to the hip for months. Don't forget you're your own person."

Without buying shoes, they left the store. It had been fun to hang out with Lucia, who had bought her a chai latte and a gluten-free muffin at a drive-thru coffee stand. Another new experience.

"Thank you, Lucia," she said, returning her friend's casual hug. "I'm glad you're my neighbor. You've been so helpful."

Each girl waved on the front steps of their own home. "We have to do this again," Lucia smiled, picking up her bags before she disappeared into the house.

Fleur closed the front door and shrieked when Cassius

suddenly appeared from the kitchen. "I thought nobody was home."

He pulled her into a warm hug. "I'm sorry I scared you," he apologized, patting her back. "Emmett told me you spent the morning with Lucia. I'm happy to hear that. Friends are important."

Glad he'd returned safely, she smiled. "It's so good to see you. Did you have a pleasant trip?"

He nodded. "The flights were on time and the hotel comfortable, but the meetings were indecisive. We should hear more soon." With an inquiring and concerned glance, he looked her over. "Did anything important happen while I was gone?"

So much had happened that her brain had trouble keeping up. She sunk down in a chair at the table, unsure of what she could share and what she should keep to herself. The loss of her virginity was definitely not something she could confide in him. "No, everything went well."

Obviously not believing her, he sat down in the chair next to hers, his brown eyes troubled. "Is this about your heart?"

She placed a flat hand beneath her breasts and felt her heartbeat calm and steady in her fingertips, withdrawing a warm smile on her face. "No, it's not that. It's something Lucia said on the way home."

Cassius waited patiently for her to continue.

"She told me people nowadays have *friends with benefits*." Pensively, she rolled a strand of her hair around her index finger. "Do you think Emmett sees me like that?"

Cassius's jaw fell open. "Benefits?" He stayed silent for a moment and then grinned. "In today's world, a lot of young people often get lost and search for personal connections through casual sexual relationships, online chatrooms, or other forms of social media. Fortunately, most of them find their way into a true and meaningful relationship, eventually. All I recommend is for you to follow your heart and your instinct, and to do what feels right, because you are the one who has to live with the consequences."

He chuckled, full of warmth. "Anyone can see Emmett loves you very much, and I recommend you enjoy to the fullest what's been given. Genuine love doesn't come easy, and sometimes it only comes once."

Chapter 38

"IT'S SO SWEET OF YOU to call, Fleur," Grandmother Barbara spoke over the phone. "But don't worry about us. Your father helped us find another apartment and paid the movers. He can sure be useful at times."

Forrest hadn't mentioned it at all, and she wondered why. *Didn't he want anyone to know he cared about her grandmother, or because he was too modest to tell anyone?* Either way, the knowledge pleased her. "Where did you move to?"

She heard something falling over, followed by Violette's excited yapping. A moment later, her grandmother came back on the phone. "Sorry about that. Violette jumped on the coffee table and knocked Chuck's juice over. It's a mess. Anyway, we moved into a low-income housing complex in Heemstead. It's close to the grocery store and the hospital, which suits us just fine."

Relieved to hear they were enjoying their new home, Fleur told her Forrest had talked to the contractor who would start the demolition of the White Castle Apartment Complex today.

"My mother told us she used to live in apartment #14, and we're going to be there in the hope that Frank and Violette hid more letters from her under the floorboards, or somewhere in the walls," she explained.

"Then maybe that crappy old building will be useful for once," Barbara cackled.

Dressed in a light coat, Fleur headed out to the gate where Forrest would pick her up, because he didn't have clearance to enter.

The soldiers saluted her with a grin and let her through. On the other side of the fence, Fleur noticed six parked cars along the road. An older woman with a baseball cap on her head sat on top of the hood of one of them, smoking a cigarette, her heels on the bumper. "Hi, Hon, you work there?" she asked.

Not interested in a conversation with a stranger, Fleur nodded and hurried past her. Instead of leaving her alone, the woman jumped off the hood. "Can I ask you a few questions?"

Fleur kept on walking. "There's nothing I can tell you," she said, her voice clipped.

"We work for a magazine called Conspiracy," the audacious woman continued, hurrying to keep up with Fleur's fast pace. "An anonymous source told us there's a time machine inside Abernathey. Since they've been in the news several times before about their controversial research, we drove out here. Do you have any comment?"

With her face wiped clean of any expression, Fleur stared at the woman. "Only a fool would believe that."

The woman flicked her cigarette butt into the dunes and grumbled. "Bitch!"

To her relief, Fleur recognized Forrest's Tesla coming her way. As soon as he stopped, she jumped in. "That awful woman questioned me about SMITS," she breathed. "And there were five other vehicles parked near the entrance."

Forrest turned the car around and drove off. "I can tell you're upset," he said. "But don't worry about it. In an hour, she'll tire of waiting and leave. And if she tries to trespass, those soldiers will take care of it. It's their job to secure the perimeter and keep curious onlookers out."

It wasn't the first time Fleur had noticed parked cars near the entrance and people strolling along the perimeter. Most of them walked their dog and minded their own business, and only occasionally someone tried to get a closer look. This time it was different, and the woman hadn't driven out just by herself. That meant her colleague was snooping around, too.

Instead of arguing about it, she let it go. "Thanks for helping Barbara and Chuck move into their new apartment," she said. "That was very kind of you."

"She's your grandmother," Forrest grinned. "How could I not?" He pulled into Sixth Street and parked his car along the road when he found the parking lot closed, the entire apartment complex surrounded with tall fences to restrict access. Inside the fence, two excavators moved around, tearing down walls and loading rubble into huge dumpsters.

Forrest walked to a mobile office unit with the name McLellan Construction Company on the side. "Jim McLellan is an old school friend," he told Fleur and opened the door.

A man with a hardhat sat behind a desk, a laptop and rolls of paper in front of him. He stood when they walked in. "Forrest, buddy. It's been a long time."

The men shook hands. "You're making good progress, Jim,"

Forrest said, pointing with his thumb toward the apartment complex.

"Demolition is easy," Jim chuckled and shook Fleur's hand. "Nice to meet you, Miss." Her hand almost disappeared into his calloused palm, his skin rough and scratchy.

"You told me over the phone your interest is with unit 14. What's so special about it?"

"One of my relatives used to live there," Forrest chuckled, trying to make light of the situation. "In her will, it says she left a time capsule hidden in the walls or under the floor. Is it possible for your men to be on the lookout? I'm more than happy to compensate you for the trouble."

McLellan laughed. "It wouldn't be the first time we would find a surprise hidden in an old building. Man, we've found cases of moonshine, a metal box filled with old bones, and a safe with money. Now, that was quite the find."

He rolled out the floor plan of the complex. "Can you show me where #14 is?"

"It's the unit on the east side," Forrest said and pointed it out.

Jim peered out the window. "I can ask Matt to move his excavator and start tearing it down if you want to stick around." He pulled a device from the pocket of his bright yellow safety vest. "Matt, can you move to the eastside?"

They saw the heavy equipment operator raise his right hand, and the excavator moved, the metal tracks grinding the pavement.

"Thanks, man," Forrest said. "I really appreciate it."

They left the office, and from behind the fence, they

watched the bucket at the end of the arm crash into the roof and tear down the wall, exposing the old living room. In a cloud of dust, the machine picked up the asphalt shingles, drywall, insulation, and wooden beams as if they weighed nothing. Within half an hour, there was nothing left of the apartment.

"How will they find anything in that enormous pile of debris?" Fleur wondered out loud, and covered her ears when the excavator rolled by, and a backhoe loader took its place.

"A ground crew will break down the pieces and sort them for disposal," Forrest yelled over the noise. "If they find anything, I'm sure Jim will call me." He took Fleur by her elbow and guided her towards the car. "Sorry, this was a waste of time, sweetheart."

"Don't apologize, because there's still a chance they'll find something," Fleur replied, holding on to hope.

After they got in, Forrest didn't start the engine. Instead, he turned towards her. "A few days ago, I told you I didn't believe your mother would have left letters at the Keizer estate. But since then, I remembered that before she disappeared, your mother was good friends with Catherine Rothchild. You know she was Kara's grandmother who lived there for many years, right? Why don't we organize a search party this coming weekend?"

Chapter 39

THE NEXT DAY, Emmett drove Fleur to the hospital for her second postoperative exam. It was rainy and Cassius had offered him the use of his car.

"Since Cassius's trip to Washington D.C., he gets pulled into a lot of confidential meetings with Commander Thornton," Emmett said, while they sat in the waiting room. "The secrecy around those meetings is causing concern among the workers, especially since they told me my internship will be cut short. I only have two weeks left."

Fleur wondered if the meetings had anything to do with the curious spectators near the entrance. On the way out, she had counted eleven cars.

Emmett crossed his ankles, his long legs stretched out in front of him. "Most employees believe it has to do with the increase of experiments, the multitude of storms bound to get noticed."

A door opened, and a nurse stepped out. "Fleur Keizer?" she asked, glancing around.

Hand in hand, Fleur and Emmett followed her into an exam room where she took her weight, blood pressure, heart rate, and oxygen level.

It didn't take long for Dr. Stevenson to join them. "How are you, Fleur?" he asked.

"Fantastic," she replied.

The cardiologist looked at the computer. "Based on your bloodwork, kidney function, cardiogram, and imaging tests, I don't see any reason for another appointment until six months from now."

"Finally, my life can turn back to normal," Fleur cried out happily.

"Until then, try to get enough sleep, eat healthy, exercise regularly, and continue to monitor your condition," Dr. Stevenson said as he walked them out.

"This was hopefully the last time I'll see my doctor," Fleur said while she studied the menu at the cozy restaurant. She and Emmett sat next to each other in a booth against the wall, each with a glass of white wine in front of them. They had something to celebrate.

"Can I get the pastrami Reuben with fries?" Emmett ordered when the waitress returned. "My girlfriend wants the same, but with a salad."

"Good choice," the waitress nodded. She took the menus and left.

Emmett raised his glass and stared deep into her eyes. "May we all get what we want," he said. They clinked their glasses and took a sip before Emmett turned away.

She followed his gaze, her eyes scanning the restaurant's décor and various paintings of sea creatures, peacocks, and other animals she'd never seen before. Other than that, there was nothing to see, and she realized he'd been unusually quiet all day. She put her hand on his arm.

"What is it that you want, Emmett?"

Dejectedly, he leaned his head against the back of the booth. "I realize you look forward to returning home, but do you have any idea what your departure will do to me?"

If her uncertain future and complicated past hadn't weighed so heavily on her mind, she could have enjoyed her current life with Cassius and her new family, and she could have allowed her relationship with Emmett to blossom. Instead, she had forcibly tried to cordon off her heart, keeping them all at a distance, to protect herself and safeguard the belief that her future lay in the past, and not here. After her doctor's visit, nothing stood in her way any longer, and with her preliminary departure date set for next week, it all became very real.

She grabbed his hand, brought it up to her mouth and kissed it, the anguish on his face tearing her insides apart. "Why don't you come with me?" she whispered.

His right leg trembled, and he crossed his legs to force it still. "Are you serious?" he said, his eyes wide in disbelief.

Nothing in the world would make her happier than to return home with Emmett. To walk the aisle on her father's arm and marry him in Heemstead's cathedral, to have children together, and live happily ever after at the Keizer Estate. "I love you and can't imagine living my life without you by my side," she spoke softly.

Emmett cupped his hand around the back of her head and crushed his lips down on hers, kissing her with a fervency that bordered on desperation. "I love you so much," he mumbled between kisses.

She responded to his embrace with the same ardor, her fingers gripping his shoulders, her tongue meeting his, seeking and probing, and longing for more.

"Two Reubens, lovebirds," the voice of the waitress interrupted their encompassing embrace.

Flustered, Fleur released her grip and lowered her arms. Any display of affection in public was frowned upon and she doubted it was any different now.

Emmett didn't care and kissed her one more time before letting go. "I always fantasized about travelling through time," he grinned. "Doing it with you would be a dream come true."

Immersed in their own little world, they ate their sandwiches, finished the wine, and left the restaurant, kissing and hugging every three seconds. When they reached the car, Emmett pressed her against the passenger door. In a close embrace, his hands buried in her long blonde hair, he whispered, "Let's not tell anyone yet."

Fleur would have agreed to anything he asked, the idea they could have a future and a life together exhilarating. "Yes, our secret," she sighed between kisses and arched up against him, his hardness fueling her desire. When his hand slid under her shirt and covered her breast, her eyes glazed over, the intensity of her need so strong that she longed to undress him in the middle of the parking lot. She hardly recognized herself. Trembling, she clung to his shoulders. "We should go home."

Emmett opened the door, and she slid inside, struggling to suppress the urge to dive into the backseat and continue their lovemaking. Next to her, Emmett clutched the steering wheel and stared straight ahead, his breathing shallow and fast.

In a dreamlike state, she sat there for several minutes until her heart rate slowed down and she no longer felt in danger of returning to that moment where she'd lost all rational thought. Embarrassed by her immoral behavior, she stared straight ahead, grateful when her phone pinged.

"It's Forrest," she said, reading the text message. "He heard from Jim McLellan. They found nothing in the rubble of Barbara and Chuck's apartment. And he's asking how it went at the hospital."

Emmett started the engine and drove off while she texted Forrest back. As soon as she put her phone away, he grabbed her hand and smiled, "Have I told you lately that I love you?"

When they approached Abernathey, there were over twenty cars parked along the road, and people walked around and talked in small groups.

"What are all these folks doing here?" Emmett grumbled.

Fleur shriveled in her seat, overcome by the premonition that the curious spectators were here for her. *What would they do to her if they found out who she was, and where she came from?*

Emmett hit the steering wheel palm with his palm. "Damn, I sure hope word about SMITS didn't get out." He slowed down to maneuver around a pedestrian. "This is crazy."

At the gate, they noticed several parked military vehicles and two soldiers immediately walked up to the car. Emmett rolled down his window to show his pass and ID. "What's going on here?" he asked.

The soldier shrugged. "Don't know."

Like everyone else, the soldiers were not allowed to talk about anything that happened at Abernathey. Sharing secret information would cost them their job, maybe even get them court-martialed.

Emmett parked Cassius's car close to the main entrance, and they entered the lobby.

"Hi, Darlene," he said. "Is Cassius downstairs?"

Darlene shook her head. "He's in Milton's office." She turned towards Fleur. "Didn't you see your doctor today? What did he say?"

"He was very pleased." Fleur smiled happily and followed Emmett into commander Thornton's office. Cassius, Milton, Adam, and Ramon sat around the shiny conference table, a newspaper in front of them.

"You must have seen the cars at the gate," Cassius said, his eyes serious.

Milton held up the newspaper. "The headline in this week's edition of the Dunedam Pioneer is *Military Presence at Abernathey Raises Concern*. The article talks about local weather shifts, strange cloud formation, and an increase in storm activity. It's bringing the locals out in droves, curious about the army presence, new fence, and SMITS."

"I was afraid of that," Emmett replied, raking his hand through his hair. "At least there's good news, too. Fleur's cardiologist cleared her for travel. He'll email you the paperwork."

Chapter 40

ON SATURDAY, the entire road to Abernathey was lined with cars when Cassius and Fleur drove to the Keizer Estate, to join Emmett and the rest of the family in the quest for the letters. They had a tool in the trunk that could locate objects inside walls.

"This scanner can detect a variety of objects such as metal, wood, plastic, and electrical wire," Cassius explained to Forrest when they arrived. "The images are sent to my laptop, allowing us to take measurements and enlarge the hidden item we located."

With the tenants notified, Forrest and Cassius started scanning the rooms in the left wing upstairs. Fleur and Emmett joined his parents in the coach house to search the loft and attic, knocking on walls and checking loose floorboards. Finn, Caro, Josie, and Arlo dug holes into the soil along the perimeter of the estate, hoping to find something that was buried. It was a long shot.

Two hours later, they all met for lunch in the kitchen at the estate. Kara had made a variety of sandwiches and a pot of hearty soup.

RAMCY DIEK

"Cassius and I finished scanning the entire left wing and attic," Forrest said to Fleur. "Do you think we should scan the walls of the right wing, too?"

Since they hardly ever set foot in her aunt and uncle's wing, Fleur highly doubted her mother would have left them there. The left-wing downstairs had mainly been her grandfather's domain, with his bedroom, boudoir and bathroom past the dining room and library. "I don't think so, but she spent a lot of time in the library."

Kara walked around, handing out bowls of soup. "Isn't that our living room now?" she asked.

The first time Fleur had walked into what used to be the library, she couldn't believe the changes. All the bookshelves had been removed and windows were installed, the always dark and imposing space where her grandfather basically lived, now light and inviting. With the major changes, it seemed impossible to find anything there.

Emmett placed his hand on Fleur's arm. "Did it cross your mind that the letters we're hoping to find might be addressed to you and not to Forrest?"

"To me?" she asked.

"Yes, we don't know if the goats and the capsules arrived, but if they did, she knows you landed in our time. Other than your room and the loft at the coach house, is there a place nobody else would know about but you?"

Fleur's brow furrowed in contemplation. "As part of the Underground Railroad, my parents helped enslaved Black people escape to Canada. They hid them in a secret hiding spot behind shelves in the cellar."

Her words piqued everyone's interest.

"Hidden slaves in our cellar? I never knew anything about it," Kara said. "Can you show us?"

Abandoning their lunch, they gathered in the kitchen where Kara opened the cellar door and turned on the light. One by one, they descended the wooden stairs and gathered on the concrete floor below. The walls were freshly painted, and a freezer and refrigerator hummed in the corner. Against one of the walls stood a washer and dryer with a basket full of dirty laundry.

"It used to be dark and damp down here, with spiders, earwigs, and sow bugs crawling around," Fleur told them. "We used it to store potatoes, vegetables, and cheese, among other things that needed to stay cool. Our canned goods were on the shelves against the back wall."

They walked to the other side and stared at the heavy-duty metal racks, overloaded with various tools, bottles of wine, rolls of paper towel and toilet paper, laundry detergent, vases, cans, and other knickknacks. It seemed impossible there could be another space hidden behind it.

"I'll get my scanner," Cassius said. "Can you help me carry it, Emmett?"

Emmett's father knocked against the drywall in various places to locate the studs.

"That's exactly where it used to be," Fleur said.

"Then let's empty the shelves and move these two racks," Forrest suggested. "If Cassius can detect space behind it, I can confirm it with a long drill, and if needed, we take down the sheetrock."

Touched by how much he was willing to do for what could

only be defined as a wild goose chase, Fleur's eyes blurred.

With many helping hands, the shelves were emptied in no time, and when Cassius and Emmett returned, the racks were out of their way. Cassius placed his laptop on a folding table and hooked it up to the yellow handheld device. "The emitted rays can penetrate most building materials," Cassius said. "To be safe, everyone must stand behind me."

He pointed the device towards the wall and moved it around until the image of a black square formed on the computer screen. "There's definitely a space behind this wall," Cassius concluded. "It measures close to six by seven feet."

"You're the contractor, Rix. How should we tackle this?" Forrest asked Emmett's father.

"For this kind of project, I use a reciprocating saw," Rix replied. "If you can start outlining the area, I'll go home to get it."

Excitement in the room mounted while they waited. Fleur found it difficult to breathe, the anticipation of what they could find tightening her stomach. "I'm so nervous," she whispered and clutched Emmett's arm with both hands.

Rix returned with an extension cord and the saw. He plugged it in and got to work, cutting upwards along a stud for about four feet. From there he started to saw horizontally.

"That should be wide enough to get through," Forrest yelled over the noise. He steadied the sheet of drywall so it wouldn't fall over and laid it on the ground when Rix reached the bottom.

The musty smell of mold and mildew emanated from the dark hole.

Rix turned the flashlight on his phone on. "Fleur, do you

want to go in?" he asked. "Or do you want me to go first?"

Fleur's mind went to the brave slaves who'd fled from their cruel owners at significant risk, and who had to trust complete strangers to help them escape. Compared to what they had to endure, this was nothing. "I'll go," she answered, and took a measured stride forward, her nerves a tangled mess.

She bent her head to step inside while Emmett and Rix pointed the flashlights of their phones into the hole. Barely able to see anything, Fleur moved around, sliding her feet so she wouldn't bump into anything. "There's something here," she said when her toes hit a hard object. Emmett followed her inside, his light outlining a square object. "It appears to be a crate or a trunk."

"Does it have handles?" Forrest asked, peeking in.

"It does," Emmett replied.

Fleur moved to the side so both men could carry the wooden trunk into the cellar, the hardware heavy duty cast iron, with beautifully crafted wrought iron details and clasps. In the bright light, she noticed her name engraved on the bronze nameplate. She could hardly believe her eyes and grateful tears rolled down her cheeks. "It's my grandfather's steamer trunk." She knelt on the hard floor and opened the lid, revealing one of the time capsules and sixty or more envelopes, all of them with her name on it.

"I can't believe it was hidden behind that wall for so long," Josie shrieked.

Fleur's head swam as she sifted through the envelopes. "These are all from my parents, and from Frank and Violette. I even recognize my aunt's and uncle's handwriting," she cried out breathlessly. It was becoming too much and with Emmett's arm around her shoulders, she started to weep.

Chapter 41

Annet, 1884

ANNET LOOKED UP from the letter she was writing. From across the table, she watched Frank read the newspaper, the permanent frown that had formed between his brows more pronounced.

"I keep telling you not to worry so much, Frank," Annet told him, concerned about the tension on his tired face. "Stress is bad for your health, and I can tell you're not getting enough sleep."

Frank let out a deep sigh. "Not worry? How can I not? The economy is in a downright panic. Banks are closing due to uncollectible loans." He pointed at the article he was reading. "Here, listen to this... *Crisis threatens to disrupt banking and payments system. An estimated five percent of factories and mines closed or temporarily down.*" He slammed his hand on the table. "Mother, we have to reduce production to stay afloat, and with so many workers lacking employment and the deflation, I don't see an end to it."

Alex stood at the window and stared at the rain, his right

hand gnarled around his cane. It was muggy and a trickle of sweat rolled down his temple, the unusually wet summer keeping the grass green and the flowers blooming.

"There comes an end to everything, Frank," he said. "This will pass too."

Leaning heavily on his cane, Alex shuffled through the library to his favorite chair next to the fireplace, his rheumatoid arthritis increasingly affecting his gait.

It pained Annet to see her husband's lined face, the swollen joints of his fingers, and the difficulty he had getting around. It had been years since he'd picked up a brush, his time mostly spent reading Charles Dickens, Victor Hugo, and Anthony Trollope. To her disappointment, the novel *The Time Machine* by H.G. Wells was still not published. Not that it mattered. The book was merely science fiction and wouldn't help bring Fleur back.

"Your father is right, Frank. Our businesses survived the Civil War, and we experienced strong economic growth in the following decade. That gave us enough financial stability to keep everything operating during the long depression, followed by tremendous growth powered by the expansion of the railroad and development of the transportation system. After this slight hiccup, we'll prosper again. That's how it goes." She had told him this already several times before, but he didn't want to accept it.

Uninterested, Frank grumbled, "So you keep saying."

Annet leaned back in her chair and folded her hands in her lap, suppressing her frustration that he him never believed anything she said. "Think about the cornerstone for the Statue of Liberty they just laid in New York Harbor, and the completion of the Washington Monument at the end of the year. Two major historic accomplishments."

The door of the library opened, and Frank's wife Isabelle walked in with their youngest child, who immediately ran to Alex and tried to climb in his lap. It reminded Annet of Fleur and Frank, who'd always vied for their grandfather's attention.

"Mother," Isabelle said. "We were in the yard when Russell Jonkers Jr. pulled up with his dray, asking to see you."

Annet's pulse raced with excitement. Nine years ago, Russell Jr. had delivered the goat with Fleur's message. She hadn't seen him since. "Please, show him into the library, Isabelle."

Isabelle shook her head. "He's delivering something heavy and wondered where you want it."

With anticipation in his eyes, Alex heaved himself out of his chair and grabbed his cane. "Let's look," he said, and hobbled to the door.

Annet recognized the ray of hope in her husband's eyes. Although they hadn't talked about the recent unstable weather, words weren't necessary to understand they both secretly hoped for a second miracle. Russell Jr.'s arrival made that hope burst out in full splendor.

"We should all go," she said.

Russell had parked his dray out front in the driveway, a bucket of fresh water in front of his draft horse. When he noticed them, he lifted his wide-brimmed felt hat, in his other hand a slice of bread.

"I'm surprised to see you, Russell," Alex said. "How are you and the family doing?"

"Just fine, sir. Just fine," he replied and walked to the back of his wagon. "My parents send their greetings." He pulled the blanket off the load he'd delivered, exposing a two-foot-long round metal object. "One of our neighbors dropped this off at the farm. They found it in their cornfield. Since they knew we're friends, they brought it by."

They all gathered around the dray and stared at the shiny metal cylinder, Annet and Alex's names and the Keizer Manor's address engraved on the side. Tears sprung to Annet's eyes. It could only mean one thing – this was more news from the future.

"It's made of the most beautiful metal and very heavy," Russell Jr. commented. Together with Frank, he lifted it out of the dray and put it on the ground.

Mesmerized, Annet knelt beside it and let her index finger slide over the engraving, the metal warm beneath her touch. She blinked her tears away and glanced up. "We can't thank you enough for bringing this, Russell. It means so much to us."

Alex reached for the wallet he carried on his belt, pulled out several coins, and dropped them in Russell's hand.

"You're far too generous, Mr. Keizer," Russell replied. He touched the brim of his hat, climbed into the seat, and drove off.

Frank studied the time capsule. "How do you suppose this opens?"

While Frank rode to town with the buggy to get the blacksmith, the gardener brought the time capsule to the coach house with his wheelbarrow. Not letting it out of their sight, Annet and Alex followed.

Henry, their coachman, immediately appeared, and inside the shop, he helped the gardener lift the capsule onto a wooden workbench.

"We hope the blacksmith can chisel it open," Alex said. He sat down on a bale of straw, both hands resting on the top of his cane.

It didn't take long for the blacksmith to arrive, who brought several sharp chisels and a hammer. Frank followed him in, carrying a saw and several more tools.

After examining the capsule, the blacksmith scratched his scraggly head. "I've never seen such metal before. I hope I can cut through."

"Do you think a fine-toothed saw could work?" Annet asked, the bottom of her skirt covered in straw and dust.

From a safe distance, she watched the blacksmith get to work while Henry held the capsule in place. She worried about the men's safety as the blacksmith hammered away, their eyes unprotected from possible splinters flying around. "Be careful," she yelled several times, the precise work time-consuming and arduous.

The air inside the shop was suffocating. Dust flew around and the smell of fresh hay mixed in with horse manure and stale sweat made it hard to breathe. The blacksmith wiped off his forehead. "A pint wouldn't hurt," he said, licking his dry lips.

Henry walked into the adjacent kitchen and returned with a pewter mug. The blacksmith gulped the entire contents down and wiped his mouth with the back of his hand before he got back to work, the progress painstakingly slow.

Alex's shoulders sagged, and from his weary face Annet could tell he was exhausted after sitting upright for several hours. Her suggestion to go home was only met with a stubborn wave of his arm. "I'm staying until we discover what's inside," he insisted, straightening his back.

"Apologies for not going faster," the blacksmith said, his lined face bathed in sweat. "I'm almost done."

With a loud bang, the top of the capsule came off and dropped to the ground. The blacksmith sent her a toothless grin. "That should do it."

Frank handed him several coins. "Thank you for your service, Mr. Hickman," he said, before he helped his father up and supported him toward the workbench. Annet had already peeked inside, too impatient to wait a second longer. She pulled out four envelopes, all addressed to them. The rest of the capsule was empty, the weight due to the large bricks of lead placed inside.

"Let's take the letters to the house and open them there," Annet suggested. She was perspiring heavily underneath her dress, her hair sticking to her forehead, and her cheeks were bright red. "We're all hot and thirsty and need to cool off."

Gloria, their housekeeper, watched them come in and immediately served cold lemonade and fresh-baked cookies in the library. "We have more news from Fleur," Annet confided to her. The longtime faithful housekeeper was like family.

"That's wonderful news," she cried out.

Left alone, Annet, Alex and Frank sat around the table, the envelopes in front of them.

"Which one shall I open first?" Annet asked. Her hand

shook nervously when she grabbed the letter opener.

"It doesn't matter," Alex replied, his voice gravelly. He took a sip of lemonade to slake his parched throat.

With great care, Annet slid the opener underneath the flap, pulled it across horizontally, and glanced inside, revealing four pictures. She placed them next to each other on the table and found her reading glasses hanging from a string around her neck. In each photo, she recognized her lovely daughter, smiling at the camera. Choked with emotion, she took in every detail, recognizing an older Forrest in one of them. She turned the picture over. On the backside, Fleur's handwriting stated, *Me with Forrest, his wife Kara, and my half-sisters Josie and Caro.* Trembling, Annet burst into tears. Fleur had found her biological father. The news couldn't have been better.

Frank picked up one of the other pictures. "This is Fleur in a hospital bed," he commented. "Do you think this is because of her heart surgery?"

Alex offered his sobbing wife a handkerchief. "Hopefully, the other envelopes contain letters that will explain," he said, his own eyes brimming with tears.

"I wish Violette was here," Annet sighed. Her youngest daughter was happily married to an ambitious solicitor in Lisk, their two young children still toddlers. She opened the thickest envelope, unfolded the stack of letters inside, and read.

My dear family,

Where do I start? So much has happened to me in such a short time. It's difficult to wrap my mind around it.

Annet's face crumbled, and she had to stop several times to collect her emotions while she read about the machine, Cassius, and her developing friendship with a young man named Emmett.

"She found somebody else to love." Annet squeezed Alex's hand in sheer delight, their love for each other as strong as ever, their bond unbreakable.

The next letter was about Forrest and the letters he'd found hidden behind *Lost in the Storm*. That he worked at Keizer Manor as the director for collections and exhibitions, was married to Kara, Caroline's Rothchild granddaughter, and that they had two daughters close to Fleur's age.

"Forrest married into the Keizer Family," she beamed, overjoyed. "Can you imagine? And Fleur found a new family and a young man she loves."

She picked up the picture of Fleur and Emmett next to his motorcycle, the familiar building of the research center in the dunes behind them. They stood in the exact location where she'd disappeared all those years ago.

"This is where it all began," she told Frank and Alex.

Gloria came in to collect the empty glasses and brought tea. The trusted housekeeper had been in their employ long before Fleur was born, and she was extremely concerned. "Is it good news, ma'am?" she asked.

"It couldn't be better, Gloria." Annet beamed. "There's more news about Fleur and I'm so, so happy and relieved."

Annet opened the next envelope. It contained a brochure of

the Keizer Museum and several quarters, dimes, and pennies, and a one-dollar bill. She handed the brochure to Alex and the money to Frank. Both men studied the mysterious items from the future, turning them over in their hands.

"Fascinating," Frank said as he examined the coins.

Annet waited several minutes before she opened the last letter and read out loud about Fleur's visit to her mother Barbara. "I can't believe it." She laughed so hard that she had to stop reading. "My mother named her dogs after Fleur, Frank, and Violette." The next moment, she was ready to burst into tears again as she read. *"I feel so much better since my surgery and like to dance all the time."*

She folded her hands and pressed her arms against her chest, her eyes spilling over. "Fleur might have died from heart failure if she hadn't been transported to the future. Instead, she has the chance to live a full life, with a husband, children. It's incredible."

Her heart hammered in her chest, all the information gradually sinking in, her feelings shifting from elation to desperation, from gratitude to sorrow. Although Fleur had received a second chance at life, she would never see her again, never meet her husband or children, never hear her voice. She put her hands over her face, trying desperately to hang on to the knowledge Fleur had survived and to control the grief only a parent could feel over the loss of a child.

"Mother?" Frank asked, laying a comforting hand on her shoulder. "Are you alright?"

"Just give me a moment," she whispered, her voice hoarse.

Frank got up, opened a bottle of wine, and poured three

glasses. "Here, drink this," he told his parents. "It may help calm your nerves."

Annet took several sips and let the tart liquid roll over her tongue, savoring the flavor, until she felt the alcohol tingle through her veins. "We have to remind ourselves how Fleur enriched our lives and that we should be thankful for having her with us for twenty-three years," she said, her voice cracked. "We should also be eternally grateful for the closure and comfort these letters will provide while we live our lives without her." She tried to smile at her husband and son. "We will find acceptance and peace of mind in these letters, and I can already feel my spirits lift and my bitterness diminish. I hope you can too."

Alex sat next to her, his hands folded, whispering words of gratitude, and thanking the Lord. Annet still didn't share his Christian beliefs but knew Alex's religion helped him through difficult times and she was grateful for that.

She picked up the letter and started reading the last paragraph. "*After I'm cleared by my cardiologist, they're going to transport me back. Please be on the lookout, my dear family. I'll be there soon. Love, Fleur.*"

With grave concern, Annet fell silent. *Sending her back*, she thought. *That's far too dangerous.*

"Mother, they can't do that," Frank cried out next to her. "Over the last twenty years, we only received one goat, and it took all that time for this capsule to arrive. What happened to the other goat and the first three capsules Fleur talks about in the last letter? Did they end up in the ocean? Were they blown to pieces, or did they land in another time?"

"Oh, honey, don't try to come back," Annet sighed. "There

are too many risks involved."

Alex gripped the table, desperation and fear showing in his eyes. 'We must find a way to contact her. To warn her of the risk."

Chapter 42

EMMETT AND FINN hoisted the trunk up the stairs, through the kitchen, and into the living room. Intrigued by the dark history of the slave era, Cassius, Kara, and Josie stayed behind to explore the hidden chamber. The rest of the family followed Fleur.

"I'm so excited for you," Caro said to Fleur, a bond with her new sister already formed. "It's like we found a treasure chest."

Images of pirates and trunks filled with gold, pearls, and other gems appeared in Fleur's mind. "These letters mean more to me than all the riches in the world ever could," she said, eager to start reading.

In the living room, they spread the letters out over the dining table. A piece of string tied several of them together. "These are all from Frank," Fleur said, placing the small stack to her right. "I believe these are from Violette."

She arranged them by handwriting, and then by the year, neatly written on the outside of each envelope.

"Somebody in your family was very organized, Fleur," Emmett commented. He stood next to her, helping her sort them out.

With all the letters in place, Fleur opened the oldest one from her mother.

"Let's give them some privacy," Emmett's mother said. "Will you two stop by later?"

"We will, Mom," Emmett replied and waved at his parents, Finn, and Caro as they headed out.

Only Forrest stayed behind. "Do you want me to leave too?" he asked, his eyes patient as Fleur hesitated.

Fleur thought it over for several seconds. "Please, stay," she smiled and motioned to the chair next to her. "Our lives have been connected since before I was born and you're my father. I accept that now and want you to be part of this, too."

Visibly shaken by her words of acceptance, he pulled her up against his chest in a warm hug. "This means so much to me, Fleur," he spoke in her hair, squeezing her tight before letting go. "Thank you." He wiped his eyes and sat down.

Seated between the two men who loved and supported her, she read.

September 2, 1884

Thank you, my dearest Fleur, my sweet daughter. What a wonderful surprise it was when Russell Jonkers Jr. delivered your time capsule a few weeks ago and to finally have closure. We couldn't be happier with the news you gave us.

There's so much I want to write to you, so much to tell. But first we want to congratulate you on your heart surgery. For years, we'd seen your health decline, until there was so little left of the vivacious girl you used to be. Tell Cassius we're so grateful he brought you to the future. He saved your life. We fully understand we would have lost you to heart failure far too soon. The knowledge that instead, you have a long life ahead of you gives us such comfort.

Emmett tore a sheet from the roll of paper towels he'd brought from the kitchen, knowing she would need it, and handed it to her, his own eyes misting over.

"Thanks." Fleur sniffled and blew her nose. "Before I'm finished, I'll probably have used up the entire roll."

I'm also very relieved Forrest found my letters inside Lost in the Storm and hope meeting him makes life easier for you. When I disappeared, I was four months pregnant and, in my letters, I begged him to find you. We're so grateful he did and want you to give him our love and endless gratitude. Be kind to him, my dear child. He's a good man, kind and generous, and I have nothing but fond memories of him.

I still can't believe he married into the Keizer family. If Kara is anything like her dear grandmother Caroline Rothchild, she'll love you instantly. Life has gone full circle.

We would have loved to have met Emmett. He looks so handsome and tough in his motorcycle clothes. But so do you! You look gorgeous and vibrant. The color is back in your cheeks, and your love for him is visible in your eyes.

Tell him to be good to you, otherwise we'll come to haunt him!

"Then I better be careful," Emmett joked.

Sweetheart, I'll keep on writing to you in the years to come, and so will your father and the rest of the family, to tell you about our lives and wish you well. I promise! But first there's something very important I need to tell you. Something of the uttermost urgency.

DO NOT TRY TO COME BACK.

I can't emphasize it enough. Please, don't. Only one goat made it over, and we don't know what happened to the second one. From your letters in the capsule, we also know it was the fourth one you sent out. We hired eight men to scour the dunes over the last few months, to find the other three. As of today, they have found nothing.

Please, Fleur, my sweet, sweet daughter, understand there's nothing more that we want than to welcome you back home and hold you in our arms, but we realize it would risk your life. Nothing is worth that.

With each word, Fleur lowered her voice until she barely spoke above a whisper. "I can't believe this." Disappointment, anger, and pain fought for control. Anger won. "How dare she tell me what to do? I'm more than capable to make my own decisions." She crossed her arms over her chest and clamped her jaws shut, her mood plummeted from exhilaration to desperation and resentment in the blink of an eye.

Forrest and Emmett gaped at her, both uncertain how to respond to the sudden change in her demeanor. They shared glances and shrugged feebly.

"Your mother has always been a woman of reason," Forrest

said, the tone of his voice sincere. "She loves you so much. I can hear it in every painful word she wrote. Fleur, all she wants is the best for you. If she's capable of sacrificing her happiness and wellbeing over your safety, she must feel strongly about the risk."

Stubbornly, Fleur stared straight ahead, upset, afraid, and hurt.

In deep concern, Forrest massaged his forehead. "SMITS's forces are too unpredictable, too unknown, and dangerous, and I have to agree with your mother. Until they figure out how to safely control them, they shouldn't gamble with your life, and neither should you." He looked at Emmett for support.

Fleur released a deep sigh. "I'm done with people deciding for me and harping about my safety. I'm twenty-three years old and can decide the future of my life for myself. I want to go home."

Emmett pushed his chair back and stood. "I think it's best to let all of this sink in."

Chapter 43

FORREST AND EMMETT loaded the trunk into the back of Cassius's car, together with the scanner and the damaged time capsule.

"I'll bring Fleur home later today, Cassius," Emmett said, watching her pace down the driveway, her shoulders raised in a defensive way.

"I understand," Cassius nodded. "She's confused and scared. Take all the time you need."

Emmett sprinted after Fleur. His long legs quickly caught up with her.

Forrest turned to Cassius. "Before you go, can we talk for a minute?"

Cassius closed the trunk and leaned up against it. "Of course."

Forrest waited until Fleur and Emmett were out of sight and then released a deep sigh.

"I have to admit my feelings about the whole thing are contradictory," he said. "And I don't want to sound selfish, but don't you agree Fleur's better off here?" He waited for a few seconds to collect his thoughts. "I only want what's best for her, and my major concern is her heart. Even though her surgery was successful, her cardiologist said that women with rheumatic heart disease have a greater chance of complications during pregnancy because of an increased pressure on the damaged heart valves. He also said that even if she would never have children, she might need a valve replacement in the future, and they won't be able to help her in the 19th century."

He kicked a stray rock out of the way and sighed before continuing. "Annet wrote that only one goat, and one of the four capsules made it. Don't you have doubts about sending Fleur back through an unpredictable vortex?"

"Just one goat and one capsule?" Cassius frowned with concern. "Any idea when they arrived exactly, so I can update and adjust my calculations?"

Forrest shook his head. "Fleur barely finished reading her mother's first letter, and I hope the other ones will tell us more."

Cassius opened the two top buttons of his shirt. The sun was beating down on them and he was perspiring heavily. "The information could be crucial to guarantee Fleur's safe return."

Then he scoffed with self-mockery. "Just like you, I love Fleur, but realize I've been selfish through the entire process."

"What do you mean?" Forrest asked.

To avoid Forrest's inquisitive stare, Cassius opened the front door of his car. "Since her arrival, I've been driven by guilt to fix the wrongs I inflicted on Annet, Fleur, and you." Ashamed, he bowed his head. "To clear my conscience, I only focused on her return, conveniently ignoring the danger involved." He slammed his fist into his palm, determined not to make the same mistake for the third time. "What you just told me changes everything."

Forrest had seen the tenacity in his daughter's eyes and knew it wouldn't be easy to persuade her. "Fleur has a mind of her own and won't agree," he warned Cassius.

"I know," Cassius acknowledged. "But in this case, defiance and willpower won't lead to victory. Only research, extensive testing, and guaranteed safety can. So far, we haven't done enough of that and can't use her as a guinea pig in our ambitious quest to dominate time."

Forrest let out an anxious bark. "I've had my doubts about her safe return for weeks. You know why? When Annet went back in time, there were records of her wedding in the convent, of her children's existence, the major role she played in the construction of Keizer Manor. According to my fathers-in-law's extensive digging into the past, the only proof of Fleur's existence is the recording of her birth."

"Nothing about a wedding or children?" Cassius said, gravely concerned. "Not even about her death?"

They heard a motorcycle start, and a few seconds later Emmet drove off with Fleur on the back. Each caught up in their own reflections, Cassius and Forrest didn't speak until the sound had died off.

"Let's hope we can convince her that the past is written, and that nothing can change history," Cassius said. He slid into his seat, started the engine, and drove off.

Chapter 44

WITH HER ARMS around Emmett's waist, they drove through the streets of Heemstead. All she wanted was for him to keep going and never stop. Finding the trunk with letters had been glorious. If only her mother hadn't started warning her about the dangers. She squeezed her eyes shut to keep from crying. She had a lot to process.

Emmett pulled over on the outskirts of town. "Do you want to go for a walk? There's a new trail around Brittania Lake. It's about four miles long."

For years, she hadn't even been able to walk one mile. Would she be able to hike four? "Yes, let's do it," she replied, up for the challenge.

Hand in hand, they walked over the newly paved trail. Benches along the way allowed people to rest or enjoy the view. They passed every single one, and she felt great.

"Look, a heron," Emmett said, and pointed at the beautiful long-legged gray bird that stood motionless as it scanned the water for food. Other birds flew around, and she recognized robins, finches, crows, and sparrows, all very common around here. It was warm and muggy, and several mosquitoes buzzed around her head. She waved them away. At least the flora and fauna had changed little.

"I'm thirsty," Emmett said at the end of their walk. "Let's get two bottles of water at the gas station, and some trail mix."

He filled his motorcycle up with gas while Fleur went inside to look around. She had her hands full of candy when he joined her.

"Chocolate pretzels, cookies, and chips?" He grinned. "Delicious." On the way to the cash register, he grabbed two bottles of water and a bag of jerky.

Several picnic tables were set up in front of the store, and they sat down. Until now, she'd avoided talking about the letters, and she didn't intend to talk about them now either, although they were constantly on her mind. All she wanted was to feel young and relaxed, and to enjoy a leisurely, carefree afternoon with Emmett, without the constant pressure and fear of having to choose between the present and the past. "Aren't you impressed I walked the entire trail?"

"I am," Emmett agreed. "Now that your heart is stronger, think about all the adventures we can have together."

His answer was a healing balm for her troubled soul, the vision of sharing the future with him lifting her spirit. "Have you ever been to a different country?" she asked, envisioning the two of them in London or Paris, or possibly even further away.

Fifteen minutes later, they drove to the Heemstead Cinema. Emmett paid for two tickets, and they watched a Disney movie. At the end of the show, Fleur was too tired to think. It had been a long and stressful day.

When he dropped her off, it was already dark inside, and

Cassius had gone to bed. Although Fleur was tempted to invite Emmett in, she was too exhausted and kissed him goodnight.

The next morning, she noticed long scratches on the floor of the living room. Cassius had dragged the steamer trunk in all by himself and damaged the floor. She opened the lid, took out the letters, and organized them in neat stacks on the coffee table.

Dressed in Javina's robe, she snuggled up on the couch, and tucked her bare feet beneath her before reading Violette's first letter.

Dear Fleur, I just recovered from the fantastic news. When I first heard about it, I couldn't stop crying. Not because I was sad. No, I was ecstatic.

The ten-year-old sister she'd left behind was now a mature woman in her early thirties, with a husband and two children. It was hard to imagine.

Engrossed in her sister's letters, Fleur kept on smiling. They were filled with funny anecdotes about her children and the turbulent relationship she had with her husband. As solicitor, he dealt with legal matters, like wills, contracts, conveyances of land, and court cases. Raised by an unconventional, progressive woman, Violette struggled with his conservative ideas and principles, but loved him enough to put up with it.

"I'm glad to see you smile," Cassius commented when he walked in. "Did you have breakfast yet?"

She'd thought he was still sleeping. Instead, he'd been at work. "Don't get up," he said. "All I have to do is heat the croissants I bought yesterday and make coffee."

While they ate, she told him about her four-mile hike and

the movie she'd seen. Then she threw a bombshell. "Cassius, I haven't told you this yet, but Emmett and I decided that he's going to join me when you send me back in a couple of days."

Cassius's smile dropped off his face. "You decided what?" His jaw tensed as he processed her shocking statement.

"We love each other, and want to stay together," Fleur added, as if it was completely acceptable to take such a risk.

"You can't be serious?" he gasped. "They will never grant us permission."

Fleur crossed her arms and clutched her elbows in a stubborn gesture. "They never gave you permission to transport me over here, either."

His breakfast forgotten, Cassius eyed her with a mixture of disbelief and mistrust, as if he thought she'd lost her mind. "I don't understand, Fleur."

"No, I don't understand," Fleur said. "For months, we talked about sending me back after Dr. Stevenson authorized it. The only difference now is that Emmett wants to go with me, and I don't see the problem. His health is better than mine."

"You're a smart young woman, Fleur, and I believe you're misleading yourself into believing that we can control the storm's powers at will. That SMITS is capable of picking you up and dropping you off exactly where you want to be, like a taxi or train. It's nothing like that, Fleur." He exhaled deeply. "Only one goat and one capsule made it, and we don't know what happened to the other ones. Those are not very good odds."

Not willing to accept reality, Fleur jumped to her feet. "It took the goat eleven years and the time capsule over twenty to arrive. I'm sure you can find the exact dates in my mother's letters, and you can update your calculations based on that information."

"You're right. It'll help. But sending someone else, other than yourself, from the present to the past will require lots of paperwork, and nobody will authorize this overnight."

"I'm counting on you to make it work, Cassius," Fleur said.

Fleur stripped, opened the glass shower door, turned on the faucet, and stepped in. With hot water cascading down her body, her legs began to tremble, and she covered her face with her hands. She had no idea what had come over her and why she'd been so unreasonable. Of course, she understood the risk involved, especially after her mother's explicit warnings. Frustrated with her own unpredictable behavior and lack of judgement, she pressed her teeth into her bottom lip until it hurt. She'd become quick to anger, cried for no apparent reason, and battled feelings of loneliness. The constant pressure, stress, and fitful nights started to take their toll. Would she ever feel normal again?

But what was normal for her, she wondered. After she had contracted scarlet fever, it had taken her a long time to recover. She'd been thirteen. Several years later, another bout of fever, combined with fatigue and painful knees, ankles, elbows, and wrists had debilitated her for several months. What had scared her most was her irregular heartbeat, and while other girls talked about boys, she'd become overly aware of every beat, noticing each flutter in her chest. It had made her feel vulnerable and her outlook on life changed, with questions of life and death and heaven and hell dominating her thoughts.

With warm water cascading down her body, she retreated in her memories to the third episode she'd struggled through, that one even scarier than the one before. Not because she was sicker, but because her malaise had gone on for much longer. Looking back, she realized she hadn't felt normal since, and it would be interesting to find out who she really was.

She washed her hair and stood under the spray until the emotional turmoil inside of her subsided. When she stepped out of the bathroom, her wet hair pinned up in a bun, Cassius was gone, his breakfast plate and coffee mug drying in the dish rack on the kitchen counter. She warmed up her own coffee in the microwave, finished her croissant, and settled on the couch with Frank's letters.

Shortly after, she heard Emmett's motorcycle. When he walked in, she crashed into his arms. "Oh, Emmett," she moaned. "I was so mean to Cassius this morning and am so ashamed." She told him about their conversation.

"Don't be so hard on yourself, honey," he said. "I remember from your discharge papers that mood swings, frustrations, and anxiety could be part of the recovery process for up to three months after the surgery. So, don't worry. It's only been two months and you're not fully recovered yet." He took her by the shoulders and squeezed them encouragingly. "Don't forget, you had quite the day yesterday, and didn't even rest."

Counting herself lucky with her supporting boyfriend, she nodded. "It's easy to blame it on my operation, but I should be able to be polite, understanding, and realistic. I'm not crazy."

Emmett laughed. "No, you're definitely not."

Chapter 45

EARLY IN THE MORNING, Fleur stood on top of a dune, with her hands in the pockets of her jeans, and stared out over the ocean, breathing in the refreshing air. In search of clarity, she'd left the house and walked through the gate into the dunes. She needed to be by herself, to contemplate and reflect, without the constant well-meaning advice of others, and make this crucial decision on her own.

A powerful wave rolled onto the beach below and chased a few food-searching sandpipers away. A second wave crashed in right behind it, the constant coming and going of water mesmerizing. She wet her lips and tasted the salty tang of the cool ocean air. It had been years since she'd been able to walk this far; her damaged heart unable to pump enough blood through her veins, leaving her fatigued, dizzy, and short of breath. Her surgery had given her new life, and she could have easily continued walking for several more miles. To prove it, she ran down the hill, kicking up loose sand until she reached the beach. Several seagulls swooped up, screeching at her. She laughed out loud at the freedom of just running and being alive. "Don't be angry," she yelled at the gulls. "You live in the most beautiful place on earth." They settled down much further down the beach, ignoring her.

She took off her sand-filled sandals and walked into the surf. The cold water pooled around her ankles. With summer in full swing and the morning sun peeking through the clouds, it promised to be another warm day. She would have taken off her clothes down to her underwear and dove into the waves if there hadn't been other people around.

It disappointed her. She wasn't used to seeing anyone here for miles. The property surrounding Keizer Manor had only been nature, unspoiled by fences, hiking trails, buoys, and signs. So much had changed through the centuries, and the increase in population was something she truly disliked. What she did appreciate were the conveniences brought by the electric network, the advances in medicine, and the new modes of transportation. If she stayed, she wanted to learn how to drive a car and a motorcycle, and further her education. Before she got sick, she had dreamed of designing homes and becoming an architect, a very unladylike profession. In the twenty-first century, women could become anything they desired, Emmett had told her. Even a doctor, detective, or astronaut, the idea of people flying into space still incomprehensible to her.

If she stayed, she could also keep on seeing Dr. Stevenson for yearly check-ups, accept the job at Keizer Manor Forrest had offered, and get to know her half-sisters and Kara better. She would have grandparents, nieces and nephews, uncles and aunts, and Cassius. He had been so good to her, so supportive and welcoming, and despite the circumstances, she enjoyed living with him. His house was tiny and comfortable, her bedroom cozy, and she thoroughly enjoyed the shower that never ran out of hot water, the proximity to the ocean, and the freedom of doing what she wanted while Cassius was at work.

She felt a blush creep up her face when she thought about how she and Emmett had ended up in her bedroom a few times, wrestling with a condom, and in a hurry, afraid to get caught while he was supposed to be at work. Oh, Emmett. What privileges she had permitted him without the promise of a wedding, while she'd barely allowed Jeremiah to kiss her, even though she'd accepted his ring. Her feelings for both men were so different. With Jeremiah, it had been about status and comfort, his family wealthy and influential, like hers. With Emmett, it was only about unconditional love and trust, the feelings she had for him fierce and forever. If he hadn't offered to go with her, she would never have found the strength to leave him behind and surrender to the frenzy of the storm for the second time. Especially not after finding her family's letters inside the trunk.

Her stomach turned upside down at the thought of subjecting herself to the dangers; her mother's warning words going off like a siren inside her head. She straightened her back and tried to swallow the fear the idea drilled into her, the torment of doubt tearing her insides apart. Although Emmett assured her that he wanted to go with her, she knew he was scared, too. He'd said he needed more time to prepare for his departure. It's not that he had to fill a suitcase, or book hotels.

But what if they decided Emmett couldn't even join her this soon? Would it be possible to postpone their departure until they granted permission and further testing improved the likelihood they would arrive in the same year she'd left? That would prevent her family years of searching, hoping, and mourning.

She took several cleansing breaths to bring serenity and peacefulness into her heart, willing it to take the place of the uncertainty and dread that had dominated her life since that fateful day when the storm swallowed her up, and then spat her out.

"Please, Lord," she whispered. "The universe creates my path. Help me read and accept the signs, follow the road that's laid out ahead of me, and surrender to what can't be changed. Not even by me."

Her eyes stung with unshed tears as she gradually made her way back. After hours of weighing the pros and cons, and delving into her deepest emotions, beliefs, and desires, she was still uncertain of what would make her truly happy, what course to follow, and what was most important to her. The familiarity of her past, her parents and siblings, her rightful place as a member of the prestigious Keizer Family, or the unfamiliar future with another family, in a fast-paced world, where she would have to earn her own money and create her own path.

Chapter 46

BY LATE MORNING, she walked out of the dunes. Although she still felt unsettled, she looked forward to the future with her newfound energy and endurance and knew with one hundred percent certainty that as long as she was with Emmett, it didn't matter if that future would be here or in the past.

At Abernathey, she noticed the long line of cars parked close to the gate had increased. And there was a multitude of army vehicles and three semi-trucks that took up the entire parking lot.

"What's all the commotion?" she asked the guard.

"I don't know anything about the trucks, Fleur." The young soldier grinned. "But all these people outside the gate are asking about you. I'm afraid word got out and you're famous now."

"Hey you, lady?" a man with long brown hair and a beard bellowed. "Is it true there's a time machine hidden inside the building?"

More people yelled questions when the guard opened the gate to let her enter. She pressed a hand against each ear to shut them out and hurried off. If she went home, this would be her last day, and life could go back to normal at Abernathey. The spectators would leave, the soldiers could go home, and the fence could be broken down. It would be better for everyone, including Cassius, who had aged visibly since her arrival. Commander Milton had been under a lot of stress and scrutiny too, and waited for her decision, the Department of Defense and the curious crowd at the gate pressing the matter. Her nerves multiplied the closer she came to the building, the weight and consequences of her decision catching up to her. If she'd only been able to sleep last night. Maybe then her brain wouldn't be so muddled.

A soldier with a hand truck passed by her. Four other soldiers stood next to a semi-truck. It had the back doors open and in passing, Fleur glanced inside the empty container box.

With her mind elsewhere, she returned the soldiers' greetings with a nod and entered the building. Another group of soldiers hung around the reception desk. Darlene immediately rushed over to her side. "Fleur, we've been trying to reach you for hours. Thank God you're all right." The kind woman had tears in her eyes. "Cassius and Milton are in his office, and Emmett is running around, looking for you everywhere."

"I didn't realize," Fleur apologized and walked over to Milton's office.

Cassius immediately flew up from his chair, unease written all over his face. "Where have you been? We were so worried."

"Sorry, I wanted to be by myself and left my phone at home," she replied. "What's going on?"

Milton waved at a chair. "Sit down for this," he said.

The grave expression on his face caused her heart to skip a

beat. "Did someone get hurt?"

Milton folded his hands in front of him and cleared his throat. "The government pulled the plug on our research and moved in this morning to dismantle SMITS."

Stunned, Fleur stared at him, unable to fully comprehend the consequences of the shocking turn of events. "They're what?" she stuttered.

Cassius lifted his shoulders in a sad shrug. "The decision is out of our, and your, hands, Fleur. I'm so sorry."

Fleur looked up into his troubled eyes. "I can't go back?"

He shook his head. "The DOD has been threatening for weeks to close Abernathey. The moment that newspaper article came out last week, they increased their demand. We didn't find out they'd decided until those trucks pulled in earlier this morning. We've been on the phone for hours trying to stop them. So far, we haven't been able to reach the Secretary of Defense for an explanation of this sudden incursion. If we can't reach him by noon, they will start disassembling the towers, and you won't be able to go back."

In a daze, Fleur gazed at the ceiling, the window, and her fingernails. "Can you please call Emmett?"

Cassius pulled out his phone and dialed. "Fleur is in Milton's office," he said. "Yes, we broke the news, and she's asking for you."

A minute later, Emmett flew into the office and took her in his arms. "I searched for you everywhere." With her face pressed against his chest, he rocked her back and forth. "Are you very upset?"

Fleur glanced at the digital clock above the door. "We still have ten minutes to change their minds."

While Milton was on hold, waiting to talk to the Secretary of Defense, he gazed at Fleur. "You're living proof of what technology is capable of today, and I have to make them understand we need several more days to right the wrong done to you. Fleur, on behalf of everyone here, I truly apologize for what befell upon you. All I hope is that you appreciate our efforts to resolve it."

A woman's voice came on the line. "Do you still want to hold?"

"Yes, I do," Milton spoke firmly. "This is of utmost importance." He glanced at the clock and swallowed hard. "Only one more minute to change Austin McConnohie's mind."

Fleur and Emmett stood at the window overlooking the parking lot, holding hands. Outside, the soldiers hung around in small groups, passing the time until the clock would strike twelve.

With each nerve-wrecking second, frustration in the room mounted, the classical music on the phone irritating everyone. "I'm sorry, sir," the woman said. "It appears that the Secretary is still in a meeting. Can he return your call?"

It was five minutes past twelve and increased activity outside indicated their time was up. "Yes, please," Milton sighed and disconnected. With his fingers buried in his hair, he gazed at Fleur. "I don't know what to say other than to apologize once again."

Fleur straightened her back. Life kept trying to knock her

over and beat her down, but she was strong and could handle this too.

Emmett wrapped his arm around her shoulders. "What are they going to do with SMITS, Commander?" he asked.

Milton opened a document on his computer. "SMITS will be moved to an undisclosed location in Alaska. By the end of the summer, Abernathey will shut down completely and be demolished. The property will become part of the surrounding nature preserve."

Chapter 47

"WHY DIDN'T YOU TELL ME the government threatened to close Abernathey?" Fleur asked Cassius an hour later.

They'd gone home to talk and sat in the living room, Fleur in her favorite corner on the couch with Emmett next to her. "Did you know?" she asked, turning to Emmett.

Emmett shrugged. "There were rumors going around, but with my internship ending in a few days, I didn't pay close attention. At least now I understand why they let me go early."

Despite all the warnings and alarm bells going off in her head because of the risk, deep in her heart, Fleur preferred to leave. Life seemed simpler where she came from; less hectic and demanding. She realized now she'd been naive, hoping they would postpone her departure until further research had improved the chance of a safe passage. With the increased public curiosity and outcry, and the pressure from the government, SMITS would be gone soon, and testing would stop, taking away the hope she would ever see her parents and siblings again.

Cassius wrung his hands and took a deep breath, his face strained and tired. "The wheels started spinning when I flew to

Washington D.C. Milton and I were able to convince them to wait until we sent you back after you were medically cleared. Every week, they demanded a full report about the progress, pressuring us to speed up the process."

Fleur remembered all the meetings he'd had behind closed doors. "If I'd known, I could have gone to Dr. Stevenson sooner instead of waiting the full two months."

"You had enough on your mind, and I didn't want to burden you with the knowledge." He mumbled several apologies, then looked her straight in the eyes. "I also didn't want it to influence your decision. You needed time."

She didn't agree. The decision of leaving or staying was so difficult that even the tiniest detail was important. "I love living in your house. What if a part of my decision-making was that I believed I could keep living here with you?"

"My sweet girl. That would have been out of the question," Cassius said with a touch of melancholy in his voice. "The moment you arrived, my career was over, and I planned to retire and move out of this house after you made your decision."

"Move where?"

"Several weeks ago, I bought a two-bedroom condominium in Heemstead where I plan to spend the rest of my days. You're welcome to move in with me for as long as you want because I've loved having you here and would have missed you so much."

Fleur knew she would have missed him, too. "I may just have to do that."

Then she thought about Lucia and Adam next door, and all the other employees. "What will happen with everybody else after they close Abernathey?"

"Ramon and Adam talked about transferring to Alaska. Darlene is retiring, like me, and everyone else will be offered a similar job elsewhere. It's the end of an era."

Chapter 48

FLEUR SQUINTED against the afternoon sun that bathed the dunes in a bright yellow light.

"This is where it all began," she said and wrapped her fingers around the chain-link fence.

Emmett covered her hand with his. "But this time, I'm here for you, instead of flying by on my motorcycle."

She leaned against his chest, feeling safe and protected. "What would your future have been like if you hadn't met me?" she asked, and then turned around in his arms to look at him.

Emmett let his fingers run through her hair. "I would have finished my internship and one more required practicum with an engineering firm to earn my bachelor's degree in mechanical engineering. Next, I would have searched for a job. But since we're not going anywhere soon, those plans are back on the table." He kissed her nose. "After today's outcome, what do you want to do with your future?"

For a while, she wrestled with her thoughts. Her mother had written that she should stay in the future, assuring her she lived on in her heart, and that she wanted to live the rest of her life knowing her beloved daughter was safe. Everybody else had written similar things. She pulled a crumpled letter from her jeans' pocket, a letter she'd read repeatedly.

"This letter is from my father," she told Emmet and read,

"*We understand saying goodbye to us will be extremely difficult. Just bear in mind that by the time you read this, we will be long gone and part of history, our pain of losing you over.*"

She briefly closed her eyes. "Since my arrival, my family lived on in my mind." Her voice croaked as sorrow threatened to choke her. "I'm struggling to come to terms with losing them all while I'm also fighting to hold on to the idea that they're still alive." Her hand balled into a fist. "I don't want to give up on them. Does that make sense?"

It didn't make sense at all, but it didn't matter. Feelings like love, hope, loss, and mourning couldn't be reasoned away. They were a part of you until time decided to take them away.

"I love you so much," he said, taking her face between his warm hands. "I want to be there for you, no matter what road you take, and will follow you wherever you want to go."

She gave him a grateful smile. "For now, there's nothing we can do but wait until SMITS is rebuilt. During that time, we have to see where life will take us."

Her gaze traveled over the research center. It was hard to imagine everything would be gone by the end of the year. If she'd learned one thing from her bizarre, unnatural experience, it would be that everything in life could change in a wink, and that you should seize whatever it offered before it disappeared. For her, clarity had come in the frenzy of a wicked storm, blasting away everything she'd believed, loved, and cherished. In return, it had given her the love of her life, a new family, and the chance to grow old. With Emmett by her side, the future looked bright and the possibilities of what to make of it were endless. "For now, I want to stay with Cassius and take that job at Keizer Manor," she said while thinking it over. "It'll make me feel closer to my family and allow me to grieve. I also want you to teach me how to ride a motorcycle. I can't wait to fly over the roads by myself."

Emmett kissed her long and hard. "Fleur, you're the most amazing woman I've ever met. You're strong, smart, beautiful, and rambunctious."

"Rambunctious?" She laughed and threw her head back. "You probably mean dynamic, impulsive, and headstrong."

"All of that too." He grinned before he went down on one knee and pulled a small box from his pocket. "Fleur, I've loved you from the moment you entered my world, and I can't imagine my future without you. Will you marry me?"

She noticed how his hand trembled when he held up a small ring and her heart overflowed with love. Instead of taking the ring, she threw her arms around his neck. "Yes, yes, yes!" Overjoyed, she kissed him everywhere until he lost his balance and they both rolled onto the ground. Laughing out loud, they found each other again, their mouths searching, their hands exploring.

"Let's not wait too long," Emmett said, his voice filled with urgency and excitement. "It's been too long since I touched you and I can't wait for us to be husband and wife." His hand slid under her shirt and stroked her back until Fleur suddenly pulled back. "Where's the ring?"

They both sat up and peeked around.

"It must have gone flying." Emmett laughed and crawled over the pavement on all fours. A moment later, he found it and put it on her finger.

Fleur held up her hand to admire the light blue aquamarine gemstone and the twisted white and rose band. "It's so pretty." They kissed again, until several brazen onlookers whistled from the other side of the fence.

"Hey, guys. What's going on over there?" they joked.

"Nothing for you to worry about," Emmett replied. He took Fleur's hand and together, they headed back to Cassius's house.

In the parking lot, they noticed an aerial lift had been set up. In the platform, attached to the lifting mechanism, two men unscrewed bolts with a power tool to take the first tower down.

Emmett stopped to look at the dangerous work. "I can't believe they're going to ship everything to Alaska."

"I didn't dare to ask this before," Fleur said. "But what's Alaska?"